OUT FROM UNDER

A Mental Maze of the Past...A Novel of Triumph!

MARK G. PLATT

authorHOUSE®

AuthorHouse™
1663 Liberty Drive
Bloomington, IN 47403
www.authorhouse.com
Phone: 1-800-839-8640

First published by AuthorHouse 4/04/2011

ISBN: 978-1-4567-4936-1 (e)
ISBN: 978-1-4567-4938-5 (dj)
ISBN: 978-1-4567-4937-8 (sc)

Library of Congress Control Number: 2011903545

Printed in the United States of America

This book is dedicated to the memory of my brother Glenn, I miss you daily, and love you always.

ACKNOWLEDGEMENTS

For their help with this book, the author is particularly grateful to Wendy McIlvride, Renne Rhae, and Laine Cunningham; to Russ and Pat Wright, Cindy Barton Steagall, Virginia Caivano, Bill and Bobbie Platt, Ed and Karen Platt, Fran Beadles, Jill Russell, Brad Green, Johnann McIlwain, Julia Daugherty, Peggy Peterson, Melinda Eaton, Anissa Lacey, Mark Terrill, Buffy Lake, and Christa Phillips; and to Jaymes Green for his never ending support and encouragement.

PROLOGUE

I t all began in the unlikeliest of places. A place where hope lies thin on the ground and redemption is most improbable. My closest neighbor created a furor this morning by smearing her own feces on the walls of her "suite", and my other neighbors greet me with blank stares, mumbled or screamed disjointed ramblings, and random violence. You see I am, once again, in a locked-down psych ward, this time in an under-funded county facility.

I have been involuntarily committed by the police for seventy-two hours under the California Welfare and Institutions Code 5150, commonly called a 51-50 hold. I'm unable to leave, after my third unsuccessful suicide attempt — two in the past four months — while my wife Ilana, whom I leapt across a table at and tried to strangle this morning, is at present, sitting in the kitchen of what I believe is my house, planning more ways to keep me locked up for just a little longer, or better yet, a lot longer. And, despite this evidence, I really don't believe I belong here.

I have a dedicated team of professionals, including a medical doctor, a pair of psychologists, a psychiatrist, a nutritionist, a social worker, nurses and sundry support staff whom I think of as "keepers" who will tell you I do belong here. "Here" is a shared room in a county lockdown facility that houses the dregs of the mentally ill, drug-addicted, and other social detritus; it is painfully obvious to me that I don't belong. The environment is hardly stimulating — think in terms of military or prison-style eating and common areas, surrounded by small shared sleeping quarters and common restrooms and shower facilities, all painted an unrelenting uniform drab color somewhere between green, brown and yellow. It's the color you get when you mix all your leftover paint together. In my family, we called it "granch". So here I am, in my granch world, with granch walls, granch furniture, granch clothing, granch bedding, and granch food. My life is regimented with a precision only achievable in an institution — breakfast, smoke break, group meeting, snack, smoke break, lunch, another smoke break, group meeting (from which I may be summoned for a private session with my dedicated team), another snack, dinner, smoke break and lights out by nine P.M.

I stand in line, when summoned, for medications then wait for a cigarette by the side door that leads to a courtyard surrounded by the buildings that make up the Riverside County Rehabilitation Center in Indio, California. I'm allowed one cigarette, dispensed by Tom, a six-foot, two hundred pound keeper whose sole responsibility is to maintain peace and ensure that all the patients are where they should be during the day's activities. Once outside, we congregate around the few concrete picnic tables placed under the sheet metal cover that shields us from the harsh sun that heats the stale, dry-as-dust air to well over one hundred degrees at this time of year. I wander along the perimeter of the courtyard which is approximately one quarter the size of a football field. As I walk, I consider where I am. A "Rehabilitation Center?" So far I haven't seen any rehabilitation — just crazy people trying to get through the day in any way they can. These people are crazy, and they have problems I never imagined were possible. NO! I don't belong here. I don't even remember how I got here. There has been a terrible mistake and soon, very soon, the warden of this asylum will realize this error and release me back to my life, back to my freedom.

Later, I stand in another line, waiting for my choice of snack — banana, punch, cookie, brownie, orange or Jell-O. At least I'm hungry. During the intake exam, the night nurse listed my weight at 120 pounds. I didn't argue but I'm sure her scale is off. At six feet tall, my normal weight is around 180 pounds. My belt, shoe laces and drawstring from my sweat pants were taken during intake to prevent me from "doing harm" to myself. My clothes hang on my body like those of a refugee fleeing the horrors of a war-torn country. Eating is good. I would look better with a bit more weight on my frame. There have been recent hushed discussions among the few friends I have left, ending as soon as I walk into the room, as my friends look at me in shock and horror at my rapid weight loss.

Yet another line, stand and wait again. All I need is a toothbrush, toothpaste, razor, shaving cream and a towel. These too are doled out by a keeper. I huddle next to the door which leads into one of the private showers — my keeper must unlock the door and wait, timing me to make sure that I don't take too long, listening for any sound that is out of the ordinary in case I try to hurt myself with the disposable razor or toothbrush or hang myself from the shower nozzle with the granch towel the County provides. I was comatose in bed for three days before the ambulance took me to the hospital and I've been here for four days so this is my first shower in a week. I haven't cut my hair for over nine months so it hangs in greasy clumps down to my shoulders. Every day I am asked if I would like to "get cleaned up." "NO" is my stock answer. I just want to be left alone. Finally I agree, just to get Tom off my back. But as I stand there waiting I have second thoughts. I'm already tired, and it takes too much energy for the simple things that most people take for granted, like bathing. Just as I begin shuffling back to my room Tom arrives. "Ready?" he asks. An indifferent nod and a shrug are all I can manage, silently indicating my indecision. Guilt, shame, and the need to please others propel me into the shower room.

I immediately regret my decision. The room is dark and the horrific smell of grime from every previous inmate hits me as if it was solid, like a bully's fist smacking me in the face. The sound of dripping water echoes as the condensation loses its grip on the ceiling tiles and hits, drop after incessant drop, the stale puddles of grey scummy water covering the tile floors. As I step into the miasma-filled room, dank and echoing with the sound of every step I take, I glance back, looking for an escape route. Tom is standing guard, he won't move, he'll keep the door open, there is no privacy, only a low wall protects me from view. Trapped and resigned, I slowly begin my bathing ritual. My toiletries are deposited on a small bench as I begin to remove my rank clothing.

Whew, the stench is potent! I'm immediately embarrassed as I realize just how unclean and unkempt I really am. How did I let myself fall so far? When did my life become so unmanageable? As I glance over my shoulder, my heart stops. I catch a glimpse of myself in the mirror. I'm scared to look closely, too afraid of what I might see, so I avoid looking into my eyes. I don't recognize the blank, drawn look on the face that is looking back at me. That guy looks horrible!! He looks like he belongs here, one of the crazy people that I see all around me every day. It's a trick, the mirror isn't a mirror at all, it must be a poster of a dangerous inmate, safely locked away to keep the rest of society from harm. Why did they put that poster where a mirror should be? Look away, just shower and leave. *You'll feel better*, I keep telling myself over and over again, like some mantra to get myself moving. Feel better my ass! Who am I kidding? That's just not possible. I'll be dead before I feel better, I just know it. Heat and moisture are the building blocks for who knows what kind of fungus, virus or bacteria. I'll never leave this Godforsaken place. I'll die here after contracting a terminal illness from the microscopic life that is thriving in this Petri dish of a hellhole. How can I get clean in this place? I concentrate as hard as I can, willing myself to hover just a few inches off the floor, like some obsessive-compulsive yogi. If I don't touch anything maybe I can escape the silent, unseen killer disease that is surely stalking me in this foul cave.

I hurry in slow motion so I can lie down. I'm tired, so very tired. I'll shave later, there's no time now, I must get back to bed. Sleep, blessed sleep! It's the only escape from the nightmare that is my life. I finally finish, pad back to my cell, and crawl into bed, pulling the blanket tightly over my head.

There is a bang on my door, "Time for group," Tom yells. "Get up!"

"Marks, you have a phone call," someone shouts. I shuffle to the nurse's station where the nurse's aide hands me the phone.

"Gregory.....its Mother. What are you doing there? Why did you do it? I need you," my mother cries into the phone, confusion, concern and desperation tinting her voice.

"I can't talk to you right now," is all I can manage as I hand the phone back to the nurse's aide. I'm not really sure what I'm doing here or why I did it. I'm too confused and embarrassed to try to explain anything to anyone at this point. How can I explain what I don't understand? I head to the group meeting and take a seat far away from the other inmates.

The group meetings are depressing, as they are designed for the lowest common denominator among us, and involve endless repeating of the "rules" for the new inmates. Since I have been here for four days, I'm asked if I would like to read the rules from the poster that is crookedly taped on the wall outside one of the community bathrooms.

"No thank you," I answer as politely as I can.

"You're gonna have to participate sooner or later," Connie encourages with a warm smile.

She is young and pretty and greets us each day with compassion that makes me feel as if she could be my best friend if I weren't me and we weren't in this place. I'm embarrassed each time I see her. In another place and time, I would strike up a conversation. She would see me as the confident, successful businessman that I have been and would like to be again. But today, I am just one of the inmates she is here to assist in their rehabilitation, down their path back into society. Finger-painting and other art therapies at an early elementary school level are the best that I can hope for. These group therapy sessions are designed to keep our hands busy and our minds thinking about anything other than why we're here and how we're going to escape.

The noise and the drama that all the other inmates create are insufferable. They yell, they cry, they wail, they attack each other and the staff and behave like crazy people. The population is transient, and length of stay varies from person to person. In the four days that I have been here, I've had two different roommates, neither of whom I have spoken to and don't plan to any time soon. I'm not here to make friends. As a matter of fact, I'm not supposed to be here at ALL!! I don't want to be friendly, and it will be easier to leave once the warden of this asylum realizes her mistake and lets me go home. I should be sunning myself on a beach somewhere in the tropics, under a palm tree swaying in the breeze, enjoying a fruity drink with an umbrella in it. After all, I'm a well educated, successful businessman and entrepreneur who has made, lost, and made again vast fortunes in my forty-odd years on this planet. I have a fabulous and stable family that has just enough eccentricity to make it interesting. I have never doubted their love, yet I've hurt them by causing grief and concern most of my life. I don't consider myself lovable, but for some unfathomable reason, they do, so who am I to complain? I take it, the love they hand out unconditionally, I need it, I crave it and it never seems to be enough. Maybe I do belong here. Where else do you send a person who causes so much trouble for such a loving family?

But no, I don't belong here. I have never run afoul of the law beyond one speeding ticket that I received when I was sixteen years old shortly after I received my driver's license. I drink very little, and am not a drug user, unless you believe Ilana — that's why I tried to strangle her this morning.

My beloved Ilana arrived shortly after group therapy for a meeting. My social worker, Lisa, struggled hard the past few days obtaining background information from family and friends. The three of us were meeting to discuss my discharge plan — a comprehensive treatment plan to monitor my "recovery" and prevent depressive drama that could lead to another suicide attempt. In my private team meeting I was given a diagnosis for the first time since I arrived, and it had a name — severe clinical depression. My psychiatrist, Dr. Brad Johnson, a handsome middle-aged man with bright, intelligent eyes and a reassuring manner had explained that after extensive discussions with my parents, friends and of course Ilana, the team determined that I have been clinically depressed for most of my life.

After a few minutes of listening to Lisa read off a list of activities, requirements, and therapy sessions, none of which I remember in detail, a familiar look came over Ilana's face. I held my breath, dreading what was coming. Ilana is a junkie. She has an addiction to methamphetamine and manipulates every situation for her own benefit. I wasn't sure what was coming but I had seen that look before and I knew it was not going to be good. Even with my preparation, I couldn't believe what I heard next.

This was low, low even for Ilana...when Lisa paused for a moment to adjust her glasses, Ilana interjected, "You know ... I'm not prepared to take him home until he admits to ... and deals with his drug addiction."

She had to be joking — a terribly timed joke. I couldn't believe my ears! Ilana was the one with the drug problem!! She was the addict!!! Although she always promised she was drug free I knew she had been using in the past year.

The earth stopped rotating on its axis. Everything went blank. I couldn't see, couldn't feel, and couldn't smell, but unfortunately, my hearing remained razor-sharp. She went on,

"He's a heavy meth addict. I think this issue should be a major part of his treatment." With a thunderbolt of clarity, I knew with absolute certainty that everything I'd been through in the past few days was for nothing. I didn't need a discharge plan. I was not being discharged today. There was no telling when I would be discharged, not with this new "information" on the table. I was shocked, appalled, flabbergasted, incensed, and furious; you name it, I felt it. Gobsmacked! In that moment I at last began to understand the depth to which she would sink, how much betrayal she was really capable of. Still reeling from this onslaught, I did what any reasonable person in similar circumstances would do. I completely lost control.

"I don't do drugs and you know that!" I yelled.

"Come on now," she began but got no further. I erupted from my chair, launched myself across the table, and landed on her chest, hands around her throat. We fell backwards, the back of her chair, or maybe the back of her head, hitting the ground with a loud satisfying thud.

Lisa hit the panic button screaming, "Code black, code black, patient out of control……."

I'd never felt better in my life.

The next thing I remember was Tom standing over my bed as he finished tightening the restraints which kept my legs and arms strapped to my bed.

"There you are, welcome back, how do you feel?"

I could hear Lisa's voice but I couldn't see her clearly. Several people stood around my bed, faces I recognized but whose names escaped me for the moment.

"You attacked Ilana," Lisa explained. "She says you have a drug problem. You should have told us. We can't help you if you're not honest with us. That's enough for now; we'll talk more about this in your team meeting tomorrow. Try to get some rest. Tom, take these restraints off right before dinner."

She lowered herself and sat on my bed, placing her hand on my cheek and said gently, "Take it easy. If you promise to behave yourself, Tom is authorized to remove your restraints. Can you do that?"

"Yes," I promised as I looked away and began to cry.

Things had gotten out of hand AGAIN. Earlier today, I was full of optimism and hope. Hope for a better life, planning my release. Finally I had information that would allow me to pull my life back together — depression. I would have to find out what that meant. Now I was really depressed, desperate and betrayed by the love of my life. I would never leave this place. I had become one of the crazy people who attacked others in random acts of violence that until now, I believed were the actions of the mentally ill, certainly not the type of action that I was prone to. Yet, here I was, strapped to my bed, wondering how my life had gotten so off course, where and when had I taken a left turn when I should have taken a right. Finding my way now seemed impossible. If I was here to prevent another suicide attempt it wasn't working. All I could think about was how to end my life, how to stop the hurt, end the pain. For the first time since arriving I began to think that maybe, just maybe, I did belong here. Maybe I should pay attention. Maybe I could learn something, but for now I would have to wait, play the game. I would tell them anything they wanted to hear. Whatever they wanted, I would comply. I had to get out of here and attacking Ilana wasn't going to help me, but it felt good. I haven't felt that good in quite a while. At least I did something. At least I took action. But it didn't work; it just put me in the category of the unmanageable. Now I had to work extra hard to prove I was ready to go home.

"It's okay, we'll talk more tomorrow, just try to get some rest."

"Lisa," I called out then paused ... "You don't believe her do you, Ilana, I mean?"

"That's not for me to decide; we'll talk tomorrow."

"Lisa," I called again stopping her at the doorway to my room, "Thank you, I promise not to cause any more problems."

"No prob…..see ya tomorrow."

CHAPTER ONE

"K enny is gone," my father said. "He's disappeared."

The call came near dawn on another perfect San Diego day. The windows were open to catch the early breezes that reached the small enclaves in the hills. On the sidewalks, my neighbors were just starting their workday strolls to the corner deli. I fumbled for my robe as my dad continued.

"His car was found on a bridge over a large ravine. You remember the place. Over the river where the whitewater is. The police found a suicide note in the car but they haven't...his body hasn't been recovered yet."

I slumped back onto the bed. My hand still held the receiver but had gone numb. Kenny and I had talked only a few days earlier. Why hadn't he said anything? I should have known something was wrong. I should have been a better brother. There must have been some hint. If only I hadn't been so wrapped up in my own damn problems.

"Uh...what?" I said.

Brilliant, Greg, I thought. *Exactly what your dad needs to hear.*

Dad sighed and repeated himself. I wondered how often he'd rehearsed those words during the search knowing he'd eventually have to make this call. As the facts repeated—*empty car...suicide note...no trace*—the walls took on a strange rubbery texture. Everything seemed to glow with its own light.

Then it sank in: this was real. Not only was Kenny my brother, he was also my best friend. And he was gone. But where had he gone? Had he

1

really jumped? Or had he faked his death to get away from his current life? And what could possibly have been so bad that he'd needed to run?

Until his body was located, I would hope for the best. Grieving was out of the question. It felt like a betrayal, like I was hammering the lid on his coffin myself. I couldn't lose hope. I wouldn't accept that he'd taken his own life.

When I tried to hang up, the receiver missed the cradle. The line stayed silent for a long moment then sent out that endless off-the-hook beep. I lay with the phone inches from my head, utterly motionless, listening to the alarm warn of a danger I did not yet understand.

* * *

I showed up at work hours late. My job was to implement total quality management at one of California's largest university hospitals. After evaluating the operations of a particular department, I found ways to cut expenses and streamline the work flow. As an extension of those duties, I installed new computer systems and kept the network operating at top capacity as needs changed.

The work was extremely demanding. No one would have denied me a few days off. I could have flown to Texas to be with my parents or simply waited by the phone as the search teams worked their way downriver. But since there was no body, there was no reason to mourn.

I focused on not staggering too much as I navigated the hall. My Abercrombe & Fitch sport jacket was thrown casually over my arm and my Church's English shoes were spotlessly shined. *Everything's fine,* my clothes said, *everything will be just fine.* My free hand ran lightly down the wall to keep me from wobbling.

When I settled behind my desk—picture of loving parents and loving brother Kenny squared neatly above the in box, desk calendar with meetings inked precisely into their time slots—my hands rested on the edge of my keyboard. There I stayed for the rest of the day. To anyone looking in, I appeared to be working. Actually the computer screen was blank. I stared only at the scenes in my head.

When I'd been very young, I'd learned the one skill that carried me through my life. I was the producer, director, and scriptwriter of my own imaginary films. No matter what happened, no matter how overwhelming my life became, I simply shot new film. My 'indies' ran at every free moment. Problem? What problem? Roll film!

He's in Barbados, I thought. *He's on a boat suiting up to dive for sunken treasure. He's in the Himalayas sipping tea in a yurt. He's copiloting Virgin's space shuttle with Brandon.* Each film was equally vivid; each scenario was equally plausible.

When someone asked if I wanted to go to lunch, I shook off the fantasies. My arms had fallen asleep from being held in the same position for so long. I sat there with my useless limbs flopped across my desk and thought about the suicide note. *Love you all,* it had said, *but can't live with the pain.*

And that was it. Nothing else, no hint of what pain he might have been feeling, no issue at which my parents could aim their anger over having lost their youngest child. Kenny had left them empty and wondering, able only to study the life they had given him as a child and the life he'd built as an adult for clues.

They'd never find it. They'd never know the reason why. But from my own memories came a real film clip, one I'd spent decades trying to destroy.

* * *

My mother's family lived in Louisiana. Aunt Louise, Uncle Conrad and their kids lived on a farm close to where my mother grew up. I spent every summer there and most weekends. Since the place was so small, Kenny stayed in the city with my dad's family and Mother stayed at her parent's place. We all got a vacation and we were that much happier to come back together when school started again.

My aunt and uncle's old farmhouse had been built in the 1940s. The roof sloped low over the wide porch where rockers and a swing waited. The downstairs was a small kitchen and living room with a full bath squeezed beside the back door. Three bedrooms had been carved out of the loft: one for my aunt and uncle, one for my cousin Shelly (the only girl), and the third for my other four cousins, all boys.

Because I was a city kid, the farm seemed like a giant amusement park. The chores my cousins grumbled about felt like adventures. From sunup until sundown we hunted, fished, camped, rode horses, and fed the chickens, hogs and cows. We tended the vegetable garden with our hands and worked the large fields on tractors. By the time I was old enough to reach the pedals, I could drive all the farm equipment and often ran the beat-up trucks around the back roads.

Shortly after my seventh birthday, my oldest cousin Dave got married. That was good news for the youngest two. Dave and Bruce, the older two, each had slept in their own beds. The youngest had shared the third bed. With Dave gone, the three remaining boys each had their own queen-sized beds.

I'd always bunked with Dave. After he left, I bunked with Bruce. Although I was closer in age to the younger two, my uncle didn't want any horsing around at bedtime. The entire family got up too early for him to have to come in six times and tell us to settle down. So I bunked with the oldest boy, who was responsible for making sure everyone else stayed quiet.

At seventeen, Bruce was a freshman, the first in his family to attend college. He was the family hero, bright, handsome and revered as the popular intellect, bound for success. I looked up to him and wanted to be just like him. Until the night I woke to find his hand down the front of my underwear.

I froze and pretended to be asleep. I didn't understand what was happening. After a while he rolled over and went to sleep. I stayed awake for a long time after that, and eventually got up to use the restroom. When I went back to bed, I stayed as far away from him as possible.

The next day and night he acted as if nothing had happened. We did the chores together and he saddled one of the horses so I could go out for a ride after dinner. I stayed out very late, hoping that when I finally got back he'd already be in bed and asleep.

He was in the living room watching TV. When he smiled, the light from the screen twisted his lips into something terrible. I cleaned up and got ready for bed very slowly, hoping to be able to lie down far from whatever spot he chose, but he still didn't come upstairs until I turned out the light.

I lay awake forever. Eventually he seemed to be asleep. As I was finally dozing off, his hand pushed past my waistband again.

Every night of every summer vacation for years afterward, Bruce fondled me. Eventually he stopped waiting until he thought I was asleep. The second he was under the covers, he'd start touching me. He also pulled my hand over to fondle him. I hated it, and I hated him for making me do it. But I didn't know how to make him stop. At seven years old, I wasn't even sure what it all meant.

For the next five years, my summer vacations were the same surreal torment. The days were spent as they'd always been, full of chores and outdoor activities. When darkness fell, the nightmare continued. I didn't understand how everything could be so precisely normal during the day and so frighteningly strange at night. This one thing Bruce made me do changed everything yet nothing else had changed.

Except me. I started pretending then. During the months of school at home with my family, I pretended my summer vacation had been fun. When my aunt and uncle welcomed me to the farm, I pretended I was happy to be there. Even when Bruce's hands were grabbing me and pressing my fingers against his own skin, I pretended it was nothing more than a dream.

The only thing I couldn't cover over in those early mental films was how I felt. I hated Bruce, and I hated myself for allowing him to do what he did. I hated the things he did to me and the things he made me do to him. I didn't know exactly why I hated them, except that what he made me do seemed wrong and dirty. I wanted Bruce to leave me alone. I wanted things to go back to the way they'd been before, without the chaos of his hands every night and the confusion in my mind every day.

Since I couldn't stop him, I treated him terribly. Maybe if he hated me he wouldn't want to touch me. When we worked in the garden, I stepped on his rows. I "knocked over" his cassette tapes and cracked every case. I even threw his baseball cap and jersey into the manure pile hours before a game.

Everyone thought I was just being a brat. I was constantly in trouble. My favorite place on earth had installed a horrifying ride on which I was trapped each night. I finally made peace just to stay out of trouble. I wanted to fade into the wall, to be ignored and unnoticed by everyone...especially Bruce. Publicly, I returned to that sweetly smiling boy who was so normal no one ever noticed what he did or said.

Inside, though, chaos reigned. I screamed at Bruce in my head. I imagined yelling at him to stop. In my 'indie' productions, I treated him the way he deserved to be treated. In my mind, he left me alone. I retreated to an imaginary theatre where only good clips were allowed. Watching my mental screen, I was insulated, protected, comforted, and completely in control.

All my life, it had never occurred to me that Bruce might also have abused my younger brother. Kenny had stayed with other relatives during the summers but often spent other vacations at the farm. He'd never seemed much different except that one year he'd suddenly given his life to Christ during a Sunday service.

Had going to God been his way of dealing with the same shame and the trauma? If he had been abused, if religion and a life of spiritual focus hadn't healed his wounds, then his death was my fault. My silence not only allowed Kenny to fall victim to that monster, it let him suffer so much he thought suicide was his only escape.

Kenny was gone, he'd disappeared, and my family was suffering because of me. Even if Kenny were alive, he'd left because he couldn't face what his life had become after the abuse—a sham that covered a well of festering shame.

Chapter Two

No one knew better than I did how desperate Kenny must have been. My own emotional stability had been steadily undermined, nibbled away each day by the shame, guilt and self loathing that had crept into my soul. I'd stayed in Texas nearly my entire life, possibly in an effort to create some stability when really I had none. The outer trappings of my climb to success were what everyone expected them to be: I graduated college, married a wonderful woman, and netted one of the highest-paying jobs Houston could offer.

Yet I struggled to understand why I was always depressed even when nothing in my life was bad enough to be depressed about. Every morning my hands tied the perfect Windsor knot and smoothed my Brooks Brothers lapels. Every evening my nose enjoyed the bouquet of a wine perfectly matched to whatever Clair put on the table. But the shell became more hollow as my insides compressed into a tiny dark star.

Clair had no idea what was happening. She knew only that I walked the same way and lived the same life but that I wasn't the person she'd married. For long stretches, days or weeks, I simply stopped speaking to her. Depression strangled me too thoroughly, and neither of us knew it. All my effort was dedicated to the public persona. By the time I came home, I had only enough energy left to sit upright in a chair. There was no way I could meaningfully interact with her. Clair was the perfect wife – kind, understanding, patient and supportive. I had it all, and it still wasn't enough.

During our separation, I was offered a job at a children's hospital in

San Diego. I had never considered leaving the area where I'd grown up but suddenly moving away seemed really appealing. Relocating would offer me a chance to start over. Maybe the new adventure would help me recapture some of that joy I'd lost so long ago.

The divorce became official on a Tuesday. That Wednesday I left for California. Oh, what fantasies ran through my head, fictions that might actually come true. I purchased a house to kick off my new life. The two-story Art Deco structure had been built in the 1940s and was immaculate inside and out. The light fixtures and stained-glass windows were original, as was the tile. It became my retreat and my prison.

* * *

As the weeks turned into months, the hopelessness over Kenny's disappearance grew. I couldn't escape the undertow of emotions that sucked me further and further out to sea. At times I would sit in my office for hours staring blankly at the wall. Work piled up, people popped in and left without my ever acknowledging them, and I didn't care.

I could only imagine what my parents were feeling. There were moments when the pain was so great I didn't think I would live through it. The *not* knowing ate at me. Was he really dead? Could it really be so final, so abrupt? Suddenly I had no idea what to say to my parents. I didn't want to talk about any of it with anyone, much less with Mother and Dad.

A memorial service had been arranged not long after the car was found. After a few days of waiting for the body to wash up—as if it were a piece of driftwood a collector might want—my parents finalized the date for the memorial.

"When will you be coming in?" Mother asked.

"I…I'm not."

A rustling sounded over the line as she passed the phone to my father. She'd never cut me off before. It felt like she'd hung up on me. Dad came on the line.

"Can you spend a day or two?" he asked. "We know you can't stay long because of your job. If you need to fly out the same day, that's fine."

"I'm not coming to his memorial. Not when there's a chance he might be alive."

He sighed. "That's an admirable thought. Come anyway. For your mother."

"I can't."

I couldn't explain it to him. What was I supposed to say? *Hey, Pops! Kenny's dead because I never told on pervy cousin Bruce.* Not gonna happen. I tapped the spine of every book on the nearby shelf, squaring each down the row as I listened to him breathing heavily, as if going through this repetitive organizational ritual could somehow restore order to the chaos inside my head.

"Greg," he finally said, "you only get this chance once."

My knees buckled. Grabbing the shelf would have knocked everything down so I sank onto the floor instead. I'd had five years worth of chances to tell someone about the abuse and decades later to clue in about Kenny. How many days were bundled into those years, how many hours, each of which had been another opportunity to save my brother's life?

I don't remember saying anything to end the conversation. I don't recall that Dad said anything, either. I think he finally just hung up.

They called a few more times before the memorial. After the service, longer and longer periods of time went between our phone calls. Kenny's disappearance, it seemed, would cause my entire family to disappear. They would erase themselves gradually, gently, drifting away on the hidden currents of a calm lake. It was worse than how the river had ripped my brother from us all.

No matter how confused I'd ever felt, no matter how often Clair failed to calm the chaos inside while we were married, Kenny had been the one constant I could rely on. Even though he'd been my younger brother, he'd always been there for me. He never pestered me to tell him what was wrong; he just called and chatted, somehow knowing the sound of his voice was more relaxing than any therapy. How was I supposed to move on as if nothing had changed? A part of *me* was missing.

Eventually I simply went to bed. When I finally got up, a week had gone by.

* * *

As I walked down the hall at work, heads popped out of different offices. As I passed each doorway, whispered conversations halted and people stared. Then the toad hopped out in front of me.

"Greg," she peeped in her deceptively gentle voice. "Glad to see you could make it in today."

She smiled sweetly and raised one acrylic-clawed hand to her face. After carefully folding those garish nails into a fist, she rubbed her lower lip with the tip of her obscenely long middle finger. I never knew if that was just another of her nervous habits or if she was always flipping me the bird.

"I've been *so* worried," she said.

I detoured around her. She hopped along behind me, croaking about reports and meetings. I'd actually been hired to replace her but for some reason human resources had kept her on as an internal consultant. She plagued every aspect of my job, acting as if my best ideas were hers and constantly sending memos to the board to undermine whichever of my policies she didn't like.

She followed me into my office. I turned toward the blank computer screen, lay my hands on the keyboard, and sat there until she finally left.

* * *

Although I managed to keep some projects going, I could manage my responsibilities at work for only short periods. It didn't help that my office had a spectacular view of the harbor, a vibrant district with seafood markets and restaurants, a cruise ship terminal and the Californian, the State's official tall ship.

I tried not to look at it. It reminded me too much of the coast of Texas where I'd grown up, where Kenny and I had swum and fished and learned to scuba dive together. Going home wasn't much better. Because San Diego's suburbs were built into canyons and hills, the neighborhoods were small and somewhat insular. They each had their own identities and the scattered business districts that served them created a small-town feel.

It was too much like where I'd grown up. Since my dad had worked at NASA, we'd lived in a neighborhood right off the back gate. Many of the top brass lived there along with a handful of famous astronauts. Since the area was also bordered by the shore of Clear Lake and Galveston Bay, the place felt like a small community tucked into a big city.

Going back to my house felt too much like traveling back to my youth. Even the hibiscus and ficus favored by California landscapers were common Texan houseplants. Everything from the smell of the salt breezes to the bright blooms of the bougainvillea reminded me of my missing brother and my failure to save his life.

On a fairly regular basis, I retreated to my bedroom and slept for days. During those periods I didn't talk to anyone, I wouldn't return phone calls, and I never answered the door. I just slept. Dust gathered on the stereo and food rotted in the refrigerator. Then one day I would swing my feet onto the floor, shower and shave, and emerge as if nothing had happened.

"Where've you been?" my friends asked. I never explained my absences or made excuses. It was as if I could pretend their questions away, pretend that the days-long gaps hadn't happened. The few friends who stuck around accepted that this was just something I did. They called it going under.

"Oh, Greg?" they'd say at parties and coffee houses and weekend trips. "He's gone under again. Give him a few days and he'll be fine."

I dove deeper with each submersion. Whenever I used the restroom, I detoured far enough through the house to hit the erase button for the voice messages. Waiting for the computer screen to pop up took a millisecond too long so I set the email to automatically delete everything from the inbox. I threw newspapers away unread and, when my neighbor placed the mail that had overflowed the box onto my doorstep, I threw that away, too.

Then I would prepare for an appearance. Inside my closet, entire outfits hung together. Suits and shirts matched with appropriate ties for work took up one wall. Blazers with khakis and pullovers for social activities filled the second. A series of recreational wear—track suits, swimwear, roomy sailing shorts—filled the shortest rod at the rear.

All were grouped exactly as I'd found them hanging on the mannequins at the store. Every season I walked through the men's department and pointed to displays I liked. I handed the sales clerk a list of my sizes along with a credit card and was home in an hour. It was the most efficient way to preserve the fantasy that I was OK.

If I looked okay, I must be, right?

* * *

Although my friends adjusted to my unpredictable absences, my employer apparently did not. One day when I'd surfaced after a particularly long dive, the personnel office called to ask where I wanted my personal belongings sent.

"What do you mean?" I asked. "I wasn't told I was getting a new office."

The woman let out a short laugh that she quickly strangled. "Mr. Marks, you've been let go. We've held your personal items here, but if you don't want to come in, we understand. I can mail them wherever you like."

"I've been fired?"

Great, I thought. *That'll make Dad really proud.*

"Yes," she said slowly. "You were let go last week. Didn't you get the message?"

Of course I hadn't gotten the voice message. Or the email or the letter. I'd destroyed them all.

"Your final check should be there already," she continued. "You'll also have to sign up for COBRA if you want to continue your health insurance and roll your 401K over to your new job. Who is your employer now?"

Good question.

* * *

Despite my lingering outrage at having been fired, I had no desire to get back to the soap opera that had been my career. The idea of not having to face the daily drama brought on by the Toad or people like her was quite appealing. Peace of mind was far more important than commanding an exceptional salary with a well-known organization. I needed to find a career that provided a nice living without being too stressful, something I could really enjoy.

Since I still wasn't quite ready for too much socializing, I signed up with a couple internet employment services. A career counselor helped me determine the type of job that suited me best based on my likes, dislikes, abilities and experience. One of the recommendations was for financial counselor or stockbroker. With my background in finance and business, the idea was intriguing.

As a broker, I'd have to seek out clients and build my own book of business. I'd have the support and resources of a large company yet be able to control my own future. I would be independent and supported at the same time. The structure gave me security plus freedom. How perfect was that?

The Series Seven broker exam was similar to a CPA exam or sitting for the Bar. Preparation required hours of study. I wasn't sure I could be diligent enough to pass. It wasn't like I was in college anymore, and study habits were a distant memory. Amazingly, I scored well. Collins & Nichols Investments, the only partnership left on Wall Street, offered me a position.

The only hitch was that the office was in Palm Springs. Moving meant starting over in a new place. I wasn't sure I wanted to start over again. Yet the relocation could be my vindication. I'd failed so miserably after coming to San Diego that making a success of myself in a new location would prove I could do it right.

Plus, the very things I loved about San Diego were constant reminders of my family, my childhood, and my missing brother. When I took a day at the ocean to think things through, I wound up running along the beach looking for Kenny among the sunbathers. The further I ran, the more I knew I'd never find him. But I couldn't stop until I was doubled over gasping for breath and blinded by tears.

It was time to go.

* * *

Palm Springs was exactly what I needed. The city was a tight-knit enclave of culture, entertainment and wealth surrounded by miles of desert. Days were endlessly sunny with none of the humidity that plagued Texas; the weather was temperate for most of the year; and never a whiff of the ocean blew through to remind me of my failures.

Until I got settled in, I rented an apartment near work. Collins & Nichols had its own building on Palm Canyon Drive. The entire edifice was redolent of financial success and conservative attitudes. The cavernous lobby greeted clients with an acre of marble floors, teak furniture polished to a dark gleam, and a bullpen filled with quiet, efficient administrative staff.

Plush offices spread out around the bullpen. Mine had a solid glass wall facing the administrative area so I could gesture for a clerk without having to put a client on hold. Corporate-owned artwork graced the walls, deep carpeting deadened any unseemly noise that might creep in, and the furnishings were all burled wood and leather. Very gentleman's club, very old-school. I had finally arrived.

Every time I walked into the building, I knew I was entering the last bastion of robber-barons...updated, of course, with the installation of a mild conscience. The company's philosophy created interesting opportunities for brokers who were motivated and who liked autonomy. For someone like me, it was heaven.

I quickly nabbed the top sales figures in California and Texas for several of the mutual funds, and set my sights on achieving more. Palm Springs had a large population of wealthy retirees, the perfect demographic with which to build my book. Soon I was on my way to being a million-dollar producer. I earned close to three hundred thousand dollars my first year and challenged myself to hit the half million dollar mark in year two.

Starting over, it seemed, had been a very good idea.

But.....in some deep, dark place from the recesses of my mind, I couldn't stop the sound of my own inner voice. *It won't last. You'll screw this up too, you know. What makes you think you deserve success? In time, it will all fall apart again, just like it always does.*

CHAPTER THREE

With all the financial moving and shaking, there was little time to think. Exactly the way I wanted it. Spare moments only allowed me to wonder about Kenny, to agonize over whether I should call my parents and attempt to patch up the relationship, to press my nails so tightly into my neck I bled whenever I thought about explaining those summers on the farm.

I was frozen by indecision, by my inability to tell the truth and face the consequences. Perhaps it was better to break from my family this way rather than introduce the idea that both their sons had been molested. I settled into a new pattern. All my energy went to work. Any spare time I had was eclipsed either by an exhausted night's sleep or a frenzy of cleaning. When my hands were busy, my endless fantasy films and an internal numbness kept me comfortably insulated from the pain.

Not long after I began mining my earthly riches, an elderly man appeared in the lobby. When he asked to speak with one of the financial advisors, the receptionist rang the broker on call that day. Fortunately, I was filling that role.

Nicholai Alexander was a strikingly handsome man who appeared to be in his mid- to late sixties. He was dressed casually in the kind of clothes I'd come to think of as the wealthy retiree's uniform: tailored yet roomy trousers, a short-sleeved linen shirt, and a gold chain thick enough to be masculine without being overbearing.

He also carried himself in a way that made me think he was used to the finest things in life. He took in my office with a smooth turn of his head then measured me with the same smooth look. He settled his approving eyes on mine and smiled graciously. When we shook hands, his grip was much stronger than I would have expected at his age. I liked him right away.

"Young man." As he spoke, his long fingers tucked under a smile that seemed amused. "I have come to the bitter conclusion that I have outlived all my friends and all my money. The only real asset I have is my house. I need your expertise to make sure I'll be comfortable in my old age."

You're already in your old age, I thought.

As he explained a little about himself and his financial goals, his amazing life's story unfurled. Nicholai was known by his friends as Nick Alexander, which was his stage name. He was a pianist and had spent his entire career entertaining in hotels and clubs, and on cruise lines. At ninety-eight...*ninety-eight!*...he still worked two nights a week at one of Palm Springs' exclusive restaurants.

He knew exactly what he wanted in terms of his lifestyle but hadn't the first clue how to manage his finances to meet those goals. I gathered as much information as I could, told him what additional paperwork I would need, and set a follow-up appointment.

For the next week, Nicholai stopped by the office every day. As we worked on solutions to his financial concerns, he told me a bit more about his life and loves. When he discovered I was still relatively new to Palm Springs and that my job had kept me too busy to make friends, he invited me to a dinner party at his home.

I was so thrilled at this new friendship I actually used a different belt with the pre-matched casual outfit I selected for the occasion. I was stepping out in style...a new style for the new Greg.

* * *

Nick's house had been built in the early 1960s when the Palm Springs Modern style of architecture had been the in thing. At that time, architects like Alexander had fueled the construction of a number of private residences in the desert. Nick's single-story house sported a roofline that was low and flat, on par with the surrounding dunes, a minimalist style with straight lines and angles.

The interior was similarly clean. The small dinning room overlooked a large pool and patio where Nick entertained during the cool evenings in spring and fall. The table sat six people and he liked every chair to be taken. Since he cooked five nights a week, a gaggle of guests rotated through his house. As suddenly as I'd been invited, I became a regular.

In addition to sampling local delicacies—cactus pear compote or braised dove with mesquite honey, for example—I met an endless stream of fascinating people. Some lived in the region; others had flown in for business or vacations and appeared for only a few nights. On the wall behind the bar hung photos signed by Hollywood's elite. Every headshot was the beaming face of someone Nick had met and charmed with his warm manner.

"At first," he explained, "any picture ended up on my Wall of Stars. Eventually I ran out of room. I had to apply some criteria to help me decide which ones to hang. What you see there are only a few of my admirers." He waved his buffed nails at the sideboard to indicate a hidden trove of additional photos.

"I decided that only people who've visited me in my home would have their pictures hung. But I ran out of wall space again. Now the person must have eaten at my table at least a dozen times."

I ogled the photos. Gene Kelly and his brother Fred Kelly, Ginger Rogers, Faye Dunaway, Elke Sommer, Lucille Ball, Eva, Magda and Zsa Zsa Gabor, Greta Garbo, Fred Astaire, June Allyson and a variety of lesser-known celebrities smiled back.

He wasn't kidding when he'd said he'd outlived his friends.

Everyone I met at Nick's table represented younger generations. Maybe surrounding himself with a younger crowd generated his boundless energy. Not only did he look like he was in his mid- to late sixties, he acted forty years younger than that. He was always gadflying about, he downed several martinis every day, and he smoked constantly.

Much of his free time was spent relaxing poolside. His body was tan and firm, and the skimpy Speedo he favored perfectly fit his personality. He seemed timeless, as if he would live forever. His main goal in life was to have fun, to seek and find joy each day. He was eternally happy and did his best to spread that happiness to others.

I'd never met anyone quite like Nick. He became like a grandfather, a very eccentric grandfather. Despite his endlessly long list of regular and occasional dinner guests, though, Nick was lonely. He had many acquaintances but few real friends. We began hanging out by the pool more often talking about everything from music to marriage.

Over time, Nick's secret began to show. During the few hours it took to host a dinner party and with everyone chatting, he was able to hide the problems caused by his advancing age. During my visits, I saw the reality. He napped often. He'd learned not to trust his memory and had developed a sophisticated system of notes to stay on top of daily life.

Soon I was recruited to help maintain the public persona. I took care of most of his grocery shopping and other errands. Eventually I began stopping by every day after work to check on him. My weekends were dedicated to helping him plan out the week's dinners and setting up deliveries so the ingredients would arrive fresh the day they were needed.

I became the grandson he'd never had. He became my surrogate family. During our time together, I almost felt human.

* * *

Although Nick's finances were in their twilight years, his network of friends had impressive portfolios…all of which needed tending. When Nick injected me into his social life, he'd also shot me directly into the core wealth base of Palm Springs. My client list expanded to include those elite who regularly flew in and out of the area that was their high-priced playground.

There seemed to be no limit to the financial rewards. I upgraded my car to a BMW 535xi, I built my own portfolio of stocks, and continued saving for a house. I had more than enough money for the down payment but was too busy to actually go looking. I was also beginning to think about designing my own home. It would be a stretch financially but well worth the effort.

On the weekends when Nick felt well enough, he loved to visit the galleries and high-end auction houses downtown. During one visit, I snapped up a trio of Salvador Dali woodcuts. Since the artist had inked them himself, each print made from the same woodcut was slightly different. They were classified as originals yet not so expensive I couldn't afford the set.

Nick detested them. The scenes were from Dante's *Divine Comedy.*

Even the angel looked forbidding. Between the subject matter and Dali's unique interpretation, they certainly weren't for everyone.

"They're grotesque," he muttered when I bid on them. After I won, he snorted, "They're *ugly*. Why do you want something *ugly* in your home?"

I laughed at him. During the bidding, I'd been caught up in the idea that I could actually own something by an artist whose works I'd always enjoyed. But when I hung them on my wall, I suddenly knew the real reason I'd been compelled to buy them. They perfectly represented my life: surreal torment followed by a strangely beautiful redemption.

The angel, haunting though she was, represented both aspects of love. She was the woman I hadn't been able to keep. She also represented hope for the future, for the new woman I might one day meet. Perhaps the scorching desert summer would crack the icy numbness that had frozen my insides for so long.

* * *

Ilana Harding burst into my office and my life one sunny afternoon. She swept in amid a flurry of designer labels—Ferragamo shoes, Prada bag, Dolce & Gabbana sunglasses—and arranged herself in the visitor's chair in front of my desk. She was tall and slim with a bust proportioned to her figure. Her blonde hair brightened her brown eyes and delicate features. She was a knockout, and all of it natural.

Out of the Prada bag poured voluminous quantities of paper. First came a file folder strapped together with tape and a pile of receipts curling under a rubber band. Binder clips strained to contain stacks relating to numerous houses, a half-dozen bank accounts, and a variety of investments. Every new delivery that hit my blotter blew the scent of high-end perfume toward me. It was intoxicating, sweet yet spicy with a hint of earthy vetiver.

Then she began to speak. Her soft, delicate voice was almost too quiet to hear over the office noises that trickled in through the door she'd left open. I had to lean toward her and really concentrate on every word. Even then I caught only half of what she said. I carefully watched her mouth shape each sound. Her lips were mesmerizing. Even though I was looking straight at them, I hadn't realized they'd stopped moving until she touched my hand.

"Are you all right?"

Her eyes searched my face. Instead of being soft like her voice, her gaze probed. She took in my expression, my clothes, the expanse of my shoulders. When she looked back at my face again, I knew she had already measured me. Judged me. I could only hope the verdict was favorable.

I took a deep breath. Fortunately my voice didn't betray exactly how addled she'd made me. "Let's have a look," I said.

Ilana had cash in the bank, a modest stock portfolio, ten income-producing properties, and a principal residence she owned outright. The mortgages on the income properties represented about twenty percent of the overall three million dollar value, and the rentals netted her fifteen thousand a month. She was interested in having her portfolio balanced so as not to be so reliant on real estate.

Nothing was filed, nothing was in order and nothing was organized. She spoke quickly, though, jumping from subject to subject. Obviously her mind was quick, razor-sharp, and always active. After a long consultation about her goals and needs, we set up another appointment. I needed time to sort through all the documentation and work up a plan for her.

As she walked back through the lobby, the security guard tipped his hat. Even the women in the bullpen shot glances her way, smoldering looks that said they never wanted to see anyone that gorgeous again. Ilana certainly had made a hell of a first impression. She'd taken over, leaving everyone forever changed in her wake. I was no exception.

* * *

Ilana and I spent several days assembling and organizing the relevant data for her investments. Each time she showed up in my office, now a daily occurrence, she produced more paperwork that had materialized since her last visit. I began to suspect that an entire room in her house was filled with random piles of documents that she doled out to me one Prada bagful at a time.

We went out to lunches and dinners while I evaluated her portfolio. Part of my duty as a financial planner was to get to know each client, their short-term and long term-goals, their risk tolerance, and any other information that would allow me to do a better job. There was nothing out of the ordinary in my meeting with Ilana outside the office.

Besides, I liked her. She was smart, successful, interesting, and a great deal of fun. There was something innocent and almost childlike about her whenever she handed over yet another stack of documents she'd found. The more we met, the more I was attracted to her combination of innocence and brilliance, charm and shrewdness. I thought it a shame that our relationship could only be professional. On the other hand, it was safe. I didn't believe I deserved someone so wonderful in my life, so the relationship had to remain professional.

We got to know each other surprisingly quickly. Ilana had been raised by her grandparents on their estate in Mexico. They had immigrated from Russia after some trouble she left unspoken. She did, however, let drop their last name: Romanovsky. Without actually saying anything, she made it clear she was a direct descendant of the royal Romanoffs.

An eccentric uncle controlled the sizeable family fortune. Again without saying so directly, she indicated that she'd parlayed a modest trust into her current holdings. She also mentioned, quite casually, that she was next in line to inherit the entire fortune. She certainly had the trappings of a wealthy past. The money and real estate came from somewhere.

Once my report and recommendations were complete, we arranged for her to come to the office to review my suggestions. The strategy I'd formulated would allow her to never have to work other than attending to her investments for one week a month. She could enjoy a very comfortable lifestyle and still look forward to a nice retirement.

Ilana listened attentively and read along as I went through the report. She asked very astute questions and seemed happy with the recommendations. As she nodded, making her blond wisps gently brush her cheeks, I realized I was going to miss her. The follow-up meetings my clients usually arranged every couple of months just wouldn't be enough. I wondered if there was some way I could do an end run around my professional ethics and ask her out. That is, if I could summon the courage to ask the question. Then that soft voice of hers wiped away my worries.

"Greg," she said, "I've been thinking it over. I really appreciate what you've done and agree with everything you're recommending. There's just one little thing I'd like you to consider."

She shifted in her seat. Her legs scissored, uncrossing one way to cross again the other. When she stopped moving, I had a long view of her thigh.

It took a lot to stop looking at the hemline of her skirt and go back to looking at her lips.

"I have enough equity in the properties to leverage," she said. "I could buy more rentals and expand what I've already got going on. Taking care of that many properties will take a lot of time and skills I just don't have. I can buy and sell houses all day long and make good money but I can't do the day-to-day stuff to run a proper business."

I nodded and thought of the stacks of paper. She probably had more towers at home that hadn't been touched in years.

"Together," she said, "we could build a really successful real estate empire. I'd like you to consider quitting your job and coming on with me full-time."

It was like Ilana had a direct line tapped into my brain. Despite my raging financial success, I'd become very unhappy working as a broker. Regardless of how many solutions I created for my clients, selling was still a major part of the job. I hated the hustle and the pressure I was expected to put on every person who walked into my office.

Part of the reason I'd put off buying or designing a house was because I'd wanted a place big enough to set up my own business. My background was strong enough that I could consult with large firms on how to improve their operations. I would offer real solutions to immediate problems without having to sell a single thing.

And here this beautiful angel was singing the exact lyrics that I wanted to hear. Managing real estate would actually be a lot less stressful than consulting. Since I'd also get to spend lots of time with Ilana, it seemed like the perfect solution. Then in chimed my inner voice: *Why would this woman want anything to do with someone like you? Do you really think you're worthy?* Although I didn't believe in myself, Ilana seemed to believe in me. I ignored the voice in my head, and decided to listen to Ilana's instead.

When I went home that night, I didn't notice that the Dali prints were a little crooked. I thought my very own angel had descended to earth.

CHAPTER FOUR

Like most partnerships, my connection with Ilana started out well. We were already good friends and we had a common goal: getting her business on solid footing. When I offered to ease the burden by putting off drawing a salary for a while, Ilana immediately offered me a room in her home in return. Within three months I'd quit my job, let my apartment go, and moved into Ilana's house.

By pooling resources, we'd keep the overhead down. I also suspected Ilana shared some of my feeling on a personal level, and moving in with her gave me a better opportunity to explore that side. Meanwhile, her real estate investments and my savings provided us with a comfortable lifestyle. A few carefully selected second mortgages and a new line of credit fast-tracked our plans for expansion. Life was looking pretty darned good. I just prayed that I wouldn't screw it up.

Even the house was several steps up from my apartment. The single-story Mediterranean home was perched on a ridge with a view of the San Jacinto Mountain. I could sit on the patio and watch the tram shimmy up the mountain. When the sun blazed off the side of the tram, the mountainside looked like it was winking.

The home's interior had an airy, cool feel with tiled floors and arched doorways. Ilana had furnished the entire place with an eclectic collection of items from the professionally-designed homes on her roster of properties. Although the pieces might have fit well in their original habitats and with their original mates, Ilana had ended up with a mishmash that left me feeling confused and uneasy.

My first task, then, was to straighten out the mess as best I could. For the first two weeks, I shoved furniture around every evening. Since Nick was needing a lot more help by this time, I spent my afternoons at his house cooking those famous dinners according to his directions. We never mentioned anything to his guests; it was still important to him to maintain that persona of boundless vitality. It felt so good to be needed.

After dinner, I'd return home and shuffle chairs, bookcases and rugs late into the night. Since the styles were so different, I could only arrange the rooms by color and texture. Even after mixing my own furniture with hers, there simply weren't enough items in any given theme to create a single coordinated room. My bedroom ended up being the only space that didn't feel like it was in a perpetual state of chaos. The Dali angel looked down reproachfully on the chaotic living room.

Meanwhile, we were interviewing contractors to help with the properties. Before we could put the rentals on the market, many needed drastic repairs. Once they were available, the units would need maintenance and ongoing repair as things wore out. They'd also have to be refreshed with new paint and carpet between tenants.

Ilana's idea had been to buy up blocks of condos and duplexes in Ontario for corporate rentals. She'd targeted units that weren't necessarily in the best shape but were close to the newly-renovated business-friendly Ontario International Airport. Renovating them herself would not only generate a faster return, it would allow her to stamp the properties with her own personal style. Marketing a branded product would go over much better with the high-end clients who were our target.

The houses she owned were a mixed bag. Some were well-maintained residences she had bought knowing the market would eventually go up; others were past glories that needed a lot of rehab to bring them back to life. Once they did, though, the profits would be enormous.

Unfortunately, Ilana was more sizzle than steak. Her real estate acumen meant she'd been able to select properties with real potential, no question there. She just didn't understand how to strip away the decay and build true quality on what remained. The ideas she had would replicate the look inside her house: quality pieces jumbled together like orphans waiting for the next train anywhere but there.

I bought some design software to help her visualize the changes I proposed for each unit. Every morning we sat over fabric swatches, paint chips and tile samples. A flair for design can't be taught but I could tone down her flashiness. Matching that with a foundation of classic elements created a look that could be sold as part of the overall package.

After hours of explaining how textures could coordinate or contrast and how color should be tied to the way a space would be used, I collapsed into bed each evening exhausted. Since Ilana often ordered out, even the lunch hour was a flurry of deliveries, six different dishes from wildly different restaurants. She'd pick at the food but rarely eat, instead feeding me more paperwork she'd unearthed.

I began to suspect she had a whole storage facility filled with mounds of contracts. No matter how much she handed over to me, the towers in her office never seemed to shrink. Even when I was running on only a few hours of sleep, I tried to keep that dopey smile off my face. She was as charming as the first day we'd met. No matter how ragged I felt, I really was performing a labor of love.

* * *

"Ilana," I said, "you have to stay. The contractors are going to be here soon."

"Oh, Greg," she said as she shuffled through the voluminous folds of her latest Prada pick, "you're so much better with those people than I am. You talk to them. They're your friends."

"You need to be involved in this. We're going to be working with these companies for a long time. You have to put in a showing, at least."

She glanced at her watch. It was so tiny I wasn't sure she ever really read the time from it but the ring of diamonds around the face looked great. "Ten minutes," she said. "Is that enough?"

I nodded. She settled into a chair with her bag piled on her lap and sighed.

Fortunately the contractors arrived a little early. I had met the two partners years earlier in San Diego. Cathryn, who got out of the first vehicle, was in her late thirties with hair a touch too dark to call sandy cut straight across at the shoulder. I went to the door as Jackson got out of the van parked behind her car.

"We've got a little situation at another job site," Cathryn said as I waved the pair inside. "If you don't mind, Jackson needs to leave soon to take care of that. I'm available for as long as you need."

"That's fine." Ilana stood and shouldered her bag. "I've got to be going myself. Greg will take care of everything. I trust him completely."

Then she leaned over and kissed me. It was only a quick buss on the cheek but I immediately flushed. That dopey smile glommed onto my mouth and my eyes did a googly dance. She was out the door before I could recover, leaving me to squirm like a love-struck adolescent under the stares of my two confused friends. Cathryn just looked at me, one eyebrow arched questioningly.

I moved everything into the office. In the time it took for us to settle in, I recovered enough composure to discuss business. Cathryn and Jackson owned a decorative concrete company that specialized in floors and custom-built countertops. Their company would be an important part of the trademark look Ilana and I had worked up for the properties. They operated primarily out of San Deigo but were flexible enough to accommodate other locations as our holdings grew.

We talked about business for the first half hour or so. When Jackson stood to leave, I realized why he was so quiet. His stride, his handshake, even the way he rose from the chair exuded confidence. Despite a little grey and the first few extra pounds of middle age, he seemed perfectly matched with Cathryn's brusque strength.

As he left for their active jobsite, Cathryn apologized again. "We certainly don't want you to feel like you're not getting our full attention," she said.

"Not at all," I said. "In fact, it's reassuring to know you're so responsive to your clients. It's the mark of professionals. Sometimes that's not so easy to come by with contractors."

After wrapping up the remaining details, a knock came at the front door. Ilana had apparently called in the lunch order that morning but forgotten she wouldn't be there to eat it.

"Cathryn, there's too much food for me to eat myself," I said. "Will you join me?"

"Sure," she said. "Nothing seals a deal like a meal!"

"Great," I replied. "Even though I've known you guys for years, I've never seen you in action business-wise before. It'll take some getting used to seeing you as my contractor!"

I couldn't help but laugh. As we picked through the mishmash of food—barbeque chicken, lentil patties and a giant Caesar salad—talk of business turned to more casual topics. Cathryn and Jackson had immigrated from Canada some years before. Their business had much more potential in the American market and, she said, they could build their own version of the American dream. I hadn't seen them for a while, so we had a lot of catching up to do.

She was amazingly down to earth. The calm, logical approach she applied to the business sprang from a personal outlook that was eternally optimistic and unendingly pleasant. Her penchant for word play popped up more often as the conversation continued, each as joyful and surprising as candy pulled from a Halloween goody bag.

Several hours later, Cathryn finally left. We'd discussed everything under the sun and reconnected easily, as old friends who hadn't seen each other in a long while. She and Jackson were solid, normal people, and I knew the kinship between us would only deepen.

As I held the door for her, I said, "It's great to see you again. It really has been too long."

She cocked her head and smiled. "You know, I feel the same way. Even if we don't work together all that much, I have the strange feeling we're going to be doing a lot more than business with you two. I'll have to get Jack together with you soon."

"You introduced him to Ilana as Jackson. I thought he preferred Jack?"

"Jackson's for business," she said. "You can still call him Jack."

As she drove away, I realized that for the first time in months, I felt calm and peaceful. Even Ilana's furniture couldn't shake my mood.

* * *

"Did you hire those people?" Ilana asked as she bustled back into the house.

"Yes, they'll be great. I gave them a very comprehensive view of what we're after, and they're sure they can provide exactly what we want."

"Do you think it's a good idea to hire friends?" Ilana asked.

"No problem. They're very professional." I replied. "Why are you so late? I just got home from Nick's myself."

"Client wanted to close the contract today." She piled her bag, her briefcase and a fresh stack of files on the chair in the dining room. "I've got to catch up on some things in the office but why don't you come to my room first?"

"Huh?" I'd never been in her bedroom except to rearrange the furniture. I wasn't quite sure what she was proposing.

She turned to me and took my hand. "Come on," she said. "Don't you think it's about time?"

"Uh…."

I trailed behind her, still unsure exactly what was going on. My heart trip-hammered with hope and the rest of my body was well along its own set of preparations but part of my brain was hitting the brakes. If she wasn't propositioning me, I could blow everything…the business, my chances with her, my life.

Before we even reached the bed she turned on me again. Her hand squeezed my crotch so hard I nearly squealed. But it was a good sort of pain. Soon we were naked and panting on the floor. She stayed on top, pounding and grinding and scratching us both to a furious, fast, frantic climax.

"Shit," I gasped when it was done. She was still sitting on me. Her weight felt good against my belly.

"Greg," she said, "I want to hire my brothers." *Where was this coming from? Why did she want to talk about this NOW, of all times?*

"What?"

Jesus, I thought. *Can't an educated guy like me think of something better to say?*

"Well," she said, "we're going to need laborers to do a lot of the demolition. My brothers can do that. And they have experience in electrical work and plumbing."

"What kind of experience? Are they bonded?"

"No." She rolled off and headed for the bathroom. "But they're family. They'll do a good job and we won't have to pay them much."

"I don't know. I'd have to know their backgrounds."

"OK. They're coming over so you can ask them whatever you like."

"When are they coming over?"

"I don't know. Soon."

Just then there was a knock on the door. More like a thumping, actually. It was so forceful the windows rattled.

"That's them!" Ilana called as she stepped into the shower. "Just let them in. I'll be out in a minute!"

I snatched up my shirt but couldn't find my underwear. I was still soaked with sweat and my arm snagged in the sleeve of my shirt. Then a tapping came at the window. When I looked up, a very tall man was leering through the glass. He waved snarkily as I dove behind the bed to pull on my pants.

When I finally made it to the door, wiping carpet fuzz from my face, I did a double take. The man had cloned himself. Ilana hadn't told me her brothers were twins. Plus, both of them looked so much like Kenny, the world stretched out like putty. I grabbed the doorframe and tried not to fall into the outer circle of hell.

They didn't wait for an invitation. They pushed past me, calling at the tops of their voices for Ilana. As I stared, I noticed subtle differences. One was a little heavier. Both had green eyes and mouse-brown hair but one had a Buckwheat-style cowlick at his crown. They were about my height, a good six feet, and their faces were lightly freckled. The overall impression was disconcertingly that of children deformed by some malfunction in their growth hormones, like giant, innocent-looking trolls.

The heavier one, I learned, was Kevin. The skinnier guy was Jeff. He handed me a gym bag that I nearly dropped when it squirmed. Inside were two teacup Chihuahuas. One wet itself when I looked at her; the other barked furiously and bit my thumb.

"Ilana's always wanted dogs," Jeff said. "Now she has three playthings."

His leer returned. I realized that my hair was pasted to my scalp and I reeked of sex. I also hadn't been able to locate my underwear and my trousers stuck to uncomfortable places. I hated not having underwear.

"Hey, just ribbin' ya," he said.

He knocked me so hard with his elbow I would have a bruise. I stood there holding my side with my cheeks blazing at every chuckle that passed between the twins. Then Jeff marched down the hall and threw open the door to my bedroom. By the time I raced in there, he'd already pulled the futon to the floor and shoved the platform away from the headboard.

"What the hell are you doing?" I tried to keep the edge of hysteria out of my voice but my world was wrinkling faster than an Armani in August.

"Ilana said to move your stuff into her bedroom. She said you like to do this design thing so all you're going to do is direct traffic."

I was thoroughly confused. And pleasantly surprised. I think. This whole romance thing was great, I'd been working toward it for all of two months, taking baby steps, and now it was moving like a firestorm. That voice in the back of my mind said, *"Slow down..take it easy"* but I shushed it emphatically. I wasn't about to turn down a woman like Ilana. I still couldn't believe that she was interested in me. If she only knew what was buried in the dark places of my mind and soul.....

The twins hoisted the bed up on end and maneuvered it through the door. Leaving that in the hallway, they returned and split up. Jeff peered behind the headboard, trying to figure out how it was attached to the wall, while Kevin unplugged my bedside lamp and muscled the entire nightstand, still loaded with my things, past me.

As Jeff produced a menacingly large screwdriver from his pocket, I realized that if I didn't jump in, my things would be trashed. For the next hour I ran between rooms, frantically trying to integrate her bedroom furniture with mine, reshuffle the layout, plan the lighting and guess at how Ilana might like to use the different spaces.

The twins took orders surprisingly well. Jeff ran his mouth the entire time, cracking jokes and cooking up strange, schoolboy pranks to embarrass me. He riffled though my underwear drawer when I wasn't looking; the next time he took a break, he made a show of wiping his brow with a pair of my hand-woven, Egyptian cotton briefs. I lunged for them but realized no amount of dry cleaning would ever make them pure. They ended up in the garbage can.

Kevin, meanwhile, stayed quiet. I got the distinct feeling that if his brother hadn't been taking my directions, Kevin would have ignored me. Nothing personal, really, but he followed his brother's lead so completely, it was weird. If they hadn't been brothers, I would have thought he was obsessed with Jeff.

Somehow Ilana managed to stay ensconced in the bathroom the entire time. When she finally swept back into the room, the new digs were complete. The extra furniture had been shoved into my old bedroom and would be somewhat functional as a guest room. I'd done the best I could but the mismatched chaos that permeated the rest of the house had taken over my new bedroom.

"So," Ilana said without more than a glance at the layout, "how'd my brothers work out? We can hire them, right?"

"Come on, buddy." Jeff poked me again, this time hard enough to make my rib ache. "No bullshit. Tell us we got the job."

What the hell was I supposed to say?

CHAPTER FIVE

The next few weeks were a dizzying kaleidoscope of sex, day trips to Ontario to start renovations on seven rentals, sex in the vacant units and any semi-remote rest stop, bleary hours spent scrabbling through a few stacks of paperwork, and still more sex. I began to feel like a service stud. Which was not a bad thing at all.

The twins hauled away most of the spare furniture from the different properties and our house. I assumed Ilana would put it in storage so she could stage her homes when they were ready to sell or rent. But the twins returned with a wad of cash that was far less than the pieces were worth.

"What's going on?" I asked.

"Oh, I sold all that extra stuff," Ilana said. "You always said it was in the way."

"Why didn't you put it in storage? If we hire a professional staging company, it'll cost more than the storage fees."

"It was too much hassle. We can afford it."

"Actually, we should watch the spending in the startup stage. We've got a lot of things to do before any of these properties will generate income."

"But this way we'll have more time." She sidled up to me and pouted her wet, wet lips. "I'd much rather spend time with you than moving furniture."

"We could have your brothers do that." My words came out heavy. She was working her hands down my pants while her teeth nibbled along my collarbone. "That's what we…uh…."

I gladly forgot what I was saying. The subject never came up again. I had fallen completely under her spell. Ilana could do no wrong, and my sense of reason was far overshadowed by the thrill of a relationship with Ilana. I just hoped I could keep up, and that she wouldn't wake up one morning realizing how flawed I was, and how undeserving of her respect and affection I believed myself to be.

* * *

One Friday we left Palm Springs heading east. Ilana had booked an entire weekend in Sedona. We really needed the break, and it was a sweet gesture. I was a little nervous the first night when she told me she'd given the twins keys to the house. But she felt safer knowing someone was home so I let it go.

We returned to find Jeff in a new Ford F-150. The paint looked a little rippled, clearly an aftermarket job. I don't know why anyone would shoot their own paint job but he claimed the dealer hadn't had the color he'd wanted. He'd gotten an extra thousand bucks off the price because he'd bitched and moaned about it for so long. I could imagine the salesman wanting to get both the truck and Jeff off his lot so a thousand dollar discount probably seemed like a bargain.

A bargain for them, anyway. When I pulled into the garage, I realized where they'd shot the new coat over the weekend. Overspray ran up the walls and the floor was still sticky with layers of primer and topcoat. When I noticed that several different colors were hidden under the screaming red he'd shot on the truck, I assumed they'd painted Kevin's car first.

They must have done some mechanical work too. Bolts and little door panel clips lay everywhere. I tried not to step on them but ended with a few embedded in my Italian leather soles anyway. A slick of oil and chartreuse-colored anti-freeze pooled at the rear of the garage near the door to the house. Stepping around it with our luggage wasn't the easiest thing but I managed.

I was furious. I understood that the twins lived in a crappy apartment with no garage but the least they could have done was clean up their mess. Ilana shrugged it off and headed straight for the office. She seemed distracted and didn't really care. She said she'd have someone in to scrub everything down.

Although I was still pretty pissed, it was her house. When I realized she was more interested in getting back to work after our break, I felt guilty. I was supposed to be the one with the better head for business and there she was putting me to shame.

When I checked the phone messages, I discovered I'd have to do a little damage control with the neighbors. A few had called to complain about all the friends Jeff and Kevin had invited over. Apparently they'd all taken advantage of the garage, and the front yard had looked like a swap meet all weekend.

I made a mental note to take a selection of gourmet coffees to everyone within eyeshot of the house. That way, even if an individual hadn't called, they'd still be placated. I unpacked quickly and joined Ilana amid the mountains of files. When she piled another sheaf of papers atop a stack I'd been chipping away, I sighed.

"Love you, Greg," she sang.

"I love you too, Ilana."

* * *

Meanwhile, I was still checking on Nick every morning. I had dropped out of many of his dinner parties but I'd hired a sous chef from a local restaurant to take over the cooking. One day I noticed that Nick's legs and feet were terribly swollen. He said they weren't painful, and didn't seem too concerned, so neither was I.

Later that evening I received a call. Nick was in so much pain he'd left his job playing piano at the restaurant that night. Ilana and I rushed to his house to find him lying on his bed moaning. Although he complained about his legs, other symptoms pointed to something more serious.

He had the urge to urinate but every time he tried, the flow wouldn't start. His doctor recommended we go to an after-hours clinic. Something was pinching off the urethra and his bladder needed to be drained. Nick was, of course, very alarmed but his primary physician would figure out what was wrong the next day.

The clinic doctors administered some medication to calm him down and inserted a catheter. Nick didn't make things easy. He refused to acknowledge the catheter. Even with the catheter in, the sensation of needing to urinate remained and he asked repeatedly to use the bathroom.

We headed home, knowing it would be easier to care for him at our house. Nick was thrilled. He enjoyed all the attention but I got the feeling he didn't really understand what was happening. At first I wrote it off to the medication he'd received at the clinic. Soon, though, it was clear that he really didn't know what was happening.

In a few short hours Nick had gone from an energetic, alert man to a feeble old codger who was losing his lucidity. We settled him in the guest bedroom where he'd have a straight shot at the spare restroom for other needs.

"I have to urinate!" he insisted. "Why won't you help me up?"

He just couldn't grasp the idea that the catheter would take care of that. After much soothing from both Ilana and myself, Nick finally fell asleep. We quietly retreated to the living room to reshuffle the next day's schedule so we could get him to his doctor's appointment. When we went to bed, I left the door open so I could hear if he called for help in the night.

A few hours later I awoke to a shuffling sound. I jumped out of bed and spotted Nick heading for the bathroom. The bag attached to his catheter was caught on the doorknob of the guest bedroom. He was shuffling so quickly the door was swinging shut.

"Nick, stop!" I yelledd.

It was too late. The door slammed, the tube pulled tight, and Nick fell face-first onto the tile floor.

Luckily he was only slightly bruised but the catheter was draining traces of blood. I made a panicked call to the clinic and was told to bring him back. By this time the medication had worn off and he refused to leave the house.

"I can't be seen in public," he sniffed, "with this bag hanging on the side of my body."

Okay, Greg, I thought, *work fast.*

On the way to the clinic, we stopped at his house. Ilana found his best pajamas and a silk robe while I dug a small leather bag with a shoulder strap out of his closet. The catheter bag went inside the leather bag then was hung over his shoulder. He took one look in the mirror and smiled. Dapper and stylish, with the bag well hidden, he was ready to go anywhere.

The doctors settled Nick down with another round of medication and pulled out the catheter. Blood gushed everywhere. Eventually they stabilized him and inserted a new catheter but not until his pajamas and silk robe were covered in blood.

While the staff cleaned Nick up, I headed to the bathroom with his clothes. I soaked and rinsed, soaked and rinsed until all traces of blood were gone. Then I went outside. By now the sun had come up and the temperature was rapidly climbing into the triple digits. I ran around the building with his pajamas and robe held over my head like a superhero too stupid to figure out how to put on his cape until his clothes were dry.

We got Nick dressed again and put him in the car. He couldn't be left alone for a minute. If I'd paid more attention, if I'd focused a little less on the business and the crazy sex, maybe this wouldn't have happened. Nick had no family and no close friends besides me and Ilana. He was totally alone. He needed me. And really, that was a very nice thing for me to feel.

We made it through to his appointment without another incident. His physician scheduled a round of grueling tests and within a week we had an answer. Nick was suffering from congestive heart failure. His heart was operating at about ten percent of its normal capacity, barely enough to keep him alive. In addition, his prostate had enlarged and was pushing against his urethra.

I took Nick straight from the physician's office to the cardio wing of the local hospital. Medications to increase the efficiency of his heart and to reduce the prostate were administered. He responded well enough that his nurse worked up a discharge plan. Nick would have to learn to live within the constraints of his condition. He couldn't have five dinner parties a week but he could return home and enjoy what time he had left.

The day before he was scheduled to be released, his body stopped responding to the treatment. He was so weak he could hardly hold his head up. Just eating a bowl of soup took more effort than he had left. After a few days, he was transferred to a rehabilitation hospital a few blocks from his home. There he would be nursed back to health.

The second Nick saw his new environment, he went nuts. He sat me down and asked point-blank if he was dying. I couldn't lie.

"Yes," I said, "but we're working really hard to get you home where you can be more comfortable."

He relaxed and settled back into his pillow. "Thank you for being honest with me," he said. "I'm ninety-eight years old. I've had a good life. Just promise me one thing."

"Anything."

"Don't let me die alone in a strange place. Take me home. Please."

"I'm already working on it, Nick. I'll talk with your doctor. OK?"

"Thank you. Now, if you don't mind, I think I'll sleep for a while."

He closed his eyes and immediately fell into a deep sleep.

* * *

Nick granted me power of attorney for medical decisions, which included his burial. He also asked Ilana to take over his finances. Although I had a better background for that task, I refused to be involved in anything dealing with his assets. I was too close and didn't want anyone to get the impression I was after his money. Although he had no liquid assets, his house was worth about half a million dollars.

Ilana agreed to keep everything in order by paying his bills and staying on top of the few obligations he had. The power of attorney gave her considerable leeway. I wasn't at all surprised; the first time they'd met, they'd acted as if they'd known each other all of their lives. I was pleased that the two most important people in my life got along so well.

I was also pleasantly surprised when they began telling each other stories about their families back in New York. I hadn't even known Ilana had family in New York. It turns out they were connected through a variety of people. Ilana later explained that Nick knew her grandmother's brother. It was natural that he'd trust her so completely.

As far as I was concerned, her taking on his financial matters was a blessing. I had my hands full with visits to the hospital, meetings with his doctors, and constant decisions about his medical care. I did what I could on the business side for our real estate but Ilana juggled much of that so I could focus on Nick.

For three weeks he was in and out of consciousness. Each time he woke up I was right there. We talked about whatever came to his mind until he fell back asleep. Fortunately the room he was in was semi-private. I paid the hospital to keep the second bed free so I always had a place to sleep.

During our talks, Nick gave me a special gift. The wisdom he'd acquired during almost a century was passed along through stories, anecdotes, and little jokes.

"In the end," he said, "it doesn't matter what kind of car a person drives or the house they live in or the job they have or the clothes they wear. What matters is only this: did you love, and were you loved?"

Tears came to my eyes. He fiddled with the oxygen tube now and then, irritated by the feel of it in his nose. I took his hand sometimes, patting it gently until he fell asleep.

I was going to miss him.

* * *

Cathryn called me from the first job site in Ontario. "You'd better come out here," she said. "You need to look at the rental units."

"I can't," I said. "What's wrong?"

"Ilana's brothers haven't been working. At least, not very hard. Jackson and I are ready to install the countertops but the kitchens aren't ready. They demoed the place but there's still mounds of garbage everywhere."

"Just do what you can," I said. "I'll take care of it later."

"You don't seem to understand," Cathryn said. "There are no counters on which to install countertops."

"What?" I stopped shuffling papers and focused my full attention on her voice.

"Jeff and Kevin demoed everything but haven't installed the new cabinetry. I don't even see any plumbing left where the sink is supposed to go. You'd better get down here and look for yourself."

Minutes later I was on the highway. The drive took over an hour one way, and that was only if I sped fast enough to lose my license if I were caught. I didn't care; I needed one thing to go right and this was definitely going wrong. I spent the entire time rehearsing the ass-chewing I'd give the twins once I found them.

Jackson stood back while Cathryn took me on a walkthrough. She was right; debris was everywhere, construction materials were piled in the corners, but not a single project had actually started. When I discovered that a structural wall had been torn out of one unit instead of the wall I'd told them to demo, my chest tightened.

"You know," Cathryn said as I leaned against the only doorframe that had survived, "Jackson and I had a bad feeling about those two. We ran a background check. You know Jeff's got a criminal record, don't you?"

I tried to say *What?* but even that wouldn't come out. Instead there was only a puff of air and something that might have been a moan.

"Yeah," Cathryn continued, "it seems like every year or so Jeff takes a little vacation at the county lockup. Nothing big, mind you, but enough."

Why wasn't I surprised? I kept breathing, or hyperventilating, while the news sank in.

"You might want to be careful around those two," she said. "We think they might be ripping you off. Maybe that's why the projects aren't done. Are you sure they haven't taken your money and spent it themselves?"

I shook my head. That, at least, wasn't possible. "I paid the suppliers directly," I said. "Jeff and Kevin were just supposed to pick the stuff up and install it. Straight labor."

"Well, maybe they've picked it up and sold it for cash."

I thought about the furniture Ilana had given the pair to sell and how quickly they'd returned…and that they'd come back with cash. Obviously they knew someone who could move stuff like that quickly. I had to find out right away whether any of the properties were going to get their cabinets and appliances.

As I started dialing the suppliers, Jackson said, "Tell him."

There was more?

"Greg." Cathryn had that look people got when they were going to tell you something for your own good, no matter how much you didn't want to hear it. "We aren't comfortable working with people like that. We'll still do the projects you've hired us to do, and we're more than happy to work with you in the future but we won't be alone in the units with those two."

"We don't know what else they might be involved with," Jackson said, "and we don't want to know."

"If you want them working on these properties while we're here," Cathryn continued, "you've got to be present."

"What?"

Well, at least that time I'd managed to actually speak.

"We know it's a long drive an all," she said, "but maybe you could rent a place here temporarily. We won't interfere in your family business but we need to protect our company's reputation, and ourselves."

I nodded. What the hell else was I supposed to do? My little voice chirped in with, *"Well, this is what you deserve, isn't it?. You knew things were going too well for it to last, and you stopped paying attention. It's your fault you know, and now Ilana will finally see you for the loser that you are."*

CHAPTER SIX

Then one day it all went horribly wrong.

After being up for days, frantically involved in whatever activity struck her fancy and absolutely uninterested in food, Ilana went to bed. She didn't bathe, she didn't talk, she didn't do anything except sleep and eat what was set in front of her. For six days she didn't get out of bed except to piss. She couldn't.

She smiled sweetly and told me it was a migraine or a heart condition or depression. After hearing a different story with each marginal awakening, I figured something was up, and it wasn't good. Cathryn and Jack's background check had turned up Jeff's arrest for concocting methamphetamine. Unlike smarter criminals, the twins apparently partook of the same drugs they sold so it wasn't a huge leap to guess what Ilana's issue might be.

The realization that I'd given up my job and my home to throw in my lot with a probable meth-head spurred me to action. On day seven, when Ilana began showing signs of long-term lucidity, I pulled a chair up to the end of the bed. When she next awoke, she was surprised to see me sitting there ramrod straight. My arms squeezed my chest to keep my voice on some even keel.

"Look," I said, "I'm not buying the migraine, heart or depression thing. It's drugs, like meth, right? And you get it from Jeff and Kevin."

"No!" She shook her pretty little head. Oily locks of hair fell around her face.

"Come on. You've stayed up endless nights filing paperwork yet not a

41

single pile has shrunk. You disappear for an hour to look at a new property and come back talking a mile a minute. You never eat then suddenly collapse into bed. You're telling me everything's normal?"

"No…not normal, Greg." She sat up and pushed her hair behind one ear. "I…I suffer from manic depressive disorder. I'm bipolar."

Her cheeks were flushed. It was the only time I'd ever seen her hesitate, the only chink in her armor of self-confidence and beauty and designer labels. Suddenly I felt guilty for believing she was a drug addict. Manic behavior followed by days of sleep certainly was a major indicator for bipolar disorder.

Besides, I occasionally "went under" myself. My up times weren't manic, of course, but I did work very hard to keep things rolling so that the down times didn't interfere too much with the overall schedule. Who was I to judge her harshly? Still, something didn't ring completely true.

"So you're bipolar," I said. "That doesn't mean you don't do drugs. So which is it, Ilana? Which problem lay you out in bed, physically exhausted, for the last six days?"

She nodded silently, staring at the floor, ashamed to meet my scowl. "It's both. I used to use but haven't for some time. Everything was going so well, you know? I'd met you, and we're putting together this business but then Nick got sick, and I can handle his bills but I'm also trying to do all the stuff you're supposed to be doing…well, I guess it just got too stressful."

She finally looked up. Tears had pooled in her eyes and slipped down as she continued talking.

"I just didn't want to disappoint you, you know? You're the best thing that's ever happened to me. We clicked right away, and the sex…." She gave a breathily laugh then began crying again. "A few weeks ago I fell off the wagon. I'm sorry."

"OK, here's how it is." I leaned back and braced my hands against my thighs. "You quit. Now. Or I quit. Now. Your call."

I wasn't in the mood for negotiations. Six days of contemplation and rehearsal was compressed into nine very meaningful one-syllable words. I wasn't so far into this situation that I couldn't resuscitate my old life. It would take a lot of hard work and I'd end up pretty much at zero sum financially but I could still leave.

"You're not kidding, are you?" she whispered.

"Nope." Another one-syllable word for her to consider.

Silence filled the void. Finally she spoke. Her voice was soft, quiet, almost hypnotic, just as it had been those first few meetings in my office. I listened just as carefully but without any lonely hormones to addle my thoughts.

"You know," she said, "when I left San Francisco a couple of years ago, I did it so I wouldn't die. My problem with meth had been around for a while. It's all tied up with my bipolar disease. I'd actually started using as a way to avoid the down cycles. They call it self-medicating."

She sighed and twisted the sheet absently. *Run!* my mind screamed. *Run fast, and run far.* I didn't need this in my life. I had my own issues to deal with.

"My doctor told me to quit or I'd die." She looked up at me, shooting those piercing, pointed, whale-harpoon eyes into my soul. "Maybe, with your help, I can quit this time. I really want to quit. I'm getting too old for this stupid kid stuff. I want my business to be successful, and it can't unless I'm on my game. But I'm scared to death to try this alone. And I just don't know what to do."

As Ilana continued talking and tears continued streaming down her face, I thought long and hard. During my career as a manager and administrator, I'd worked with, supervised and worked for a variety of people. The most remarkable had been the ones who'd recovered from addiction. They were survivors, and had developed a strength of character that comes only by battling through and triumphing over adversity.

I respected that. I always had. But I'd never known anyone who was actively suffering through that process of kicking their addiction. I had no idea what lay down the road for either Ilana or myself. I could stick it out or bail. Help her strive toward becoming one of those remarkable people or let her founder.

"Here are my ground rules." I interrupted her but she looked more relieved than upset. "And notice that I say 'my' ground rules...not yours or your brothers' or your doctor's. These are my rules. You'll play by them or I'm leaving the game. Got that?"

She sniffed delicately and nodded.

"No more drugs. Not for your use or for sale. If I find any, it's over. If the twins bring drugs into this house, I'll assume they're for you and it's over. And no substituting alcohol or prescription drugs for meth; addiction is addiction. Got that?"

"Thank you! Greg, I love you!"

Who was I trying to kid? Ilana loved me while I believed I was unlovable. It would take a lot more than a drug problem for me to let that love go and end the relationship. She loved me, and in my mind, that gave her a pass on most things I wouldn't tolerate in anyone else. I just needed to be loved that much.

She threw herself across the bed and draped dramatically across my shoulders. I held her gently, patting her back and rubbing her arms. She wept for a while then inched down to open my zipper with her mouth. It was the best kind of make-up sex: the kind where I got all the rewards.

As she disappeared into the shower, I moved the chair back into the dining room. Addiction forced its tentacles deep into a person, and I clearly understood the possibility that Ilana might waver back into occasional drug use. As long as she continued to improve overall, I'd stick it out. Arranging treatment for her bipolar disorder would be a big part of helping her stick with it.

In one sense, I breathed a huge sigh of relief. This diversion kept the focus away from my screw ups at the rental properties. It bought me time. Time when Ilana would still think I was worthy, even if just for a little longer. She might have a drug problem, but I was broken from the inside out. She was so busy with her problems, and if I could keep it that way, maybe she wouldn't notice how incompetent I could be.

Of course, it was easy to line up all the details into orderly steps and projected outcomes. Yet somewhere inside was a nagging feeling that I'd just made one of the biggest mistakes in my life. From her perch on the wall, the Dali angel frowned at me. I turned away and ducked into the office, unwilling to meet her gaze..

* * *

It took a lot of maneuvering but I finally got permission to take Nick home. A hospital bed, a shower chair, a bedside potty, and a slew of other equipment and supplies were ordered. Hospice counselors trained me on the few needs he had and how to make him comfortable. A home nurse began visiting him so he'd see familiar faces when the caregivers came to the house.

I was making good on my promise. He'd never been left alone. Even during Ilana's six days of slumber, I'd never left Nick's side for more than an hour at a time. When I had, the hospice nurse had always been there in case he woke up while I was gone. Half the time I called from my cell in case he was asking for me. No matter what, he wasn't going to die alone in a strange place.

A delivery truck was scheduled to stop at the house around noon. Ilana was in Ontario that day performing an open house on the first property we were presenting to the market. She had potential buyers coming to look at the house, so obviously couldn't be there while the hospice set up the equipment.

As I stood at the end of Nick's bed, putting off my departure until the last possible minute, he woke and sat straight up. "Take care of each other," he said. "You and Ilana… be good to each other."

I patted his hand. I was so relieved that he'd woken up. Now he would know why I was leaving and that I'd be right back.

"Nick," I said, "I'm going to the house for just a few minutes to get everything situated. When I come back, I'm taking you out of here. Ilana will be in later tonight and we'll have a nice dinner together. Will you be OK for a few minutes while I'm gone?"

"Of course. Go! Take care of what you need to. I'm anxious to get out of here." Dazzling me with that performer's smile, he settled back and promptly dozed off.

Ilana's house was only a few blocks away so the trip home took less than ten minutes. I was worried. I'd never cared for someone in Nick's condition, and was afraid I wasn't up to the challenge. As I obsessed over every detail—how would he react to my helping him use the bedside toilet? Would he insist on being in the tiny office with us when he got lonely? What if he became too sick to eat?—my mobile rang.

Nick was dead. He'd passed without a whisper, simply nodded off while I stood there and, moments later, completed his journey to the other side.

I was instantly angry. Why had I left? I'd promised he wouldn't die alone in a strange place. Why hadn't I waited just another minute? Why hadn't I hired someone to meet the delivery truck?

I rushed back to the hospital. The room looked so different. The monitors were all switched off and the oxygen tube lay on the pillow. The space was entirely still, suspended between the life that continued just outside the door and the weight of Nick's empty body.

I sat on the chair next to the bed, staring and not daring to touch him, for the longest time. Some time passed; it didn't matter how much. Finally I put my hand over his. The flesh was cool and still supple, the skin as paper-thin as ninety-some years of life had worn it.

The funeral home staff arrived. I couldn't stand to leave him alone again. I stood inside the doorway listening to the soft rustle of sheets, the murmured instructions from one mortician to another.

I spent the next several days making arrangements for a memorial service and burial. None of it seemed to stick in my head, and I finally printed up a to-do list just so I could remember which things I'd already done.

I was suspended between numbness and guilt. One would sink me into my own grave; the other would devour me every day I continued to live.

* * *

Given Ilana's history with Nick and the fact that he'd signed over power of attorney for financial affairs to her, it didn't seem odd when she came up with his will. What did surprise me was its contents. His house, his only real asset, was left to Ilana and I was named executor.

I'd never been the executor of an estate, so I hired an attorney and we filed the appropriate paperwork to have the will probated. Everything moved along smoothly until a judge heard the case. Just before he made his ruling, an attorney rushed into court.

"I'm sorry for being late, Your Honor," he said. "I was tied up with another court matter down the hall. I represent the Wilson family, Mr. Alexander's sister."

"And why are you here?" the judge asked. "Is the Wilson family contesting Mr. Alexander's will?"

"Yes, Your Honor. We have reason to believe the will presented by Mr. Marks is a forgery."

I couldn't believe it. Someone had just said my name and the word *forgery* in the same sentence in a court of law. This was my payback, the cosmic lightning bolt that would punish me for not fulfilling Nick's last wish. I immediately began hyperventilating and adjusted my tie. Hopefully I wouldn't have a panic attack right there.

Cindy Wilson was Nick's estranged sister. They hadn't spoken in over twenty years. How would she know what Nick's wishes had been? And what made her believe the will was a fake? My attorney and I had a lot of investigating to do…and it would all begin with Ilana.

I sat hard in my chair. Fortunately it happened to be right behind me; otherwise I would have simply buckled to the floor and wrinkled my Corneliani suit. With the thump of my ass hitting the hard wooden seat, a single moment of clarity broke through the confusion.

I had done my part. I had made a promise to Nick to take care of him. I was exhausted, upset, sad, and just beginning to realize the depth of my loss. The last thing I wanted was to be embroiled in a legal battle with a family I didn't know for a house I didn't want.

My attorney suggested I resign as executor and let the court settle the matter. Otherwise, it could cost me thousands of dollars in legal fees. Nick's possessions had never been important to me. Only he had mattered, and now he was gone. I wanted to sit with those good memories, to cry the tears he deserved to have shed, and to eventually move on.

I got up and walked out. Ms. Wilson could have everything, right down to the muck at the bottom of the pool.

CHAPTER SEVEN

As Ilana and I left the courthouse, I realized what a monumental gift Nick had given me. He'd been a surrogate family, a friend when I'd been alone, and a teacher who'd shown me how the tiniest things could hold vast meaning. His life had been one long lesson. Now his death would teach me something else: how to let go.

It all came back to Kenny. I'd hurt my family terribly by not attending the memorial service. They'd said their goodbyes...and they'd done it as a family. My absence had created a second hole in their lives. I'd let everyone down because I'd been too selfish to just go.

It would take me some time yet to stop looking for Kenny around every corner and I'd still do a double-take whenever I saw Ilana's brothers but mourning for Nick just might teach me how to mourn for Kenny. The sooner I dumped the extra baggage in my life and got on with that, the better.

But Ilana wanted to fight. She was angry that I'd removed myself as executor.

"Why are you so upset?" I asked as we drove home. "It's not like you visited him there as a child or anything. If his sister gets the house, so what?"

"I want that house in my portfolio." She tapped her flawless nails on the door panel. "Do you know how much I could get for that place?"

"Is this all about money?" I turned a corner a little too sharply. "Don't you have any respect for the friendship Nick gave us?"

"Of course it's not about the money, Greg. It's about the house, and

Nick, and his life." She lay that perfectly manicured hand on my chest. "I want to restore that house to its original beauty. Then I'll find the perfect buyer. Someone who'll appreciate the house, who'll host dinner parties there and make it a home. Like Nick did."

Tears burned in my eyes. I slowed to the speed limit as I took the last turn into our neighborhood. "You mean that."

"Of course I do."

She leaned over and purred in my ear. She felt so damn good I actually thought for a second about calling the attorney.

"Look," I sighed. "If the court rules the will is legitimate, you'll inherit the house. Otherwise, there isn't much you can do."

"But you can." She sat up straight and looked at me.

I shook my head. "They've already raised questions about the will being a forgery. I can't stick my nose into that without raising more suspicions. It's best I stay out of it."

"You don't love me." She pulled away and looked out the window. Even when I parked the car, she continued sitting there.

"Ilana, I can't get involved. We're building a business. If they investigate me, they might tie up my assets. They won't find anything but that doesn't mean they won't ruin me in the meantime. Besides, we don't want to get a bad reputation before our company even gets off the ground."

"What about all that stuff in Nick's house? What's going to happen to that?"

"There's nothing of value there. It's just a few pieces of furniture that won't fetch enough at auction to cover the cost of moving and storage."

"Those photos are worth something," she said. "All that Cindy creature is going to do is sell them. At least if we get them you can keep a few as mementos."

I reached over to take her hand. God, how she loved me. She'd been thinking of my feelings all along.

"I don't know what Nick's sister will do with all those pictures," I said. "But they're not him. Yes, it would be nice to have something as a keepsake but I have the most important thing, my memories."

She snorted. "We could go there tonight. We could take just a few of the ones he stored away. No one will ever notice they're missing."

"I can't believe you're suggesting we break into Nick's house."

"Oh, it wouldn't be illegal," she said. "I have a key."

"Taking something without permission is still stealing--"

Wait, I thought. Now things were getting strange in an eerie, trapped-in-a-movie kind of way.

Nick had given me the key to his place once we'd moved him in with us. Ilana was always off in Ontario or outlying counties scoping out new properties so I was the one who retrieved whatever Nick needed from his house. He'd told me several times not to lose the key because he'd never bothered to have a spare made.

"How did you get a key to his house?" My voice was measured but my insides twisted like rubber bands.

She rolled her eyes. "Greg, I had financial power of attorney, remember? I needed access to his place to pick up the mail."

"No, you didn't. The mail was on hold at the post office and you only had to pick it up once a week. I'm the one Nick told where to find the checkbook and account ledgers. I'm the one who got them out of the house for you. So how did you get a key?"

"He gave it to me. Nick. The owner of the house. Remember him?"

I gripped the steering wheel. The next-door neighbor kept looking through her window, probably wondering why we were just sitting there in the driveway. The homeowner's association had sent me a letter about the weekend the twins had spent souping up their friends' cars so I guess the board was still checking up on me. I ignored the prying eyes and focused on not exploding at Ilana.

"Nick did not give you a copy of his key," I said slowly. "There was no extra copy to give you. He told me that several times."

She laughed and squeezed my arm. "I made a copy using the one he gave you! God, Greg, you're so silly sometimes. I can't believe you can be so smart and so lost all at once!"

"When?"

"What do you mean when?" Her hand radiated a chill through my sleeve.

"When did you have a copy made? I didn't give you the key so you must have taken it when I wasn't looking."

She spoke patiently, like someone would to a small child. "Greg, my love. Of course I took it when you weren't looking. You've been so stressed out taking care of Nick and the business. I know I haven't been around much to help out but I promise I'll make it up to you."

Her hand slid down to my trousers. I was too tired to care.

"Tonight, then?" she murmured into my ear. "We'll be in and out. I know just which photos to take."

I shook my head. "Forget the photos. Forget everything. The court-appointed executor will look into all the details. He'll sort out the paper trail. You'll either get the house or you won't. Either way, it never would have mattered to Nick."

"He'll sort out the paper trail?" she asked. "What paper trail?"

For some reason, Ilana seemed very nervous. Ilana twitched in her seat, her eyes opening wide. Her long, thin fingers clutched her Prada-of-the-week like the sinewy talons of a bird of prey.

"He'll look at the will you provided and the one the sister's attorney has. They'll check with the notary, the attorney of record, all those details. Eventually they'll figure out which paper is real. If they're both real then they'll decide which one is more recent. That's the one that will be recognized by the court." I turned toward her. "You seem worried about something. What's going on?"

"Nothing," she snapped. "I just don't like to think of that woman touching Nick's things. She won't know what that house is worth."

"I thought you said this wasn't about money."

"It isn't!" she screamed. "If you loved me, you'd help me!"

Her words were like the slap of icy river water against my face. I was as horrified, feeling as if Kenny had spoken the words himself through Ilana. Because, in fact, if I had loved him enough, I would have helped him.

Ilana whipped open the door and skittered inside. Just for a second, with her hair flipping back like the crest of an angry bird and the whir of those skinny legs, I thought of Wile E. Coyote and Beep Beep the Roadrunner. If Ilana was the roadrunner in this production, that left me playing the fool. Only this cartoon wasn't funny at all.

* * *

It didn't take long for the executor to develop many questions and concerns about some of the spending on Nick's accounts shortly before he died. According to the credit card bills, Nick had purchased a dozen

Dolce & Gabbana sunglasses in one shot. At a few hundred dollars each, that single charge amounted to thousands.

It was small compared to other charges. It seems he'd bought five thousand dollars worth of new patio furniture. And a car stereo. Oh, yes, and some fine jewelry, really a modest four figures for a pair of earrings. Oddly enough, he'd bought all these things after the doctors declared him dead.

My attorney provided this information by phone. I had taken the call while relaxing on Ilana's patio furniture. Her brand-new patio furniture. Since she was sitting across from me, it was hard to ignore the fact that the sunglasses perched on her nose, also new, were Dolce & Gabannas.

While my attorney rattled off the extensive list of purchases, Ilana looked up from the latest issue of Vogue and smiled. I tried not to stare at her as if she'd suddenly grown rubbery and strange like Dali's angel. In a way, she had. She'd taken advantage of Nick at a time when she was supposed to be helping him. He'd trusted a false image. I'd trusted a false image.

When the attorney hung up, I sat there with the phone still glued to my ear. Ilana would want to know who'd called and I felt so sick, I thought I'd vomit if I tried to speak. I'd failed Nick so thoroughly. I should have paid closer attention. Did anyone in Ilana's family ever know him? I was involved with a thief. If she'd done that to Nick, what would she do to me? Finally I closed the phone.

"Who was that?" she asked.

"The attorney. Ilana, where did this patio furniture come from?"

"Desert Imports. Do you like it? It's French."

"No. I mean, how did you pay for it?"

"Oh, you're such a bean counter!" She leaned forward to touch my face. Her eyes sharpened when I pulled away. "What did your lawyer tell you?"

"That there was a load of fraudulent charges on Nick's credit cards. Cards you were responsible for paying off, cards you were supposed to cancel and destroy."

"Those were not fraudulent charges." She sat up straight. God help me, she was actually offended.

"What, you're going to say Nick told you to go shopping after he died? Have a nice spree on him?"

"He doesn't have to pay for them," she said witheringly. "He's dead."

"It's still stealing!"

"No, it's not! Nick's dead! I'd never do anything to hurt him!"

I spoke one word at a time. "It's. Still. Stealing!"

I shouted the last word so loudly one of the neighbors came out onto his deck to see what was going on. Ilana waved pleasantly; after a confused wave in return, the neighbor retreated inside.

"Nick wanted me to have these things," she said. "He felt he owed me something for helping with his finances. We were waiting until he felt better so we could go shopping together but that never happened. I was just doing what he wanted me to do."

I stared at her. The sun hovered just over her shoulder and made it painful to look at her but I couldn't stop. As I blinked against the glare, her face began to change. Her jaw elongated along with her nose until they had merged into a glossy beak.

The roadrunner, I realized, was nothing more than a cuckoo that ran along the ground. Everyone knew the cuckoo left its eggs in other birds' nests. Wreaking havoc was in its nature. And there I was, as ridiculous as a coyote perched on someone else's eggs.

Ilana's peculiar brand of love was killing me. It was a slow death, strangling my spirit and eating away at my physical health. I needed professional help. Without another word, I stood up from the table and walked to the garage. I heard her voice receding into the distance, but it was only the dove-like *coo, coo* of the roadrunner coaxing me back

So, have I had enough yet? Kenny's dead. Or missing. His absence left a gaping wound in my heart. Not knowing was killing me. Nick's death? Just salt in the wound. A constant reminder of my own failure. I failed Kenny. I failed Nick. Ilana screwed Nick over, and that happened on my watch. That was the last straw. I was hopelessly in love with someone who, at best, had no moral compass and at worst, was an out and out criminal. Love? Maybe the wrong word. Need? Who knows. I knew intellectually that she wasn't good for me, but somehow, emotionally, she filled the gaping maw of need and desperation that I had become. I couldn't imagine life without her there to fill the hole in my soul. In fact, I couldn't imagine life at all.

In an instant, I was engulfed in a tsunami containing every emotion I had ever felt in my entire life. I was pounded relentlessly by surge after raging surge of shame, anger, frustration, grief. Tossed about like a cork, I was hit from all sides by the swirling mass of flotsam and jetsam of past events, and the feelings that accompanied them. I was drowning, pounded to death by my own memories. I needed to breathe. I needed air. Or I would die.

At that moment, death was preferable to the struggle. I could imagine, actually feel the quiet and peace that death would offer, and moved toward it, drawn like a moth to the flame. I had to act, and I had to act immediately. This pain HAD to stop. It hit me, clearly, in an instant. Death was my answer, my salvation. The cure for the guilt, shame, and helplessness that was slowly killing me. I needed to speed up the process. I couldn't wait a second longer. I needed relief from this horror NOW.

I drove to the nearest emergency room. The place was pretty empty that time of day so I walked right up to the triage nurse.

"Hello," I said calmly. "My name is Gregory Marks. I've worked in hospitals for nearly twenty years so I know how things work. Don't fuck with me. I need enough morphine to kill myself, please."

"Well, Mr. Marks," she said smoothly, "let's see what we can do for you. Will you please follow me?"

Folding her clipboard under one arm, she escorted me to a private exam room. As she settled me on a gurney, I said, "Oh, and I'll need a few sterile needles, as well."

"No problem," she said. "We'll fix you right up."

It was a perfectly reasonable response to a perfectly horrible day.

CHAPTER EIGHT

The emergency room physician admitted me to the psych ward for observation. When people said certain kinds of things, hospitals tended to take serious action and ask questions later. For the four days of my hospital stay, I was seen by a psychiatrist and prescribed medication for depression. My release was accompanied by instructions to follow up with a therapist on an outpatient basis.

I knew I wouldn't follow up. I'd gone to the hospital to die. What an idiot. I couldn't even get that right. What had I been thinking? That they'd just hand over the morphine as I'd asked? I slunk out of the hospital as invisibly as possible, embarrassed at how stupid I'd been. And I sure as heck wasn't about to discuss that with any therapist.

Although the hospital had an attendant at the ER entrance who would have parked my vehicle, I'd taken it to the garage myself. My emotions had been stretched so tight I couldn't bear the thought of a single ding or dent showing up on my car...even if I thought I'd never see it again. I'd parked far enough away from the door that it would likely have few people parking next to it.

I couldn't find it. I walked the top level four times then searched the entire garage. Although I'd been confused when I'd arrived, I had definitely parked in the garage. I called Ilana and asked her if she'd picked up my car during my hospital stay. When she said no, I reported it stolen.

I wandered aimlessly around the house for days. I just couldn't get myself into gear. The hospital stay had been peaceful in a way, a sanitized retreat where I hadn't had to do anything except sleep. The doctors had lectured me about eating more, of course; I'd already lost so much weight I was starting to look like a model…or a meth addict. But I didn't want to eat and picked at the meals just to keep them off my back.

When I got home, I picked at the gigantic meals Ilana ordered, but never ate anything there, either. I knew I'd have to make a decision soon about my life with her. I couldn't do it right away, though. My heart was still mourning Nick and my brain was still throwing Kenny's face up to me. Ilana's words kept coming out of his mouth: *If you loved me, you'd help me.* But it was too late. I couldn't help a ghost.

Just when I thought my life had hit a new low, the police called. They'd found what was left of my car in San Bernardino. Apparently a chop shop had bitten off every saleable part like piranhas after a cow. The only reason they knew it was my car was because they'd found the frame and matched the VIN to my vehicle.

Criminals could be so stupid. The idiots who'd stolen the car had reported their sixteen-year-old daughter missing. When the police came to the house to investigate, the frame of my car was sitting in plain sight in the back yard.

The daughter returned from her afternoon at a friend's house but not before the police had noticed the stacks of car parts from a variety of vehicles leaning against the fence. Interestingly, Jeff and Kevin lived in San Bernardino. Ilana talked to them almost every day. Surely she'd mentioned my hospitalization during one of those conversations.

The car had probably seemed like easy money. And no harm done, they probably thought; I had once been insured to the hilt. But to cut expenses, I'd cancelled the comprehensive and theft portions of the coverage. The twins probably figured I'd come out better because the insurance would pay for a new vehicle. It had been intended as a victimless crime, just like Ilana's use of Nick's credit cards.

I couldn't think about it. A car was nothing; my ability to go on living was everything. This time, I'd get someone to help me sort out the mess my life had become.

* * *

When the hospital released me, Ilana was everything I needed her to be. Up until that time we'd been lovers, yes, but in that oversexed, pinpoint excitement kind of way that starts nearly every relationship. My feelings for her had grown strong but I wasn't about to let her in on how far I'd already sunk into her pool. Even though the sex was powerhouse through and through, I was still afraid the feelings weren't entirely mutual.

Ilana proved how deep her love was for me that first week. She understood, she listened, and she didn't push me to do too much right away. She let me get back to normal at my own speed. I didn't give much thought as to why I'd been in the hospital. I just wanted to forget the entire situation and get on with my life. If you don't talk about it, it doesn't exist, right? Roll tape, just like when I was a kid.

So of course I didn't take the medication. I didn't need medication for a condition I didn't have. A mental illness? No, not me! My life had hit a huge bump, sure. But I'd already figured it all out. Nick deserved mourning; Ilana had made some crappy decisions trying to honor Nick's wishes; and the police couldn't find any evidence that the twins had anything to do with the car nabbing. Time would heal all that; medication was unnecessary. The crisis was over.

I did go to therapy, though. I thought I might need someone to talk to in the future. I still had a stack of woes as tall as any of Ilana's paperwork: my savings were shrinking at an alarming rate, I couldn't afford to buy a new car, my parents stayed well behind the boundaries I'd set for them, and…

And. I was working my ass off to make a better life. But somewhere inside was this howler monkey of a feeling, a hopelessness that dragged at my arms and pulled my eyes into my head to look at all kinds of strange pictures like me going to jail for Ilana's crimes. Me being shot by her brothers during a burglary. Me dying in a hospital, forsaken and alone.

Me in the river.

I started out, at the therapist's suggestion, with three sessions a week. All he did was listen to me ramble on about how hopeless my life was. He very rarely said anything. When he did, it was far from a pearls-of-wisdom-slowly-granted kind of thing. Instead it was box-top psychology, like something you'd hear on a daytime talk show. *So you feel pretty down,* or *You've been a success in the past. Can you create that for your personal life?*

Duh. Double duh. I'm paying for this?

Finally I just stopped going. That helped address one of my problems, anyway, by keeping more money in my pocket. It was the most efficient thing to do.

* * *

"So," Cathryn said. "I heard you were in the hospital. That you'd asked for enough morphine to kill yourself. What was that all about?"

My head snapped back and my tongue tried to crawl down my throat. *Don't answer. If you don't talk about it it doesn't exist.* I thought even as the world stretched into odd shapes around me. I had driven into Ontario to work in the back bedrooms of a rental while Jack and Cathryn did their thing in the kitchen.

The work was meant to move the business forward and keep my mind occupied, thus solving two problems at once. The entire time my hands were busy, though, my mind chewed over my problems like a starving coyote at a parched bone. *Why can't I make this work?* I kept thinking. I knew life couldn't all be blooming flowers but was I really doomed to an emotional desert?

And now, out of the blue, came this question. From Cathryn, no less. She was a very intimidating woman, at least to me. She was strong enough to plow through just about anything life dealt her. We'd known each other for years, so knew each other well by now. But I still wasn't sure I wanted to go there with her.

Right from the start, she'd been forthright with her observations about my troubles. Blunt, even. While other people might have been offended by her directness, I found it frightening. And a relief. Maybe I was just a sucker for punishment.

"Sucks failing to off yourself, doesn't it?" she asked. "Makes you feel like a bigger loser than before you went there."

"It wasn't a real attempt," I mumbled. "That was the fastest way to get help."

"A little melodramatic, wouldn't you say? Kind of like Ilana?"

I was getting annoyed. *I don't have to explain anything to you,* I thought. *It's my life so back off, lady!*

I shuffled through my toolbox as I regained my composure. Did she think she was my therapist or something? I still felt as though I had to defend myself. Ilana even. I felt like an idiot, and that was the last thing I wanted to be in front of Cathryn. I hadn't even earned her respect, really, and I was rapidly losing any ability to do so in the future.

I threw the screwdriver back into the box and rounded on Cathryn. I stood there, taking deep breaths to launch into different explanations then abandoning them. They all sounded so ridiculous. How could I get her to understand what I felt for Ilana?

"Our relationship is…complicated," I finally said. "I'm not sure I understand it, much less can explain it. There's a lot to complain about but what couple doesn't have trouble?"

"The kind of trouble that drives you into a mental ward? Plenty!"

I shook my head. "There's a lot more to it than that. Besides, Ilana's been really great this week, very supportive. It's different now. More like…."

I wanted to say more like a marriage but the words wouldn't come out. They seemed too real, too hopeful. Clair had banked on me and I'd crumbled when nothing was wrong. I couldn't risk letting my relationship with Ilana be overtaken by the current trouble. Our lives would have to be pretty settled before I'd even consider proposing.

"More like what you and Jack have," I finished.

She laughed. "Yeah, Jack and I are practically joined at the hip. That doesn't mean he'd let me take him down if I sink, though."

"I'm not going to take Ilana down." My voice was so fierce it surprised even me.

"That's not what I meant." She looked at me strangely. "Don't let Ilana drag you down."

"She won't," I said. "She's made some bad decisions but we're past that now. Nick's family settled with her out of court. I told them how much Nick had meant to us both. His sister wanted out of that situation as much as we did, so Ilana got a certain amount of money in exchange for not contesting their version of the will. It was less than the property was worth but it was a good compromise."

"Yeah, those investigations can tie up estates for years," Cathryn said. "I'd pay her off, too."

"It wasn't a bribe!" I flushed more with embarrassment than anger. "Ilana was heartbroken over giving up that property."

She was about to say something else but Jackson interrupted. We all knew he was pulling her out before the discussion went any further. He didn't do that often but at this point, he might have thought I'd fire them if Cathryn said anything else. I wouldn't have but I was relieved to stop defending my choices. We all went back to work in our separate rooms and didn't speak for the rest of the day.

* * *

When I got home that night, Ilana was in bed. I knew right away something was wrong. Normally she came home, paused only long enough to order more takeout or heat up leftovers from lunch, and disappeared into the office. I could hardly keep up with her sometimes, and often went to bed before she did.

Sometimes I'd wake early the next morning and find her already up. She'd even throw on the clothes she'd been wearing the day before until she was ready to leave the house. Then she'd shower and change, looking gorgeous as usual and making me ache with anticipation for her return.

"Are you all right?" I sat on the edge of the bed.

"I'm not sure," she mumbled. "My chest hurts and my arm is numb, my left arm. I think it's my heart."

I was alarmed and shocked. How could she have heart problems when she was so young? Maybe it was just indigestion. She couldn't possibly be about to die. Could she?

"My family has a history of heart disease," she continued. Her words were breathy from the effort of speaking. "I've inherited a bad heart. The doctors diagnosed it when I was a teenager, but there was nothing to be done about it. My grandparents thought about sending me to America for treatment but…."

"Don't worry, Ilana." I cupped her pale, drawn face in my hand. "I'll take care of you."

The next day, I lined up an appointment with her doctor. When she went in for a battery of tests, I couldn't help but think about Nick and how familiar it all seemed. I began to think my life had gotten stuck in a single groove. If I didn't figure out a way to make it skip forward again, everyone in my life would die of heart failure one right after the other.

I was frantic to make her life easier. I stood in on a few open houses Ilana had already scheduled, met with a corporate representative to survey the rental units that were still under renovation, and fielded the dozens of phone calls she got every day. The work on the units was handed over entirely to the twins. That, of course, meant shuffling Cathryn and Jack's work schedule to keep the four of them separated but somehow I managed.

When I wasn't handling Ilana's side of the business, I waited on her. She slept endlessly and seemed groggy whenever she woke, exactly like Nick. She at least had an appetite, although it was mostly for sweet things like ice cream and tiramisu. I chopped nuts on top of the desserts to get some protein in her, thinking that anything was better than nothing.

After about ten days, she got better overnight. One day she was in bed moaning and the next she was up, dressed and ready to take on the world.

"Where's my Blackberry?" she asked as she bustled into the office.

I hung up the phone, stunned to see her so pristine in her designer suit and heels. "Here," I said.

She scrolled down through the messages I'd been unable to answer. "You didn't delete anything from my brothers, did you?"

"No. I didn't read them, either. They knew you weren't well and would get back to them when you could."

"OK." She deleted a text message and snagged her attaché off the table. "Gotta go."

"Wait! Ilana, don't you think you should take it easy for a while? Maybe we should think about how to reorganize the business a little to take some of the weight off you."

"My doctor and I have that covered," she said over her shoulder. "Don't wait up! I've got a lot of work to catch up on!"

The door banged shut and she was gone. I felt like I'd been caught in a whirlwind again. Although caring for her had been stressful, this was different. She'd quite effectively sucked all the energy out of the room and taken it with her. I had forgotten how exhausting her nonstop activity could be.

Ilana could be kind, compassionate, caring, giving, generous, thoughtful, encouraging, and above all, magnetic. She had an unbelievable capacity to win people over. Time and again clients, corporate representatives and the neighbors were mesmerized by her personality. She really was hypnotic.

Why was someone as wonderful as Ilana interested in a loser like me? I was so entranced I collapsed on the couch and slept for two hours.

* * *

Barely a month after Nick's death, Ilana was scheduled for an angioplasty. The procedure would mechanically widen her narrowing coronary arteries. Doctors would be inserting a balloon to open the blockage that was slowing the blood flow to her heart. Although a fairly common procedure, it was nevertheless serious.

She was adamant that I tell no one. She didn't want her family to worry. Besides, she thought the twins might try to take advantage of the situation somehow. She'd claimed many times that her entire family was after her money and that none of them could be trusted. With suspicions about the twins still lurking in my mind, I agreed that keeping things quiet was the wise choice.

I drove her to the hospital and waited while she was prepped for surgery. Over two hours later, the nurse came out and said she'd been given a sedative. I could see her briefly as she was wheeled to the operating room but soon she'd be out cold.

As they pushed the gurney down the hallway, she rolled her head to look back at me. In a slurred yet unmistakably clear voice, she called, "Don't you think it's time you proposed?"

Swoosh! The double doors shut behind her.

I stood there with my knees trembling. Any doubts I had about whether she was committed to the long haul disappeared. I vowed to never doubt her again. If she made it through the surgery, I'd never hold back my feelings again. Life was too short.

Ilana's angioplasty went off without a hitch. I doted on her during her recovery and arranged every detail of our life. She lay propped up against pillows with the most exclusive bridal magazines spread like dainty centerfolds across the covers and pointed to what she wanted. She ordered the flowers, set up the catering, and reserved a private room at the best restaurant in town.

We even brought a tailor to the house to fit the gown. Ilana was weak and leaned heavily on me during the fitting but was so brave. We were engaged, life was good, the business was coming together, and everything was perfect. At last, all my hard work was paying off. Soon I'd settle into my real life. The nagging doubts would never bother me again.

I didn't think about Kenny. I couldn't, not yet. I hadn't even had time to visit Nick's grave. But I would. Then, finally, I'd lay the dead to rest and be able to focus fully on the living.

When I stepped into the living room, Gus was switching his gaze back and forth from the Dali angel to me and growling. I wondered whether Ilana's brothers had given her those dogs just to keep an eye on me.

CHAPTER NINE

Ilana recovered wonderfully. That whole month we…well, mostly me… worked hard to keep up with her investment properties. She scanned the papers from a dozen nearby cities every day looking for other units to add to our inventory. Every Friday I spent an entire day on the road making the initial drive past houses to eliminate the ones we obviously wouldn't want.

We began entertaining. Dinner parties, cocktails and pool parties filled our weekends. Cathryn and Jack were regularly invited but couldn't attend more than a few events due to the drive. I offered them the guest room but they usually turned that down. Jackson often had other engagements, and I assumed they were potential clients who could only clear time to meet with them on the weekends.

Ilana was sleeping well and her bipolar disorder seemed to have disappeared. She'd gone into therapy around the same time as me and said she'd gotten medications that knocked it right out. I never saw her take anything but assumed she was too embarrassed to make a show.

Meanwhile, the depression that had plagued my entire life seemed to be in check. My world didn't stretch out into a Dali nightmare anymore and the leering angel was now simply a piece of art that brought me pleasure. Gus continued to growl at her at odd moments. After I threw him outside in the midday heat half a dozen times, he quit.

The one sticking point was the twins. They were like the two stooges of home repair. They quickly painted two bedrooms in one of the rentals yet when I went to install the hardware, it was clear they'd applied the primer over the topcoat. For their second attempt, the color was rolled so unevenly the rooms needed to be painted again.

I bought a sprayer. The sprayers use more paint but were fast and easy to operate. The twins broke the compressor the first time they used it. Rather than tell me, they loaded the paint into spray bottles and shot an entire room with a drippy, streaky mess. They attached the crown molding so there were visible gaps between it and the ceiling, they didn't tighten the plumbing enough to prevent leaks, and their drywall work always needed to be heavily sanded and smoothed.

In short, they were making me nuts. But Ilana's health was still in a delicate state. The last thing I wanted was to worry her. Besides, she'd said they needed a second chance after Jeff's criminal convictions. They both had some abilities but needed a crash course in job skills. If I could help them, I'd be helping Ilana.

In the long run, I'd also be helping myself. I was, after all, engaged. These guys were about to become my brothers-in-law. The thought was actually somewhat unsettling. But I was committed to Ilana, and to my new life of prosperity and happiness. Who wouldn't want a shot at the American dream? It was so very, very close.

And yet so very far.

* * *

My desk at the house sat at a window facing the street. One day as I looked out, two trucks with long trailers pull up. *Sudden Moves* was printed on the sides. "Hey, Ilana," I said, pointing out front, "who's moving?"

She glanced outside, shrugged, and glided out of the office to the rear of the house. I had already gone back to my work when the doorbell rang. A county sheriff and an overweight, balding man stood at the door.

"Good morning, sir," the sheriff said. "We're issuing this Notice to Vacate."

"What?"

He barely looked up. "By virtue of the Writ of Execution for Possession of Real Property, eviction, issued out of the Riverside County Superior Court—"

"No, wait--"

"You are hereby ordered to vacate the premises described as 3434

Avenida Del Oro, Palm Springs, California. You have fifteen minutes to vacate. Do you have any questions, sir?"

Did I have any questions? Of course I had questions! Several hundred, in fact! My mind went blank. I couldn't breathe. I just stared at the sheriff and the fat man wearing unpleasantly grimy shorts.

"Ah," I finally managed, "I think there's been a huge mistake. There is no landlord for this property. It's owned by my fiancé, Ilana. Hold on, let me get her."

When I tried to close the door, the sheriff moved his foot inside.

"Sir," he said in that irritatingly measured voice, "you have fifteen minutes to leave the premises. The clock has already started. You can call the number on the back of this form and deal with the details once you have left the premises."

"Ilana!"

I looked everywhere but couldn't find her. By the time I returned, the sheriff and the short guy were standing in our living room with three other men.

"Wow, look at this place!" one of the movers said. "We've never done one as nice as this." He lifted a painting by Peter Max off the wall.

"Hey, be careful with that!" I squealed. "It's an original! It can't be replaced! What are you doing?"

"Sir." The sheriff moved between us. "I told you to vacate the premises. These men work for the owner of the house. They'll pack and remove your belongings. As I have explained, you can claim your property from the landlord."

I began walking in circles. All I could think was that all of our beautiful possessions were being touched and fondled and made dirty by the hands of people I didn't know. Ilana and I had been collecting art glass and had a large collection of original Kosta Boda crystal. It was all in danger if not treated gently. How could this be happening? And where the hell was Ilana?

In the bedroom, I grabbed Gus. He sank his teeth into my middle finger and held on, growling furiously. Gizmo was cowering under the bed so I pulled her out by the scruff of the neck and tucked her into my armpit. I shoved two pair of underwear in my pocket and snagged the dog bed on my way to the garage. After dumping everything into the front seat of the Explorer, I turned to find the sheriff blocking the side door.

"Time's up," he said. "I'm gonna have to ask you to leave."

"But all I have are the dogs and their bed." I waved at Ilana's SUV so forcefully blood droplets sprinkled the window. "You can't expect me to leave with nothing."

"Sir, I'm not gonna ask you again. I have already been lenient with you. Please leave peacefully. I would hate for this to get out of hand."

"But I don't even know where Ilana is. Where am I supposed to go? What about my fiancé?"

"If she shows up here I'll explain the situation to her. Please leave."

As I moved to the driver's side, I looked around the garage. It was full of tools I'd collected since I was a teenager. The brand-new table saw I'd assembled two nights before sat next to its own packing box. With my luck, the art and paintings would be packed in the same box as the tools.

I wrapped my finger in the only thing I had, a pair of my underwear, and hit the garage door opener. As I backed down the driveway, life twisted like that surreal putty again. A dozen or so people stood on the front lawn unfolding boxes and taping up the ends. An equal number of neighbors had assembled across the street. They yammered and gestured. Some held their hands over their mouths and shook their heads.

I'd become a public spectacle. Not only were the entire contents of my life and the house tipping into the abyss, there was an audience. Even my humiliation couldn't be kept private. I tried to put on a brave face and waved as I pulled down the street. They gaped back, looking confused and offended. Not until I turned the corner did I realize I'd given them all a fat, hand-woven Egyptian cotton finger.

I wanted to call Ilana. Since my mobile phone was sitting on my desk, the only way I could manage that was to hunt for a payphone. The cell phone revolution had left the only functioning payphones in drug-infested neighborhoods and dirty convenience stores. I'd have to use the ruined underwear to wipe down the receiver before it touched my ear.

The dogs, at least, had made themselves at home. Gizmo lay in the bed while Gus stood at the window watching life go by. Then a voice came from the cargo space behind the back seat.

"Pull over and let me out," Ilana said. "It's fucking hot back here."

I slammed on the brakes, ran to the back and flung open the rear hatch.

"What the hell?" I said. "What are you doing back there?"

"Oh, chill out, Greg. I didn't want them to know I was home." She smoothed her hair and looked very nonplussed.

"I don't understand. You *knew* they were coming? What the hell is going on, Ilana?"

"Get in the car," she sighed. "We can talk about this on the way to a hotel. We have to find a place to stay and figure out when we can get our stuff back."

"Yeah, but what about the house? Who are those people?"

"Boy, you can really be dense sometimes." She flipped her hair again and flounced around to the passenger's side. "I lost the house in foreclosure, you idiot. Who do you think they are? Someone bought the house at the foreclosure sale. I've been trying to buy it back so you wouldn't find out but I guess they got tired of negotiating. We've been living there without paying rent."

"You lost the house?" The world was disintegrating into a series of dots at the edge of my vision. "Why didn't you tell me? We could have moved. We could have…hell, I don't know! We could've done something! You left me to deal with this while you hid in the back of the car?"

"That about covers it." She settled the dogs in her lap and leaned over to shut the door. When she realized I was standing in the way, she rolled her eyes. "Get over it, Greg! I was embarrassed, OK?"

"Embarrassed? You just lost your house. Everything we own is locked up in there. We're gonna have to pay them just to get it back and all you can say is 'I'm embarrassed?'"

Ilana had lost the house, yet she was calm. I had nothing to do with this, yet my self-control was slipping away.

"Knock it off," she said. "I made a mistake, OK? Just get us to the nearest hotel so I can make some phone calls."

Fortunately nothing else came out of her mouth. Slowly, oh, so slowly, my brain started working again. I would have preferred that it stay on hold. Instead, it took inventory. Everything I owned had been stripped away. My ability to earn money and provide myself with some security was being packed into boxes destined for who-knew-where. The woman

I was supposed to spend the rest of my life with had disappeared during the crisis.

I felt violated, as terrified and alone as I had those nights Bruce had busied his hands under the covers. The feeling made me sick. The more I thought about those strangers in my house, the more dizzy I became. I whipped the SUV into the parking lot of a hotel a few blocks from the house.

Would my entire life be viewed through the dirty filter of those years on the farm? Would I constantly carry that duel burden, the filth left by Bruce's touch on my skin and the dark sorrow of Kenny's death on my heart?

When we got up to the room, there were no phone calls or discussions, no arguments or accusations. After settling the dogs, we both went to bed.

* * *

When we woke up, Ilana began explaining. The foreclosure, she said, was the result of her not paying attention to business and personal affairs while she'd been doing drugs. By the time she got off drugs and started paying attention again, the foreclosure was well under way. She did what she could to stop it but the angioplasty and her prolonged recovery interfered.

She'd been tormented the entire time she'd been ill thinking about the house. She hadn't told me because she'd been too embarrassed to admit she'd screwed up so badly. Since she'd been working with the buyers to assume the mortgage again, she thought she could work something out. Her plan had been that I'd never find out, I'd never have to worry.

"Greg," she sniffed as tears rolled like tiny pearls from her eyes, "you've worked so hard to make the business work...to make our lives work. I couldn't let you down. I couldn't have you wondering if I knew anything about real estate. If I couldn't handle my own house, you'd wonder how I could do anything for our business at all."

Here she bent over, holding her stomach as if suddenly ill. "Oh, Greg," she moaned, "don't you see? I did it for you! For us...for you!"

All the tension drained out of my arms. It all made perfect sense now.

We were a team. I took her hand and settled the engagement ring gently at the base of her finger.

"Together," I said, "we'll make sure this never happens again. I don't claim to be perfect but I'll always do my best to be understanding and supportive. But you have to tell me, Ilana, you have to let me know when problems come up. That's what marriage is about…handling things together. OK?"

She sniffed and looked up with hope shining behind her tears. She nodded and collapsed into my arms. Soon we were rubbing and kissing. We pulled off only enough clothes to consummate our recommitment as quickly as possible. I barely noticed when Gus nipped my ass.

The next day we moved into one of the rental units that had just been vacated. The condo was located in a questionable neighborhood. Palm Springs didn't have much actual urban decay but this area had been hit somewhat hard by the foreclosure spat during the sub-prime mortgage crisis. The neighborhood was poised to make a comeback but for now was less than desirable.

The condo had itself been a small but pleasant unit at one time. A series of renters had taken their toll, though, and the place seemed gray with built-up grime. I couldn't focus when I worried about whether the crusted food on the counters harbored *salmonella* or *e. coli* so I bought an extravagant amount of cleaning supplies. While I scrubbed and rinsed, I kept one ear tuned to Ilana's phone conversations. If something sounded like it was going to explode, I wanted to make sure we worked on it together.

How could I possibly have ended up here? I was deathly afraid that this was simply a way-station on my long descent into hell. Next I'd lose what little was left in my savings to a bank failure. The Feds wouldn't make good on the insurance because by then we'd be evicted again and they wouldn't cut a check to someone who had no permanent address.

Ilana and I would live on the streets of Palm Springs. We'd carry the dogs around in a little plastic hand basket we'd steal from one of those discount retailers. We'd be so poor the only shopping we'd do would involve the five-finger discount.

We'd eat dinner at midnight out of trash dumpsters behind pizza joints and fast-food chains. The saturated fats would clog Ilana's heart and she'd die in my arms during a dust storm. Gizmo would die soon after that from a broken heart, and Gus would try to get revenge by gnawing at my jugular every time I managed to doze off in some alley.

I'd fall prey to other homeless people and be raped now and then. I'd sell my body to the horny businessmen who flooded the convention center by day and wanted to fill their lonely nights. I'd steal all the little soaps and shampoos from their hotel rooms then walk around with my pockets bulging with sample-sized crumbs of the life I used to have.

And I'd still be a public spectacle. The neighbors who'd known me in my glory would see me panhandling downtown. They'd drop a fistful of coins into my filthy hand, careful not to touch my skin, before hurrying away. They'd congregate around their pools and shake their heads, muttering about poor Greg and how he'd let Ilana die, how he couldn't even provide enough food to keep a teacup Chihuahua alive.

The dirt in the condo wouldn't come up. My arms were swathed in industrial gloves up to the elbows as I slopped out one caustic cleaner after another. Scrub brushes, scouring pads, and a series of toothbrushes to push the built-up grime from the cracks wore out but the grey patina stayed. I nearly cried from frustration.

There was also a strange red blotch on the wall...spaghetti sauce? Blood?...shaped like the Grim Reaper. It seemed to move whenever I didn't look at it directly. I'd whirl on it, spray bottle drawn like a chemical gun, but never could catch it creeping closer.

Pitiful Greg, it said. *Used to be a have. Now he's a have-not.*

CHAPTER TEN

"Get dressed." Ilana swept into the bedroom and hung our dry cleaning on the closet door. "We're going to be late!"

"For what?"

She pulled an outfit from the suit bag. I was moderately horrified to see it was a tuxedo. The tuxedo itself was relatively non-threatening; what it represented, though, sent a shockwave through my chest.

"The wedding, remember?" She stripped the plastic off her gown with a flourish. "It's today!"

I hovered in the middle of the empty room for a moment. Then I rushed to the bathroom and tried to vomit. But I hadn't had anything to eat for almost twenty-four hours. I hunkered over the toilet dry heaving until Ilana banged open the door.

"What do you think?"

She twirled in the doorway then struck a pose. For some ungodly reason she'd applied a heavy layer of shimmery eye shadow across her lids with a dollop of crimson at each corner. Her gown was a designer original, nipped tight at the waist then flared behind in a bustle that trialed a narrow froth of pleats like a tail. Her shoes were so pointy the tips were like talons.

I was marrying the roadrunner.

"Meep-meep!" she said triumphantly.

"What?" I managed around more retching.

"I said, meet me at the church!" She grabbed her tiny white handbag, a beaded wonder coated with freshwater pearls then paused at the door.

"Oh, and Greg," she said with a hint of irritation, "try to look presentable. This is my special day!"

Then she swept out of the room, leaving me to hear the echo of the door banging shut.

I was already dressed by the time I realized she'd taken our only vehicle.

* * *

Taxis are hard to come by in Palm Springs, so I walked the twelve blocks to the church. Maybe it was the heat. Maybe it was exhaustion, or the stress, or the dirt, my current state of homelessness or the cummerbund squeezing my gut down into my groin but I wasn't much in the marrying mood. I showed up, though, and was relieved to see Cathryn and Jack already in the pews.

Cathryn immediately came up to me. "What in god's name is going on with you?" she said. "You look like crap!"

"Oh, thanks," I said. "It's this cummerbund. Wrong style for my form."

"Cut the jokes, Greg. You've lost twenty pounds and are whiter than a fish belly. What's the matter?"

"Well," I said as I leaned against a nearby pew, "Ilana lost the house in foreclosure, we're living in a filthy condo, the dogs have a nicer bed than we do, and I'm wearing dirty underwear."

"OK, sit down." She guided me toward a seat as the music started.

"Got to go." I pointed weakly down the aisle to where Ilana was shooting me *get over here* looks. "It's her big day, you know."

Ilana's brothers were seated near the aisle. They kept looking at me and snickering. I stared at them, really too exhausted to move my eyes or head away. I couldn't quite figure out the joke. Then Jeff blew his nose noisily several times. Finally he took the direct route and fished out the offending booger with his little finger. He grinned and wriggled his newly dressed pinky at me.

Cathryn, meanwhile, had summoned Jack. He and some guy I'd never met came over. They each took one of my arms and escorted me down the aisle. I was too weak to protest. I tried to stay focused on my lovely bride but kept getting distracted by all the decorations. With each new sight, my brain tallied the damage.

White silk runner for the aisle: $3,500. Lotus petals to cushion my dear fiancé's feet: $750. Origami swans folded from hand-pressed paper made from papyrus grown on the Nile: $2,250. Catering for the special dinner afterward, minister's fees and gift, the gown, the tux, the shoes, the pearl bag, the veilofTibetiansilk the firstprintingoftheGuttenbergBiblefromwhichtheministerreadourvows (*Ridiculous!* my brain screamed. *We aren't even religious!*)…I was panting by the time I reached the altar.

Jack stayed by my side in case I toppled. But I managed to turn toward Ilana, to look into her blazing eyes, to remember that she did, in fact, love me very, very much, and …*Snap out of it, Greg!! You're just nervous. You're marrying Ilana, you fool. Don't screw this up!!!*. When I reached for the ring, which had been tied with a satin ribbon around Gus' neck, he sank his teeth into my thumb. I never flinched. I placed the ring on Ilana's finger, streaking her hand with my blood.

All things considered, not a bad ceremony.

* * *

The wait staff rotated through the private room like clockwork. Trays of local and imported appetizers, cocktails, entrees, and wine that changed with every course appeared and disappeared. I was still mentally blown, like I'd been in a car wreck or survived a hurricane.

Jeff leaned across the table. He didn't bother to swallow first so I watched the shrimp he was chewing turn to pulp as he spoke. "You were punked, you know."

"What do you mean?"

"Jeff--" Ilana said.

"No." My voice was suddenly sturdy. "I want to hear what he has to say."

Cathryn, Jack, and the mysterious stranger fell quiet. Jeff and Kevin exchanged glances and snickered.

"You were punked to end all punkings," Jeff said. "I always knew my sister was evil but God, this one beats anything she's pulled off in the past."

"Jeff!" Ilana held her fork in a menacing way.

"She spent weeks planning that setup at the hospital!" Jeff roared with laughter. "I never thought she'd get permission to do that in a real facility but by God, she did!"

"Do what?" I thought about all the doctor's visits we'd gone on, about the hours I'd spent in the waiting room near the lobby. Had something happened behind closed doors?

"That whole heart thing! It was all a joke!"

He stuffed another shrimp in his mouth and blew tiny chunks of it out as he kept laughing. A wet lump of it landed dangerously close to the open wound Gus had inflicted. I didn't care.

"Ilana?" I asked.

"Greg." Her voice was pitched low again, forcing me to pay much closer attention than I wanted. But I did. God help me.

"I...I love you so much, Greg. I had to do it." She began twisting her napkin in both hands. "You were so...closed to me. I wasn't sure how you felt. I wanted so much for you to propose but it didn't seem like you were ever going to ask. I...I had to know. I had to plan for my future. We were either going to be together or not. I had to know!"

"So you thought faking a heart condition would...what, be incredibly romantic?"

"I thought it would draw us together." She managed to look hurt, as if she were the injured party. "And it did, Greg. You were so wonderful to me all during my recovery!"

"Recovery...." I was about to explode. But I didn't want to do that in front of my friends. "How...."

"Maryann!" Ilana said cheerily.

Maryann lived across the street from us. From our old house, that was. The foreclosed house.

"She works at the hospital," Ilana said. "She and some of the other nurses thought it was a fun idea. They helped me arrange the whole thing!"

"What about all those checks I wrote to help you pay your medical bills? You said you had a cash flow problem."

Her face pinched down and she managed to look even more hurt. "I

75

put that into the wedding fund. It helped pay for all this. Don't worry, I paid for much more of this than you did."

She threw down her napkin and pushed out her lip. I picked up my glass and drained the rest of the wine. A silent waiter instantly refilled it and I considered downing that glass, too. But I had to think.

OK, so I'd been punked into proposing to Ilana. She'd been devious and underhanded, had fooled me and roped others I knew into fooling me. But was that such a bad thing? She'd gone through a lot of trouble to take a shot at something that might have backfired. And although I'd promised myself to be totally open with her, had I actually been fully available to her? She hadn't trusted my love enough to tell me about the foreclosure. Was I holding up my end of this relationship?

As the wine flushed through my veins, I felt a rush of warmth. It didn't matter. What mattered was that I was starting my new life with my new wife. I wouldn't let a practical joke, as terribly unfunny as it might have been, come between me and the happiness I'd worked so hard to achieve.

"Ilana," I said, raising my glass, "here's to our future."

The tension around the table drained away. Cathryn still shot me sideways looks but after a third glass of wine, I hardly noticed.

* * *

Returning to the condo jolted me out of the warm fuzzies. I loved Ilana, yes, and Ilana loved me but as they say, love don't pay the bills. I paced around the empty living room for a while, calculating how quickly we might lay our hands on some cash.

My savings were down to practically nothing. I had planned to cash in my 401K to purchase a new car but it looked like a used vehicle would be the wise choice. Ilana had a potential buyer for the one property that was almost done. The rest of our assets suddenly looked like deficits. They would all require more infusions of cash before they'd be ready.

I had one ace up my sleeve. In the few spare hours I'd squeezed from my schedule, I'd started up a high-end design business. My first line was a series of sturdy leather boxes with handles. They were intended for men to use the same way a woman used a purse.

They were very masculine, and had originally been inspired by Nick's need for a discrete way to handle his catheter bag. If one elderly man needed an unobtrusive way to carry a medical device, how many other guys were looking for ways to carry other things around? Give someone a Blackberry, a microcomputer and maybe a pager, and poof, he looks like a geek with all that crap hanging off his belt.

The leather boxes solved that in a rugged yet sophisticated way. Each came with handles and removable straps. Many of them looked like smaller versions of a briefcase but I'd worked up a whole range of sizes. The smallest ones held a single credit card and clipped inside the waistband to foil thieves while traveling.

I hadn't bothered marketing them to any place that didn't have a national distribution system already in place. I thought big right from the beginning, and my approach had immediately borne fruit. One of the biggest cable shopping channels agreed to manufacture and sell the products under the label To Go Boxes. The contract paid enough up front that I might be able to work with the buyers of Ilana's house to get the property back.

The paperwork was, of course, now packed away in an unmarked cardboard box. The minute we recovered our things, I would dig up the papers and overnight them to the cable company. Along with the signed contract, I also had to deliver a prototype for each To Go Box along with design specs. All my drawings were in my computer so it would take only minutes to print those out.

The prototypes were a little more tricky. I'd have to unload all my tools and set them up in the living room then make a sample of each design. It would take time away from the real estate properties but it was the fastest way to put sure money in our hands. With all this spinning through my mind, I didn't respond when Ilana came up behind me and slipped her hand under my shirt.

"Greg," she purred into my ear. "Husband. Your wife needs attention. Now."

"Not now, baby." I sighed and turned around to hug her. "I'm really exhausted. Can we celebrate tomorrow?"

"No." She loosened the cummerbund and tickled my sides. I hated being tickled.

"Really, Ilana, I'm not in the mood."

She pulled at my clothes. She was surprisingly strong…or maybe I was eating so little and worrying so much that I had become surprisingly weak. As one hand unbuttoned my shirt, the other twisted into my waistband.

"You're my husband," she said. "You have to provide for me. Make sure I'm not hungry. And Greg, I am so very hungry."

Her tongue flicked along my jugular as if tasting me, as if readying that pointed beak for a bloody plunge. It never came. Instead she nibbled my nipples, pinched the flesh edging my armpits, and ground herself against my crotch. As she pushed me to the floor, I managed to gasp, "The tux!"

After folding the clothes neatly atop the bathroom sink, I padded back into the bedroom. The stain on the living room wall loomed through the doorway. We didn't have a vacuum cleaner so the rug was still layered with filth the tenants hadn't bothered to clean before they'd vacated. I rapidly lost any desire to continue.

Ilana pounced on me from behind. She'd been waiting for me to come out of the bathroom like a stalker. Or a rapist, really. Her hands and mouth were all over me, squeezing and sucking while her body…oh, her body. Wriggled and rubbed. Squeezed and hugged. I was helpless and crumpled to the floor with her on top.

I'm not sure how much noise we made but it must have been a lot. When the blood finally started flowing back to my brain, the neighbors beside us were banging on the walls. Ilana lay beside me with her head snuggled against my arm.

"Oh, Greg," she sighed, "I loved you."

"What?"

Did she just say loved, as in I used to but I don't anymore?

She laughed. "I love you, silly! We're married now."

I couldn't help but feel it would have been better if she'd sliced open my throat with her sharp beak. I was covered in the kind of carpet dirt that smelled musty and I tried to calculate how many sloughed skin cells from strangers were sticking to my body. Millions, no doubt. And then there were the dust mites that fed off the cells, and the dander of other people's pets, and maybe dried blood particles from when jolly renter man killed harpy renter woman in this very unit, on this very spot….

I raced for the bathroom. Ilana called after me, asking if I were sick. I was but not in that way. I turned the shower as far to one side as it would go and jumped in. The stream started out icy and climbed to searing. Although steam rolled up in clouds and I went through two travel-sized bars of soap—*just like the ones I'll steal from hotels after I start whoring!*—I couldn't seem to get clean.

Chapter Eleven

We spent over five thousand dollars to get our stuff back from the company that handled the eviction. In addition, we had to prepay a month's rent for the storage units where they moved our belongings when everything was released. Once everything was settled, I went to put our own locks on the storage units. I wanted to grab some clothes and check that everything had made it.

The door opened to utter chaos. Everything had been thrown around. Furniture was piled on top of boxes that had been crushed or sagged under the weight. Obviously much of our glass collection had been broken. We'd also mysteriously acquired items that didn't belong to us.

It took me a week to sort through everything. Predictably, Ilana remained in bed as I headed to the storage unit each day. Quite a number of things were missing. Most of the missing items, interestingly enough, were mine. Among the casualties were my computer, my safe, one of the Salvador Dali originals, two other original paintings, all my tools and equipment, and most of my clothes.

When I studied the Sudden Moves manifest, I finally read the address. Their headquarters was in San Bernardino…the same area where Ilana's brothers lived, coincidently, and close to where my car's remains had been found, also coincidently.

I cursed myself for having been so stupid. Ilana had said her entire family was after her money. If they couldn't get it by badgering her for loans or gifts or cash, it looked like they were going to extract it any other way they could. And I knew exactly who was responsible for heading up those crimes: Jeff.

Jeff was the one who'd worked up a rap sheet beginning at an early age. He'd been in prison a few times, always for minor offenses, and didn't seem to care if he did another tour. He was laid back one minute then screaming crazy the next. He scared me sometimes, and he definitely had the balls to cook up different schemes. Not enough brains to make the schemes very good but that also didn't seem to matter.

Kevin, meanwhile, was the quiet one. He didn't seem to have much idea about what to do with his life without Jeff. He shadowed his brother so closely that the few times I saw him without Jeff, he seemed lost. Maybe he was obsessed but I didn't care to explore their interpersonal relationship.

I had much more pressing problems than deciphering whether they were really to blame or even whether I'd see that stuff again. The only thing that made any difference to me was that my computer was gone. All my designs had been saved on its hard drive. I'd been so thrilled with my new life and working so hard to keep everything going, I'd never bothered to burn a backup.

Silly me. Feeling secure.

All the prototypes were missing. Why, of all things, had the thief stolen my To Go Boxes? How much could they possibly net at a pawn shop? Since all my tools and equipment had also been stolen, starting over meant starting from less than zero. At least Wile E. Coyote had been able to order anything from the ACME company with near instantaneous delivery. I didn't have even that.

The contract wouldn't wait while I ramped up the entire design process again. Reluctantly, I sent the shopping channel a letter explaining the situation. I never heard back from them, and their deafening silence screamed *loser!* every time I thought about it.

So I very efficiently stopped thinking about it. Ilana asked a few times when I was going to get the prototypes worked up so we could get the optioning check. I finally told her I'd decided the design business would take too much time away from our real estate business. She knew about the thefts, of course, but I put a positive spin on the outcome.

It had nothing to do with a husband protecting his love from harsh reality. It had everything to do with Greg protecting himself.

I smiled and nodded my way through the conversation. But my insides buzzed with anxiety. With the loss of that potential stream of income, I became even more dependent on Ilana.

I had to make this thing work. I had to make *everything* work.

* * *

The next morning I was up early. I had a therapy session with a new doctor. There was just too much to worry about not to try this talking thing again. I wasn't sure what to expect, really, but anything had to be better than that first guy's dead-fish look and his ridiculous questions-that-weren't-questions.

Ron's greeting was a high-energy handshake and a glossy smile. I was encouraged and put off at the same time. He certainly had more life than the first therapist but he seemed too...polished. Like he'd been a televangelist in a previous life and had fallen into counseling as a backup plan.

"So, Greg," he said as he settled me into a chair. "May I call you Greg? You can call me Doctor Ron."

"Uh...all right." *Doctor Ron? Is this Sesame Street? How about you call me Patient Greg?* I said none of that.

"What brings you here today?"

He listened for, oh, maybe five minutes. Then he held up his hand, leaned back toward his bookshelf, and whipped a copy of his latest book into my lap.

"It's called *The Black Hole of Money,*" he soothed. "I wrote it for people like you who can build their fortunes but whose mindset won't let them keep it. You can purchase it from the receptionist, if you'd like."

"Great." I put the book on the side table. "That's only what's been going on recently."

"Please." He waved beneficently. "Continue."

I talked about my prior marriage and the moves I'd made between jobs and cities. He leaned back again, never breaking eye contact and *mmm-hmmming* while his fingers located a DVD. He snapped the program into my lap like a Frisbee.

"Here's my seminar on change," he said. "I call it *The Black Hole of*

Security. It's about how we think new things are dangerous but they can actually be open doors to opportunity. A therapeutic bargain at $49.95."

"Uh…OK." I put the DVD on top of the book.

He waited but I refused to read the blurb on the back. No doubt it was a lovely blurb that he'd paid some overpriced marketer a thousand bucks to write. I still wasn't interested. Finally he smiled. That polished gleam was starting to look strained.

"Please," he said, "continue."

"The real problem," I said, "is about my brother Kenny--"

A CD sailed through the air.

"The Black Hole of Brotherhood," he crowed, "a wonderful lecture about brothers. I have another that deals with sisters. Do you have any sisters? You can get a discount when you buy the pair."

"My brother," I said while placing the CD pointedly on the growing stack, "committed suicide."

"Ah."

His brow wrinkled. His hands pressed together. After the tiniest of moments, he leaned toward the bookcase on his left and gently fished out a shrink-wrapped package.

"The Black Hole of Suicide," he said quietly, "a book and DVD set for those mourning this terrible act of self-harm."

I didn't touch it. Somehow he reached the exit before I did.

"I'm here for you, Greg," he said as he held the door. "My DVDs and books can be there for you any time, day or night. Oh, and we take credit cards."

He put on his hopeful-plus-compassionate face and stuck out his hand. I didn't shake it and I didn't look back.

He can kiss, I thought, *the Black Hole of My Ass.*

* * *

When I returned to the condo, it was nearly noon. I detoured around the overgrown shrubs and eyed the dead grass that lay in the ridiculously small area set aside as patio space. One side of the fence had been knocked down ages ago and I could see Ilana through the sliding glass door. She was standing at the island in the kitchen pulling delivery boxes from a grocery bag.

"We've got to get out of this place," I said as I walked in. "It looks like a slumlord owns this unit. We've got to get it fixed up and rented."

"I'm so glad you agree!" She pushed aside the food and spread a handful of papers across the counter. "Everything's ready for you to sign."

"What? What everything? What do you want me to sign?"

"Our new house!" she beamed. "Greg, it's all ready. All you have to do is sign for this mortgage and we can start building tomorrow!"

"Building what? Ilana, what have you done?"

Apparently, she'd done a lot. The moment she'd risen from bed after the week of mourning her old house, she'd worked on securing a loan using my credit. We were married, after all, and she'd used the power of this freshly minted legal bond to set up the mortgage. It was for an astonishingly large amount.

"Why do we need all this?" I asked.

"For your dream home!" She draped herself around me. "Oh, Greg, I've had this idea for such a long time. I've been looking and looking for the perfect house for us, something that meets your high standards. I was going to sell my place to make the down payment when I found the right home. But it doesn't exist...yet."

"Let me guess," I said heavily. "We're going to build it."

"Yes!" She flapped a few papers at me. "I've already lined up the contractors. Cathryn gave me the names of reliable companies--"

"You've been talking to Cathryn behind my back?"

"I wanted it to be a surprise. Surprise!"

"Does Jeff know?"

She stepped back. "No. Why?"

I shook my head. "Never mind. What are you thinking?"

She talked a mile a minute. She was never as lively or as beautiful as when she was excited about a project. It made me feel good about my life. Nothing mattered...not the book-pushing therapist or the lost design business, not even the temporary crash-landing in slumville. Ilana wasn't a roadrunner, she was a phoenix. Together we would rise from the ashes.

When I started looking over the plans, though, two things immediately became apparent. First, the design was utter chaos. Although the blueprints had been drawn up professionally, the rooms were jumbled together. The living space stuck out to one side like the end of a barbell, and the foyer looked anemic. Ilana had tried to set up a house that would take advantage of the world-class view she planned to locate but nothing flowed.

We worked through the issues bit by bit. I knew generally what would work but I really needed to see the building site first. Ilana carted me to a series of properties that hadn't been developed. She told me to select the one I liked best; she'd already knocked out the locations she didn't like. I finally narrowed my choices down to one.

California provided a wonderful environment for this type of project. The home was designed to take full advantage of the weather, the light and the view with a covered outdoor living space. Part of the yard backed up to a butte with the rest heavily bordered by existing growth that could be tamed. The yard would end up being so well screened we could wander in and out naked if we wanted.

Once the design process started in earnest, I began having doubts. Ilana wanted a spa and I preferred stone tile to the cheaper porcelain for the bathrooms. Lofted ceilings cost more than standard construction but we had to bring the feeling of the outdoors inside. I thought the project would be too expensive.

Ilana told me not to worry. Her properties were beginning to move and she could afford three homes at that price. We certainly seemed to have a strong enough cash flow based on how quickly her spending had ramped back up to its old level.

After some additional reassuring, I cut loose. The house would be my sanctuary. Since we'd lost a lot of the furniture to theft or damage, we could start over there, as well. Ilana gave me complete control. The entire place would be calming and classy, the perfect start to our new life. *Maybe,* I mused, *the eviction was a good thing.*

The final design was a masterpiece. At roughly 4,500 square feet, the entire structure flowed in a U shape around a courtyard-style patio. Floor-to-ceiling windows would let in light and draw the eye to the beauty of the golden landscape. Doors would open from three sides of the house to the patio. The living room, a long hallway, and the master bedroom would all look out into the backyard. Tucked behind a low screen of bushes would be a guest cottage that would double as an office.

Since the mortgage was obtained using my credit, the house was entirely in my name. Ilana had asked about transferring the property into both our names once the deal was closed. I was reluctant to do that as long as I was carrying the mortgage myself. If the debt was all mine, I wanted the asset to be all mine.

Besides, every other property in our real estate business was solely in Ilana's name. Rather than sloughing through all the paperwork, effort, and legal fees to transfer everything into both our names, we'd agreed to let my portion of the balance sheet grow naturally as we acquired more properties. Our home would be the first property toward balancing out our individual holdings.

Since the loan Ilana had arranged was for so much, we were able to fast-track the building process. I spent nearly every day on site helping the contractors handle the little fires that popped up during every construction process. Cathryn and Jack were in and out at different times working on the house and the guest cottage. To keep the transition from the interior to the exterior space seamless, I had them put in the concrete patio, too. Soon Ilana and I were ready to move in.

* * *

Weeks later, an intense pain woke me in the middle of the night. The feeling was so extreme and jolted me awake so quickly at first I wasn't sure what was happening. I thought Ilana really had turned into the roadrunner and was stabbing me with her beak. As my brain kicked into gear, I thought I was having a heart attack. The pain was too intense to figure out where it was coming from.

When I moved a little, the stabbing sensation concentrated just above my waistline. As spikes radiated up from my back, my hand flopped around trying to wake Ilana. She wasn't in bed. When I tried to take a deep enough breath to call out for her, the pain clamped onto my ribs. All I could do was lie there and moan.

"Greg?" She appeared in the doorway. "Are you awake?"

I couldn't really communicate. "Pain," I groaned, pointing to my side. "Awful pain. Help."

She hoisted me out of bed. "Really, Greg," she said as I groaned louder.

I wasn't sure if she was complaining about my hollering in her ear or if she was worried that I'd still not managed to regain any of the weight

I'd lost from the foreclosure anxiety. At any rate, it didn't matter. Nothing mattered except the pain.

Somehow I staggered to the car without collapsing. Ilana drove me to the emergency room where I was taken to a bed screened by curtains. As I lay there, unable to stop writhing from the constant burning jabs, the screams and moans of other patients grated on my nerves. When one of the nurses came to my bed, I grabbed her smock.

"Nurse," I panted, "please do something for that poor soul who's screaming."

"Mr. Marks," she said gently, "you're the one screaming."

"Oh." I nodded as if that were a perfectly reasonable explanation. "In that case, do something about my pain, *please!*"

Once the IV was in place, the morphine calmed me down enough to rest. My body was so wiped out I slept through the rest of the ER visit. I missed a trip to radiology for X-rays. I missed the doctor explaining to Ilana that they'd found seven large kidney stones. I missed the nurse giving Ilana the prescription for painkillers with instructions to follow up with a urologist. I even missed the drive home.

The next few days were a fugue of sleep, pills and pain. The follow-up visit with the urologist, the same doctor I'd met while caring for Nick, confirmed the diagnosis of kidney stones. However, the urologist was more concerned about an infection in my gut. When the blood tests came back, he scheduled a colonoscopy. By then the kidney stones were better and things were getting back into a routine.

The day after the colonoscopy, I left on a trip. To save money, I'd purchased a used car from an old friend in Texas. I'd fly out, enjoy a few days with my friend then spend the Christmas holidays driving the Blazer back to California. It wasn't as fancy as my BMW but it was cheap, it would hold all the tools I needed to renovate and maintain our properties, and it was mine.

On the return trip, I enjoyed watching America unroll. The long tracks of farmland probably would have bored a lot of people but I reveled in the view. It was also very peaceful to be driving by myself. I hadn't realized how exhausting Ilana could be with her endless projects, her whirlwind plotting and planning, and the chaotic way she did everything.

I shook my head, wondering how she'd ever gotten as far as she had in real estate. But people loved agents like her...charming, always on, always revved up in high gear. I could put on a public face when I needed to but preferred to sit in the serene beauty of my house and work quietly.

My cell phone rang. It startled me; I hadn't been in areas that could pick up service for much of the trip. When I answered, I was surprised to hear my doctor's voice on the line.

"Greg," he said, "you have to come into my office as soon as possible."

The urgency in his voice was unmistakable.

"What's going on?" I asked. "Is the infection worse than you thought?"

"You have colon cancer," he said. "You need to be in treatment immediately."

There was a long pause while I tried to find a place in my brain for this particular piece of information. Finally I said, "I'm in Arizona. I'm traveling and just crossed into the state. I wasn't planning to be back in California for another few days."

"Drive straight back to my office," he said, "now. We have to establish the treatment regimen. If you don't get in to see me, you won't make it to your next birthday."

"Yeah, right," I said. "My birthday's in June, you know."

"I know," he said. "Drive fast."

I drove. Fast.

CHAPTER TWELVE

Because I thought colon cancer was a private matter, I didn't tell anyone about it. I insisted Ilana keep that confidence, as well.

"But why, Greg?" she asked.

We were sitting in a patch of sunlight in the dining room. Although breakfast was spread out on the table—a host of pastries and fruit she'd picked up during an early-morning run—neither of us were eating. Me because I was worried and Ilana because...well, because she never ate.

"Why do you always order so much food?" I asked. "We never eat everything you order."

"I want to make sure you have a variety," she said. "People will help us if they know you're sick, Greg."

"That's exactly what I don't want." I started flipping bear claws into the to-go box. *Ugh! A crappy, waxy, cardboard to-go box! Not a leather To Go Box! Never to be! Never!* I nearly squashed an éclair in my fist.

"Ilana!" I snapped. "All this food goes to waste!"

"Take it to the contractors," she shrugged, "like you always do. Now, if I tell Cathryn and Jack about your cancer--"

"Don't tell them!"

I stood and sent the chair squawking back toward the wall. I glanced down at the floor; I almost didn't care if the legs had damaged the finish on the concrete floors. Then I neatly tucked the chair under the table and folded the lid onto the pastry box.

"Ilana, my love." I bent forward and touched her face with the one finger that hadn't picked up any gooey icing. "No one can know. Especially not Cathryn and Jack. I don't want anyone worrying. I don't want anyone hovering. You know, and that's all the support I need."

She touched my hand. "Oh, Greg," she said, "you're so wonderful."

I kissed her. She smelled like the desert, scented with pinion and dust. It was a dry and windswept kind of smell, like she'd been gliding over the sands and had tucked the first breath of dawn into her feathers.

* * *

The treatment plan consisted of two rounds of radiation treatments, each six weeks long. Besides getting well, one of my priorities was to finish off as many of the rental properties as possible so they could start producing money. I still wasn't drawing any income and until something hit, my now-miniscule savings would continue to suffer.

The days I had no appointments were spent in Ontario; the days I did go in, I'd run errands beforehand or make calls after. Everything went well for a while. I was surprisingly productive, and although Ilana kept asking if I needed anything, I was able to take care of myself. I floated through the first round of radiation with few side effects.

The second round hit me hard. It started the day after the first appointment. I was getting ready to drive to Ontario when I started sweating and nearly threw up. I couldn't eat that morning, of course, and managed only to pick at some crackers at lunch.

The worst symptom was the profound fatigue. I couldn't seem to get my head out of the fog long enough to think clearly. Instead I pushed my body to do whatever task sat in front of it: hold the steering wheel; pick up the hammer; drill the hole.

Scrambling to hold my life together was bad enough but to be exhausted and nauseous while scrambling to hold my life together was just not fun. Soon I was taking long naps at the work sites. Sometimes I actually made it out to the car; most of the time I'd hunker down in a corner intending to rest for a few minutes and wake up an hour later when one of the workmen came by.

Cathryn and Jack woke me a few times to ask if I was all right. I told them I had a stomach flu and that I just needed to rest for a while. Many days I asked them to stay late to meet a different contractor or to pass on a check to someone so I could go home early. I was so relieved to have their friendship. Without their support, many of the jobs would have come to a complete halt.

A few weeks into this, Cathryn and Jack showed up at the house. I woke to hear their voices in the dining room. At first I thought I was dreaming. When the fog finally cleared a little, I panicked. I thought we had invited them to dinner and I'd forgotten they were coming. I stumbled into the closet, banging my toe and generally making a racket as I tried to find something to wear.

Although Ilana had her own closet, lately her things had been creeping into mine. She was just too overwhelmed with all the extra chores she had to manage while I was sick so I hadn't said anything to her. As I pushed through her clothes looking for mine, I noticed something strange. It took a minute to register but when it did, the shock brought tears to my eyes.

Her stuff was all knockoffs. At a glance the labels belonged to designers but a closer reading proved them to be copies. The Oscar de la Renta was misspelled and the Carolina Herrera was a synthetic blend. Even most of her handbags, the Pradas she consistently and covetously rotated through, were fake. The logo was real but had been ripped off last year's bag and attached with a wire to the knockoff.

Ilana knew our business needed time to grow. She knew my savings would be empty by the time the medical treatments were done. She knew she'd have to support me fully soon, and had cut her spending as a way to prepare. That she would give up what meant so much to her and her ability to woo clients, that she'd switch to patent leather and polyester for me, touched me deeply. I wept as I placed her knockoffs gently back on the shelves.

God, I thought, *how she loves me.*

Although I managed to stop crying, I wasn't terribly successful getting dressed. Ilana had been picking up the dry cleaning but she didn't know which pants went with which shirt. Instead of ready-to-wear outfits all hung neatly along the pole, there was a sea of chaos. Colors were mixed together, lone shirts were stuffed among the trousers, and not a single belt had been matched to its pants. Half the things had been crushed together and were too wrinkled to wear.

I couldn't deal with it on a good day. Now, with radiation regularly being shot into my gut, I was beyond coping. I worked my legs into some khakis the dry cleaner had neglected to press, pulled on a shirt but forgot to button it, and located a pair of socks and some loafers.

When I appeared at the dinner table, everyone stopped talking.

"Sorry I'm late!" I tried for chipper but sounded like the last howl of a road-killed coyote. "Ilana, what's for dinner?"

I gave her a kiss and fell into a chair. I looked around and noticed… nothing. Nothing was cooking on the stove, I didn't see the delivery menus Ilana normally left by the phone, and no coffee scented the air.

"Can I get you a drink?" Ever the gracious host, I hoisted myself up and shuffled to the bar.

"No, thank you, Greg," Cathryn said. A touch pointedly, I thought, but I wasn't sure why.

"Jackson?" I waved grandly at the liquor to cover the fact that I could barely stand. "Brandy, perhaps? A cigar?"

The joke fell flat. Jack shook his head.

"We'd better be going." Cathryn nodded at Jack as they stood.

"Wait. What? We haven't eaten yet. Ilana?"

"They can't stay, Greg. It's all right."

She patted my hand and escorted our guests to the door. Jack took both Ilana's hands in his as Cathryn spoke in low tones. There was a lot of head nodding, looks shot my way, tight smiles topped by piercing eyes. I wanted desperately to sit down but was afraid that if I stopped leaning on the bar, I'd pitch face-first to the floor.

So I waved, a limp smile pasted to my face, my eyes tearing up from the nausea, wanting them to stay and sit by my bed as I fell asleep and wanting them to leave so they wouldn't see me collapse.

I knew I'd tell Cathryn but after…after the doctor proclaimed me well, after the radiation had stopped stirring my guts into a terrible storm. She was a good enough friend that she'd understand why I hadn't told her during the treatments. She was a good enough friend to deserve an explanation.

But later. For now, I was sticking with the flu story. That was good for at least another week.

* * *

The World of Concrete loomed. After the To-Go Boxes idea had collapsed, Cathryn had said she and Jack were looking to expand their business. They'd seen how I worked during the construction phase of the house and asked me to join forces with them.

It was a fantastic idea. Although I still didn't know Jack well, I was positive Cathryn wouldn't be with him unless he was a stand-up guy. Before we finalized the plans, I'd attend the World of Concrete expo to make sure I knew what I was getting into.

The annual expo was set in Las Vegas. Although at lot of the attendees were regional, a surprising number of vendors and participants flew in from around the world. The weekend was filled with seminars and lectures, and would be a crash course for me. Although there wouldn't be much down time, I was looking forward to spending the days and evenings with my friends.

Ilana, meanwhile, would head north for a short visit with her mother and stepfather. She'd leave a couple of days before the expo and wouldn't return until I did. I told her to invite the twins to stay at the house over the weekend. That way, if Jeff's criminal buddies found out we were gone, he would have to answer for any "burglaries."

The ploy had already worked for the couple of surprise getaways Ilana had booked for the two of us. Despite having married into a family with criminal elements, with a little cleverness, the damage could be controlled. Of course, I always told the twins they were free to work on their cars *inside* the garage and not to invite so many people over that their vehicles wouldn't fit in the driveway.

I'd probably have to ramp up efforts to keep the pair at bay once Ilana inherited the family fortune, of course, but that wasn't an issue yet. Meanwhile, I was starting to feel pretty capable and in control. If I could handle the twins, surely I could handle my own life. I might even get Ilana on solid enough footing that she'd relax a little and not stay up every night working late.

To my surprise, the twins turned down the offer to stay at our house. They had other plans, a business deal that needed their immediate attention. I didn't want to know what kind of "business" those two were into and didn't ask. I told the neighbors the house would be empty that weekend and to call the police if they saw anything unusual…like two guys loading our things into a van.

The day Ilana left, the side effects of the radiation and my stubborn work schedule caught up with me. I fell into bed, exhausted and blessedly alone. I slept for hours, waking only to make an obligatory first-evening poke at a meal before returning to bed. My body and mind relished the recovery of peaceful, uninterrupted sleep.

Sometimes, when kids were playing outside or the neighbor cranked up his stereo while cleaning the car, I left the television on to drown out the noise. The murmur of soap operas and daytime talk shows was a soothing sound. It reminded me of staying home sick when I was a kid and sipping 7-Up all afternoon.

After the first day, I didn't even get up to eat. I slept, and slept then rolled over and slept some more.

Unfortunately, I slept through the World of Concrete.

* * *

Eventually Cathryn got hold of me. I just happened to be in the kitchen pouring a tall glass of water. The cool liquid soothed my body in a way nothing else could. When the machine kicked on, I heard her voice. I was so focused on shuffling over to the phone I didn't really listen to the message she was leaving.

"Hello!" I was panting from the effort but had caught her before she hung up. I was so pleased to hear her voice…until she started talking.

"Where the hell have you been?" She wasn't shouting but she sure wasn't using her inside voice.

"Catching up on my sleep," I said. "I know I'm a little late for the expo. I'll be there tonight."

"Greg, the expo is over."

"What? It's only Friday. I know I'll miss the networking dinner but I can catch up."

"It's Monday. Hello!"

I slept for…four days? Jesus!

"You never picked up at the house and your cell phone went right into voicemail," Cathryn said. "I even tried your email."

Well, the phones were both at the other end of the house and I certainly hadn't returned emails in my sleep. "Look, Cathryn, I wasn't going to tell you this--"

"Oh, don't worry, you don't have to tell me," she said. "I already called Ilana. She gave me an earful!"

"Oh. Well, I'm sorry you had to hear it from her. I was going to tell you--"

"When? After I'd already told all my business associates about our plans? After you decided to blow off the World of Concrete and embarrass Jack and me in front of people who've known us for years? Well, good job, Greg. The damage is done."

"Why are you being so hard on me?" I was starting to get angry. "I'm sorry but I think under the circumstances you might cut me a break."

"Cut you a break?" She was really furious now. "Why? So Jack and I can fill in for you while you stagger home or collapse in a back room somewhere? What makes you think I want to nursemaid you through your drug binges?"

"Drug binges?" Now it was my turn to shout. "What the hell are you talking about?"

"Oh, don't play Mister Innocent with me, Greg. Ilana told me everything. That's why you've been so wiped out lately. You're strung out on something, taking uppers to keep you going and crashing whenever your own little party is done."

I was shaking so hard I slid down the wall. "Cathryn," I gasped, "it's not true."

"It's not? Well, what is it then? The stomach flu? Male anorexia? Because from where I'm standing, it looks like a touch of the junkie bug."

"I...Cathryn, I have cancer."

"Don't you even lie like that!"

I'd never heard her so angry. Now I knew why Jack was such a quiet guy...he'd have to be pretty low-key to keep off Cathryn's radar.

But it didn't matter. There was only silence on the line, her breath and mine butting heads in some electronic world.

"Cathryn," I said, "it's true. I'm in treatment. It's almost over but I just don't have the strength right now to deal with this. I'll show you the hospital bills when they come in, if you like. But you have to believe me. It's not drugs."

"You're in treatment?"

"For cancer," I said.

"Yeah. For cancer."

She didn't believe me.

"All right, Greg," she finally said. "I don't know much about this entire situation. All I know is what Ilana told me and what you're telling me now. You don't seem like the druggie type but what do I know?"

"You know me," I whispered. "We're friends."

"Yes," she said. "And because we're friends, I'm going to give you the benefit of the doubt. If you do have cancer, I'm sorry for that, and for yelling at you. Whatever kind of treatment you're getting, I hope it sticks. Because if you do drugs in the future, it's over."

"What's over?"

"Everything."

"Our friendship?"

"Everything."

Well, that was pretty clear. I nodded then realized she couldn't see me. I managed to say OK and we hung up. I was too exhausted to get back to the bedroom so I crawled onto the couch and stayed there until Ilana came home.

* * *

When my loving wife finally arrived, she kept me at arm's length. She managed to stay very busy with work, phone calls and errands. I thought she felt guilty for lying to Cathryn, who also seemed distant. I thought she was angry because I'd missed the conference.

Cathryn and Jack, I decided, would get over it. They'd see me when I finally got back to work and would realize it had all been a strange mix-up. I was so used to Ilana's chaos by then it didn't really occur to me they might have any other reaction. Besides, the friendship was strong enough to carry us through.

Ilana, however, needed to be pinned down. I finally caught her on her way out the door one day. Quite literally, too. I had to grab her arm to keep her from whisking away on yet another urgent errand.

"Why," I said evenly, "did you tell Cathryn and Jack I was on drugs?"

She seemed surprised. "Greg," she said with complete sincerity, "you told me not to tell anyone you had cancer!"

"So it seemed logical to tell people I was on a drug binge instead? Did that seem like a good cover story?"

She rolled her eyes. She actually rolled her eyes!

"Greg," she said patiently, "have you looked at yourself lately? That flu story didn't last past the first two weeks. Cathryn and Jack kept finding you passed out in the bedrooms of the rentals. You weren't very coherent, your clothes are hanging off you and...well, your personal hygiene hasn't been up to your usual standard lately."

"My...personal hygiene?" I wanted to laugh and wrap my hands around her skinny little neck.

"Yes, Greg. It's not my fault you didn't want anyone to know."

So. It was my fault.

I staggered back to the bedroom and turned on the TV. Maybe I could drown out my marriage, too.

CHAPTER THIRTEEN

About a week later, I found a document on the floor next to Ilana's desk. It contained notes on the structure of the new business Cathryn, Jack and I were attempting to start. The proposed structure gave equal ownership to Ilana, Cathryn and Jack. I, however, was listed as a manager.

I hadn't even known Ilana was interested in joining the new venture. I'd assumed she was already overloaded with moving the real estate properties. Besides, she'd brought me on to her company because she hadn't wanted to be bothered with the day-to-day workings of the rentals and the corporate side. Since the concrete business was going to be a slew of similar details, I couldn't fathom that she'd want a piece of the action.

But I also couldn't understand why no one had told me she was getting involved. I thought it must be a mistake. They must have all assumed I was going to be listed as one of the owners and had simply forgotten to include it in the notes. The attorney who drew up the papers wouldn't know that, though, so I tried to clear things up over dinner.

"Oh," Ilana said as she spooned a dainty portion of chow mein onto the bread plate she insisted on using for dinner, "Cathryn decided you're too flakey. She thought it would be best if I shared ownership instead of you."

"Flakey? Why flakey? She doesn't still believe that drug stuff, does she?"

Ilana shook her head. "You didn't show up for the expo. They think maybe you aren't committed to this industry."

"I have *cancer,*" I said. "I think that's worth a free pass this one time."

"She knows that. But Greg, look at it from their side. If you're too ill to work, they need to protect their interests. We'll start up the business this way and see how it goes. If you prove yourself, we can discuss adding you as an equal partner later."

"If I prove myself? What, if I live long enough? Or if it turns out I'm not a dirty junkie?"

"Don't be so bitter!" She shot me a piercing look. "Come on, Greg, cut them a break. They're professionals. They need to know we're professionals, too. Besides, we're married. You'll benefit from my share of the business even if you aren't on the papers."

I had doubts—slowly creeping, foul doubts—that Ilana had generated this particular idea. The end result was the same, though. She was in and I was out. Not only had she closed the door to my financial independence, she'd taken my place as both business partner to and friend of Cathryn and Jack.

I was trapped. I was working for Ilana managing her modest real estate empire...still without pay. She'd tried so hard to get me to put the house in her name when it was built and had only backed down when I'd gotten testy. The let's-put-future-properties-in-your-name-to-balance-out-the-holdings had been poisoned meat thrown to a starving dog. Or coyote.

She wasn't about to share any part of her business with me, not the real estate holdings or the concrete company. I was just her hired hand, a workhorse she kept fed and watered in a fancy stable. All my future held was more exhausting work, blame for jobs that were never good enough, and more struggle with staff, including her brothers, whom she also never paid.

I felt the betrayal so deeply it was almost physical. Enough, as they say, was enough.

* * *

All my friends had stopped talking to me. Even the neighbors wouldn't look me in the eye. I guess they all believed Ilana's lies. I fell into a vast, deep, depression. Every day I struggled to find a reason to get up and drag myself to another radiation treatment. Ilana never—not once—offered to drive me to an appointment.

If a spouse, a significant other, can't be counted on during something as traumatic as cancer, could anyone? I'd allowed Ilana to so alienate me from my acquaintances that guilt and a fear of being disbelieved prevented me from asking for help. I wondered if the cancer would get the best of me. Before long, I wished for it.

In spite of my health, the depression and myself, I stayed relatively productive. I had no choice, and the movement kept my mind and body occupied. I was in charge of maintenance for the rental properties. Although everything was in Ilana's name, I tried diligently to do my part regardless of how tired and listless the treatments made me.

Besides, the routine offered me some comfort. I'd created this much of a life; wasn't there at least some hope it could still be salvaged? Would all that work just disappear because I'd screwed up a single weekend? If I quit now, what would Cathryn and Jack think? I had to keep going. I had to preserve what little was left of my life…assuming I would even have a life after the doctors had taken their shot.

I continued spending most of my time away from Palm Springs. We'd picked up a few extra properties in a satellite suburb about eighty miles away. I worked with painters, carpenters and subcontractors to renovate three houses…and, of course, I managed Jeff and Kevin. My days were consumed by laboring until I passed out. After a comatose sleep I went for another radiation treatment then worked until I dropped again.

Finding help for the renovation projects became more and more difficult. I could never get Ilana to pay anyone. The payroll checks she wrote consistently bounced. She always had some excuse…one property hadn't closed escrow yet, the deal on another had fallen through. She brimmed with intentions, fewer and fewer of which panned out.

Of course, I was the one who had to deal with the angry employees and cursing contractors. Good, hard workers walked off the job. Soon there weren't any companies in the phone book that didn't hang up when they heard my voice. The work force shrank to the twins and myself. The more things crumbled, the harder I pushed to hold everything together.

If I just kept going, I thought things would eventually turn around. We'd start drawing steady income off the rentals and could talk through the legal side in a calm, rational way. By this time, my savings were completely gone. I'd switched to a local bank that allowed me to keep a savings account open with a balance of five dollars. Some days, I was desperate enough to think about taking out that last tiny amount.

Then one afternoon I arrived on a job site. I'd put in weeks of my own time and had cycled through another series of workers. The last team had been great, putting in long hours and coming back week after week despite the paycheck issues. Suddenly the tide had changed. Five burly guys had stopped hanging drywall and laying carpet to load all my tools into their van.

"What's going on?" I asked. "We're not moving to the next site until this one's done."

"We need to eat," one said. "We're taking our pay today. Materials, tools and equipment."

"It's the least you owe us," another said.

"Look, I know it's been difficult but I'll pay you myself."

"You've been saying that all month," the first guy said. "We're tired of waiting."

They went back to loading the van. When I tried to take a box of screws off the pile, all five men surrounded me. A crowbar, a hammer, a shovel and a nail puller were brandished in a very threatening way.

Just then, a familiar Ford F-150 with a crappy paint job screeched to a halt in the driveway. One of the workers had to jump out of the way. Jeff got out, smiling broadly and holding his hands out like any good politician. Kevin, meanwhile, folded his arms and lurked ominously near to the largest two workers.

"What's up, fellahs?" Jeff said. "Looks like a tea party, only I wasn't invited!"

"We want our pay," the leader said. "All the checks bounced and this guy's nothing but promises."

With some smooth talking, a few crude jokes and a well-placed hangdog expression, Jeff convinced the mob I had nothing to do with payroll. His sister owned the houses, he said; she was responsible for the money or lack thereof. I was only a hired hand, just like any of them.

Shit, I thought. I wasn't just an employee. I was one of the owners. I was her husband.

I opened my mouth to protest. Then I realized this was probably not the time to argue the minute details of my business arrangement with Ilana. Jeff convinced the guys to be happy with what was already in the van. They grumbled a bit but got into the vehicle, still clutching their tools as if ready to resume the fight.

"Thanks, guys," I said as the van disappeared around the corner. "I don't know what might have happened if you hadn't shown up."

"We got your back, bro!" Jeff clapped my shoulder so hard I winced. Kevin grinned and we all went inside.

* * *

"Where's the money?" I kept my voice down but didn't disguise the edge of anger.

Ilana looked at me with those wide, innocent eyes. *A well-rehearsed expression,* I thought.

"Greg, what money?"

"This money."

I slapped a sheaf of paper onto the desk. I'd run some rough calculations using what I knew we had plus the money from the payoff from Nick's family. A lot of it had gone into renovations and investments, yes. She'd also maxed out the line of credit at the bank but hadn't added any new properties to our roster. None that I knew about, anyway.

"That's a lot of money to go through in three months," I said.

She picked up the loan paper by one corner. "You know I bought those properties here in town."

"With the settlement money. This is a separate loan you took out after that."

"For the business." She dropped the paper onto the far corner of her desk.

"Not for the business."

"Greg, what's gotten into you?"

"I've been looking through the files--"

"You've been snooping?"

"I've been looking through the files on our business. Ours, remember? Yours, and also mine? You leveraged all the condos for this new line of credit. The papers say it's for a property but you don't have any new ones. So where's the money?"

She fingered her cell phone for a long minute. "Greg," she finally said, "I...."

She sighed and leaned back. "I didn't want to tell you this. I wanted it to be a surprise. A birthday surprise. I bought a vacation property for us."

"Where?"

"Sedona."

"When did you have time to go to Sedona to look at properties?"

"Over the Christmas holiday. Then, when I told you I went to my mother's place, I actually went back there to close. That's why the twins weren't here, either. They went out to start the renovations."

"You're lying."

"I'm not lying!"

She stood and began pacing. She clutched the cell phone in one hand and waved her other around. "Why would I lie to you, Greg? Whatever do you think I'd get out of it?"

"Let's see. You lied about Nick's will. You lied to Cathryn about my so-called drug addiction when you're the one who was an addict."

"That's not fair!"

"You lied to get me to propose! You manipulate every situation for your own benefit, and I'm just one of your dupes!"

I was so hurt. Angry, yes, but deeply hurt. I stood there, completely bare, hoping for once she'd say the right thing. Just once.

She stopped pacing. She took two steps toward me and leaned her face close to mine. She was absolutely furious. "I did it all for us," she said.

"You're lying."

My voice was flat. I was completely deflated. I had given her everything and had nothing left.

"If you're not lying," I said, "show me the property. Let's drive out to Sedona right now and you walk me through it. No phone calls along the way, no running a few quick errands before we go. Just you and me, right now."

She hesitated. She glowered fiercely and turned away.

Then she punched me.

I never saw it coming. She must have punched me with the fist holding the cell phone because it felt like a two-by-four hit my cheek. My head rocked back and smacked the doorframe.

"Goddamn it!" she snapped. "I broke a nail!"

She stormed out. I heard the car backing down the drive and that infuriating double-beep she always hit to let me know she was leaving. I was alone, so utterly alone, in a dream house that had become my prison.

* * *

I woke up in the ICU. Just like Nick, I had a catheter and was hooked up to IVs and monitoring devices. I wasn't sure why I was there but obviously I was in trouble. I had no memory about what put me there and could only guess what had happened. Ilana hadn't punched me *that* hard.

The nurse arrived. She explained that Ilana had found me on the bedroom floor and called 911. I'd taken several bottles of pills. The empty containers lay on the nightstand with a note that read, *I can't do this anymore. I can't take any more pain.*

It was a perfectly reasonable response to what had not been a very good day.

After receiving this momentous news, I must have nodded off. When I woke again, Cathryn was sitting beside my bed.

"So," she said.

"A needle pulling thread," I replied.

"Well, I can see you're gonna be all right. Nothing wrong with this guy!" She touched my hand. "I'm glad to see you're back in the land of the living."

I nodded and pointed to the door. The nurse was bringing in a tray of food. I wasn't sure how long I'd been in the hospital but I was ravenous. When Cathryn pulled the cover off the plate, her lip curled.

"Hope you'd like to lose even more weight," she said. "I'd starve on this food."

My dinner consisted of a very sad hamburger, fries, and a small bowl of corn. The lettuce, tomato and onion sat next to the bun along with packages of mustard and mayonnaise. Although I was practically drooling, I didn't have the strength to feed myself. I lay there looking helpless.

"Would you like some help with that?" Cathryn asked.

"Sure."

She spread the mayonnaise on the top of the bun. When she tried to squeeze the mustard onto the same piece of bread, I grabbed her arm.

"You like mustard," she said.

"Everyone knows it goes on the other side of the bun. The meat goes on the bottom piece with the mustard and the lettuce sits next to the mayonnaise."

Apparently I could be compulsive even in the ICU.

"You're the boss," she said.

Cathryn smiled and looked over at Ilana. She'd been sitting in the corner the entire time and was clearly impatient.

"Greg," my loving wife said, "since Cathryn's here, I'm gonna step out. I'll be back later."

Before Cathryn or I could respond, she was gone. A dark look shadowed Cathryn's face while she glowered at the door. Then she turned to me and smiled again. "One bun-mustard-burger-lettuce-mayo-bun, as ordered."

I chomped through the burger in five huge bites and washed it down with warm iced tea. The beverage looked cloudy, obviously concocted from a mix. It didn't matter. I would have eaten horsemeat.

The fries were next. My lean coyote belly started working on the food and between each fry, I dozed off for a few seconds. Then I'd snap awake and continue eating as if I'd been conscious the entire time. Twenty minutes later, all that remained of the fries were a greasy spot and a lukewarm memory.

The corn was gulped down next. When I put the spoon down, I asked Cathryn to push the limp strawberry cake close enough to gobble down.

"Oh, no, young man," she said. "You can't have your dessert until you finish your entire meal. There's corn left in this dish."

"Are they whole kernels or partial kernels?"

She peered closely. "Partial kernels, I guess. Why?"

"Everyone knows partial kernels don't count." I sighed heavily. "You know, I don't understand corn."

"Well," she said matter-of-factly, "corn grows on a stalk. It's actually grass. They have corn that's for popcorn, they have corn that's feed for pigs and cows, there's sweet and yellow corn for humans, and there's even corn called hominy. That's what they make grits out of."

I shook my head. "I was just thinking of green beans. Who is they? You keep saying they have…."

I fell asleep.

It was a brief respite before the next storm.

CHAPTER FOURTEEN

The next day I woke up in a semi-private room. I had no idea what that entire exchange with Cathryn had been about. We laughed about it as I recovered. Eventually she said, "I'm glad you're getting help. I can't imagine how scary it must be to have seizures."

"What?"

Was she talking about the overdose? Had I been having seizures when Ilana found me?

"Ilana told me you've been having seizures lately. Greg, you've got to get off those drugs."

"Cathryn, I'm not a drug addict. Ilana. Ilana!"

"She's not here now. Look, Greg, you have to know something. I'm your friend and I don't bolt on friends easily. But this drug thing…you've got to get that straightened out."

"I'm not an addict!"

The room was spinning around me. My heart was racing and I could have ripped open Ilana's throat with my teeth. I must have passed out because the next thing I remember, I woke up alone.

The day I was discharged, Cathryn drove me home. Ilana was off working on some property or spending whatever was left of the loan she'd taken out; it didn't matter. What mattered was that Cathryn was going to stick around until Ilana came home. She and Jack wanted to make sure everything was set up so it was more convenient for me. Until I got some of my strength back, I was going to be hanging around the house a lot.

When Ilana walked in, Cathryn stood to go. I grabbed her arm.

"Wait," I said. "There's something I want you to hear."

I got everyone to sit down in the living room together. Ilana was nervous; she knew something was up but had no clue what it might be. She kept checking her cell phone and looking at the office as if she had something urgent to do. She wouldn't squeak out of it this time, though.

"Tell them." I leaned against the back of her chair. I swayed a little but I was on my feet.

"What, Greg?" She plastered that innocent look on her face again but her eyes were sharp, black points.

"Tell them you lied."

She flushed the tiniest bit. "What do you mean?"

"Tell them why I've been so tired lately. Tell them that what you said before was a lie."

Her face shifted. A casual observer might buy the puzzled act but underneath I saw a flitting moment of cunning. She was racing around mentally, darting under cover and pecking out little worms hoping to distract the coyote and his friends.

"What lie, Greg?"

"About the drugs."

"Greg, I told them you were abusing meth."

"Right."

She shot Cathryn a quick look. I waited. She shifted and sighed, looking very much the put-upon spouse. I was determined to break down that façade.

"Look, Greg," Jack said, "we don't need to hear anything more. You're in treatment. That's all that matters."

"Tell them." I leaned over Ilana. "Tell them!"

"Tell them what, Greg?"

Her face turned up toward me. There, in her smile, was triumph. Cathryn just had to see that. She had to know what a devious mind lay behind that beautiful exterior.

"Tell them I'm not a drug addict!"

"Greg," Cathryn said.

"It's all right." Ilana folded her hands primly in her lap. "He's not a drug addict."

"Tell them you lied."

"Greg!" Cathryn started to stand but Ilana held up one manicured hand.

"I lied," Ilana said.

"Tell them why I've been collapsing lately."

"What do you mean?"

"Tell them about my treatments."

"Your treatments?"

"For cancer!"

"You want me to say you have cancer?"

"Ilana!"

"OK, Greg," she soothed. "Cathryn, Jack, Greg is not a drug addict. He has cancer."

"OK?" I looked at the pair. They seemed utterly unconvinced. And I was utterly worn out. I began to sway dangerously. Jack stood and caught my arm.

"Why don't I help you to bed?" he said.

I nodded. As I shuffled into the bedroom, I realized I was leaving Cathryn and Ilana alone together. That probably wasn't good but I passed out the second I hit the pillow.

* * *

Ilana wasn't around much the next week or so. That was fine with me; I spent the time shuffling between the bed and the kitchen shoveling food and sleep into my body in massive quantities. Since I left the television on for company, I also found some tiny outlet for my anger.

During the day, the channels were filled with a parade of yell-at-the-cheating-spouse talk shows. A stream of cross-dressing, gambling-addicted, on-the-down-low, kleptomaniacal, panty-obsessed, toe-sucking mutants made me feel like I wasn't the only one stuck in a bizarre relationship. My favorite programs were the ones where the hosts goaded the guests into duking it out. They were doing what I would never allow myself to do... lose any pretext of control.

Instead, I ordered my life. As my strength grew I dusted and mopped, scrubbed and squeegeed. When everything was clean I took a toothbrush to the grout and ran a toothpick through the joints where the kitchen sink met the countertop. I lifted miniscule spots out of the area rugs and combed the hand-tied fringe with my fingers. It was a perfect low-impact exercise regimen that moved my body and calmed my mind.

When there wasn't a single thing left to clean, arrange or organize inside the house, I went to the office. Papers were stacked everywhere, and I hadn't a clue what they locked us into or where the money might be going. I'd have to get back to the properties soon but I could slip in a little time here and there reading through the mystery files. I had to if I wanted to find out what Ilana was really doing.

As I sat at her desk, I didn't know where to begin. I shuffled through her inbox and found letters that were months old. I looked through all the desk drawers but didn't find any stray slips of paper or furtive notes. Finally I pulled open the lowest drawer, the one that held files. It would take the longest to go through but might be where she'd stick something important.

To my surprise, the drawer appeared neat and somewhat organized. The hanging folders were filled with slim files, each printed in her hand. Even with the first glance, I recognized the addresses of the condos she'd earmarked as corporate rentals. But I didn't spend more than a second considering the files.

I was too busy staring at the knife.

A rather long knife lay lengthwise across the tops of the file folders. This wasn't something from the kitchen block or even a pocket knife someone might carry for little fix-it jobs; this was a street weapon intended only to draw blood. Copious quantities of blood. The message couldn't have been more clear.

Stop asking questions or else.

* * *

As soon as possible, I got back to the rentals. At first I only spent an hour or two at the properties but soon felt well enough to get some real work done. In addition to all the repairs, keeping up with the twins took a great deal of energy. They loved to work at looking busy without actually doing much. They could never be left on their own without the entire unit being in jeopardy. Cathryn and Jack still didn't trust them so I couldn't even go to lunch and leave Jeff or Kevin there.

After months of hand-holding, pleading, cajoling, begging and threatening, I finally fired them both. Ilana went insane. Oddly, she seemed more panicked than angry. When I asked her what the big deal was, she kept saying, "They need a second chance." Well, I'd given them a second chance, and a third one, too.

It didn't matter. The new appliances had been installed, the faucets and doorknobs had been polished. The properties became available one right after the other, like a satisfying row of dominoes I had set up myself. Now it was up to Ilana to knock them down with corporate contracts, high-end rentals and a few vacation gigs. She'd get out of debt, I'd get some income, and we could both rationally tackle all the strange things that had happened.

It didn't work out. Ilana did nothing. The condos stood empty and the homes clicked through daily cycles of automatic lighting but she never committed to renting or selling a single one. I kept mowing the lawns, trimming the bushes and pitching out the sales notices college students tacked to the doors. Nothing showed, nothing sold. We were at a dead halt, as were my finances.

I stayed home for a while, intending to enjoy a much-needed rest. If she wasn't going to do anything, I could at least take a few days to regroup. Just as I was beginning to relax, there was a loud thumping on the door. I knew that sound well by now. It was the twins.

I didn't want to open the door but I did. Whenever Jeff got pissed off, he screamed the most outrageous obscenities. At different job sites, I'd heard a lot of tirades against this buddy who'd smoked all his weed or that neighbor who'd let their dog piss on his truck tire. He had his own mental dictionary of disgusting phrases he'd invented, all of which could come out in long streams. The last thing I wanted was our neighbors getting an early-morning earful of that filth.

I opened the door. The sense of doom was already overwhelming.

"Greg, buddy!" Jeff grabbed me by both shoulders as he shoved inside. "Look, we got thrown out. We need a place to crash."

"The guest room's in the back." Ilana popped her head out of the bedroom and waved to Kevin. "Stay as long as you like."

"Wait!" I didn't want either of them, least of all the convicted felon, living in our house. "What happened? Why'd you get kicked out?"

"Oh, the landlord's brother's coming back into town next week. He had a place lined up but the guy's a deadbeat. He can't pay the first and last month's rent. So we're out, the brother's in."

Kevin headed into the guest room while Jeff retrieved some of his things from the truck. I knew they had split up to make sure I didn't lock them out. The Ford was stuffed with clothes, stereo equipment and gummy work boots. I imagined the bedbugs, lice and filth they trailed through our house with every load.

I couldn't stand to watch. I went into the kitchen to make coffee. They hadn't been there long enough to infest anything but I was already starting to itch.

* * *

Having the twins as houseguests turned out to be worse than I'd feared. Every morning when the pair woke up, they coughed and sniffed and blew their noses into their bed sheets. Jeff kept it up while he showered, blowing his nose into his hand and washing it down the drain. Kevin had cleared his sinuses by then but hawked and spat while he showered.

Every time they shaved, it looked like the can of foam had exploded. Shaving cream spattered the mirrors, the toilet, and the silk-and-papyrus wallpaper I'd hung in the guest bath. They never rinsed the sink or the tub, and the first time I went in there to clean it myself, their whiskers clogged the drain.

"Just be glad I didn't clog the toilet, buddy," Jeff said as he walloped me chummily on the shoulder. "I can take some monster dumps!"

I clutched a bottle of bleach and a plunger. The industrial rubber gloves I wore went past my elbows. Did I look like someone who enjoyed scatological references before breakfast?

Most days the twins actually left the house. They claimed to have a job, although they wouldn't or couldn't say what it was. I imagined it mostly involved standing on the street corner. Often they arrived home in the middle of the afternoon, devoured the delivery Ilana had ordered, expelled rolling belches to compliment her on the choice of cuisine, lit horrifyingly foul cigars they claimed were to cover the smell of their farts (which smelled equally horrifying but at least didn't cling to the upholstery) then lay in the sun scratching themselves.

Their second outing didn't end until late at night. They often rolled

112

in well past midnight, waking me with the bang of the front door. Jeff apparently couldn't shut the door any more gently than he could knock on it. When I asked about their odd hours, Jeff just grinned.

"Split shift," he said.

Then he hawked up a huge wad of mucus and swished it noisily through his teeth. I nearly ran to the bathroom to vomit.

I nearly vomited a lot those first two weeks.

* * *

After a while, Ilana began complaining that she didn't want the twins staying any longer. She said she'd already asked them to leave twice but they'd refused. I marched into the guest room and told them they had twenty-four hours to pack up and go. If they didn't, I'd call the police. Jeff barely noticed me; Kevin glowered.

At the appointed hour, I dialed 911. When I hung up, I heard that double beep. Ilana was backing her car down the driveway and she drove off just as the police pulled in. The officer looked suspiciously like the sheriff who'd evicted us. I tried to keep a grip on my anger and my sanity while he tried to sort out the conflicting stories.

"I want them out," I said.

"Our sister lives here," Jeff said. "She told us we could stay."

"She wants them gone." I turned to the twins. "She already asked you to leave twice."

"May I speak with your wife?" the officer asked. "I need to verify what you're telling me with her."

"She's not here," I said. He gave me a look. "She left while I was calling 911. She knows what's going on."

"Why would she leave in the middle of this?"

"She...."

Tends to disappear when the heat's on, I thought. *Darts off whenever her plans fall apart.*

"She doesn't like confrontation," I said.

Kevin's mobile phone rang. It was Ilana. The policeman asked to speak with her. After a few nods and *um-hmms,* he handed the phone back to Kevin.

"Mrs. Marks says you signed a lease and are paying rent," he said to the twins. "Do you have a copy I can look at?"

"There's no agreement," I said. "I don't know anything about any agreement!"

"Do either of you have a copy of this lease?" the officer asked again.

"Sure," Jeff said. "Hold on a second and I'll get it."

I was dumbstruck. Within seconds Jeff returned with a lease agreement and an employment contract. The papers said the twins would work for Ilana in her real estate business in exchange for room and board. The agreements were dated the day after they'd arrived. Ilana had never said anything to me about the agreement.

Once again, I was left holding the bag.

"I'm sorry, officers, for having wasted your time. I have obviously been misinformed."

The two officers looked more impatient with each passing second. As they left, Jeff and Kevin smirked. Kevin headed back to the guest bedroom…excuse me, their room. Their bought-and-paid-for room. In my house. My prison.

Ilana arrived. How did she know the precise moment the police left? Had she been parked around the corner? She ignored me and went directly to Jeff and Kevin's bedroom. I banged on the door a few times but they ignored me. The three of them talked for half an hour before Ilana finally came out.

"You should have told me," I said.

"Oh, give it a rest, Greg. It was all a misunderstanding. Everything's fine now. They forgive you for calling the police on them."

"Forgive me? I called the police because that's what you and I agreed on. Why would you let me do that when you had an agreement with them? Why didn't you tell me?"

"Because I knew you'd react just as you are right now. You don't want them here, so you're making me choose between them and you. I won't do that!"

By then she was shouting. Why, I wondered, was I being punished? What crime had I committed?

"I've never asked you to choose," I said. "You're the one who complained about them being here. What was that about?"

"Oh, so this is all my fault? I can't just throw my brothers on the street, you know."

"I don't know what to say. All you had to do was tell me you had agreed they could stay here."

"OK, I agreed that they could stay here. Now can we just drop this?"

She headed toward our bedroom. I grabbed her arm. "We're not done yet!" I shouted.

A vice grip squeezed my arm. The twins had appeared and Kevin was apparently trying to see if he could crack my bones with one hand. "You're done," he said. "Let her go."

I released my grip. Kevin, however, kept the pressure on until Ilana banged the bedroom door shut. Jeff leaned against the wall and smirked until Kevin finally let go. Before they banged their own door shut, Jeff put his arm around me and leaned in close. What he whispered chilled my heart.

"I," he rasped, "know how to make napalm." Then he strutted away, throwing another smirk over his shoulder.

I stood in the middle of the living room. What the hell had just happened? Had she planned all along to turn the twins completely against me? Were they additional weapons—bigger, more threatening weapons—she'd use against me if I didn't stay in line? Or was this some sick joke on Jeff's part, a show of machismo in line with all the mucus hawking?

I was shaking. I was stuck with her family in my home. My entire life had washed away. First Kenny had been swept off by the river, then Nick by a century of years. Now my autonomy and any illusion of control had been stripped away.

I *was* being punished…because I hadn't told anyone about the abuse, because I had failed to protect my brother, because I had abandoned my parents. My life from then on would be nothing but more abuse, more slavery to a wife who had her brothers on a choke chain. If I didn't follow orders, she'd turn them loose on me. Or she'd do me in herself.

What was the point? Who'd choose to live this way? I still didn't have the final verdict on the cancer so that potential death sentence still loomed. The only control I had left was how the end would come.

I found a bottle of muscle relaxants and swallowed ninety pills. I slipped under the covers of my bed for the last time. As I relaxed, gave in and gave up, I looked at the time. Eight-thirty Thursday night. Close to dusk. A fitting time to die. My stomach started to ache but before anything felt very painful, I drifted away.

CHAPTER FIFTEEN

I woke up Sunday morning. Ilana was shuffling around the room banging doors, slamming drawers, and generally making a lot of noise. She seemed pretty pissed. Was she mad that I'd tried to kill myself again or that I'd been unsuccessful? I'd probably never know for sure.

I was still pretty groggy and couldn't walk on my own. I asked Ilana to help me up. She yanked me out of bed, shoved me into the bathroom, and left me on the toilet. I didn't have enough strength to sit upright so I slumped forward until my chest rested on my knees. I stayed there for two hours until she finally returned.

"Are you through yet?" she demanded.

"Hospital," I mumbled.

She called an ambulance. She must have given the dispatcher some sob story because a police officer also responded to the call. It was the same officer who'd shown up after my first overdose. He recognized me and remembered the prior attempt. He placed me on a 5150 hold, a seventy-two hour involuntary commitment under the California Welfare and Institutions Code 5150. I was headed for psychiatric treatment whether I wanted it or not.

As the EMTs wheeled me into the ER, Ilana told the nurses I had no insurance and that I was out of my mind. They shot me full of anti-anxiety medication and tried to keep me quiet until I could be transferred to the county lockdown in Indio.

I went ballistic. Ilana had told me she was going to get a soda from the vending machine but she'd already gone home. I was angry that the staff

117

refused to look for her and repeatedly screamed out her name. As I begged and shouted for them to stop, I was strapped to a gurney and loaded into an ambulance.

On the twenty-minute drive to Indio, I quieted down. By the time the ambulance pulled up to the facility, I was resigned to the fact that I would be locked away for as long as was necessary. My destiny was in the hands of a few doctors and a small staff of dedicated county employees.

My loving wife was already home tucked in our bed.

* * *

Indio was an unlikely place to heal. Hope lay thin on the ground and redemption was improbable. My closest neighbor created a furor every morning by smearing her own feces on the walls of her "suite." My other neighbors greeted me with blank stares, mumbles or disjointed rants shrieked at full volume. All mixed with more than a smattering of random violence, of course.

The county facility was grossly under-funded. I bumped around the plastic tables and chairs, unable to leave, while my wife enjoyed breakfast at the mahogany table with hand-turned legs. I squinted through the wire mesh inside the heavy shatterproof windows while she basked in the view from our wall of glass. Planning, no doubt, more ways to keep me locked up for a little longer. Better yet, a lot longer.

Despite the fact that this had been my third suicide attempt, I really didn't believe I deserved to be locked up. A dedicated team of professionals disagreed. Housed among the dregs of society—the mentally ill, drug-addicted, addled social detritus—it was painfully obvious that I didn't belong.

That silly chant from Sesame Street, *One of these things is not like the others, one of these things does not belong,* ran endlessly through my mind. Every day I "worked with" a medical doctor, a pair of psychologists, a psychiatrist, a nutritionist, a social worker, nurses and sundry support staff whom I thought of as keepers.

"One of these things does not belong," I rasped at them faintly.

They never got it. Cathryn would have. I wondered where she was and hoped she wouldn't come to visit. I didn't want her to see this place. I especially didn't want her to see me in it.

The environment was hardly stimulating. The facility looked more like a military barrack or prison than a place where anyone would get well. The eating and common areas were surrounded by tiny shared sleeping quarters. All the areas had been painted an unrelenting drab color somewhere between green, brown and yellow. It's the color that appears when all the leftover paint has been mixed together. My family called it "granch."

So there I was in my granch world with granch walls, granch furniture, granch clothing, granch bedding, and granch food. My life was regimented with a precision only achievable in an institution—breakfast, smoke break, group meeting, snack, smoke break, lunch, another smoke break, group meeting followed by another snack, dinner, smoke break and lights out by nine p.m.

At any time, I could be summoned away from this regimen to attend a private session with my dedicated team. "Why do you think you're here?" they'd ask. "What do you think you should do to get back home?"

Divorce my loving wife, I'd think. *Pluck out her feathers. Burn down all the investment properties and collect on the insurance. Run the twins off the road.* Any one of those solutions would have taken far, far more energy than I had. Even talking was too labor intensive so I stared at the doctors and waited for them to release me into the common areas.

I stood in line for medications then waited for a cigarette by a side door. Everyone smoked in a courtyard surrounded by the buildings that made up the Riverside County Rehabilitation Center. I was allowed one cigarette at a time, each dispensed by a six-foot, two hundred pound keeper whose sole responsibility was to maintain peace.

Once outside, the dregs and I congregated around a few concrete picnic tables. A sheet metal cover shielded us from the harsh sun but nothing could protect us from the stale air or the triple-digit heat. I wandered the perimeter. *A rehabilitation center?* I thought. So far I hadn't seen any actual rehabilitation. Just a bunch of crazy people trying to get through the day.

I didn't belong there. I didn't even remember how I'd gotten there. Someone must have made a terrible mistake. Soon, very soon, the warden would realize the error and return me to my life.

What there was of it.

* * *

Four days later, I stood in another line waiting for my choice of snack—banana, punch, cookie, brownie, orange or Jell-O. At least I was hungry. During the intake exam, the night nurse had listed my weight at 120 pounds. I didn't argue but her scale was obviously off. Normally I weighed around 180. I'd lost some weight but there was no way I was that thin. That would make me skeletal.

My belt, shoelaces, and the drawstring from my sweatpants had been taken to prevent me from "doing harm" to myself. My clothes hung from my body like I was a refugee fleeing a war-torn country. Eating was good. I'd look better with a bit more weight on my frame. Cathryn would be happy.

Yet another line, stand and wait again. All I needed was a toothbrush, toothpaste, razor, shaving cream and a towel. These too were doled out by a keeper. I huddled next to the door to one of the private showers for today's keeper to unlock the door.

It was Tom. He waited in the doorway, timing me to make sure I didn't take too long, listening for any unusual sound in case I tried to hurt myself with the disposable razor, stab myself with the toothbrush, or hang myself from the shower nozzle with the granch towel.

Since I'd been comatose for three days before being committed, this was my first shower in a week. It had been months since I'd cut my hair so it hung in greasy clumps down to my shoulders. Every day at Indio someone had asked if I would like to get cleaned up. Finally I'd agreed just to get them off my back.

As I stood there, I regretted the choice. I was already tired and simple things like bathing took energy I just didn't have. As I shuffled into the dark shower stall, the horrific smell of every previous inmate hit me like a bully's fist. The sound of dripping water echoed as condensation pattered into stale, scummy puddles.

Keeper Tom was posted outside. He wouldn't move and he kept the door open. Only a low wall shielded my lower half from view. My toiletries stood guard atop a small bench as I removed my clothing. Whew, the stench! I blushed when I realized just how unclean I really was. How had I let myself fall so far?

As I glanced over my shoulder, my heart stopped. I didn't recognize the blank, drawn face looking back at me from the mirror. That guy obviously belonged in lockdown. I turned away and minced into the shower.

I'd be dead soon, I just knew it. Heat and moisture were the building blocks for who knew what kind of fungus, virus or bacteria. I'd die in Indio after contracting a terminal illness from the microscopic life thriving in this Petri dish of a hellhole. How could I get clean when the very building was diseased?

I hurried in slow motion. I was tired, so tired. I'd shave later, there was no time for that, I had to get back to bed. Sleep, blessed sleep! It was the only escape from the nightmare. I finally finished, padded back to my cell, and pulled the blanket tightly over my head.

* * *

There was a bang on my door. For a throat-clutching second, I thought Jeff and Kevin had hunted me down.

"Time for group," Keeper Tom yelled. "Get up!"

The meetings, designed as they were for the lowest common denominator among an already low-function group, were depressing. The rules were endlessly repeated for the new inmates. Since I'd been there four days, the counselor asked if I would like to read the rules from the poster taped crookedly to the wall.

"No, thank you." I answered as politely as I could. The effort it took to speak at all was astonishing.

"You're gonna have to participate sooner or later."

Connie encouraged me with a warm smile. She was young and pretty and greeted me each day with a compassion that made me feel like she could be my best friend if I weren't me and my vacation hadn't been booked at Club Indio.

I was embarrassed each time I saw her. In another place and time, we would have struck up a conversation. She would have seen the confident, successful businessman I had been and would like to be again. But that week, I was just one of the inmates she helped down the faded path back to regular society.

Finger-painting was the best I could hope for. Apparently that was less than satisfying to the other inmates, as well. The noise and drama they created were insufferable. They yelled, they cried, they wailed, they attacked each other and the staff, and generally behaved like…well, like crazy people.

In the first four days I had two different roommates, neither of whom I spoke to. I should have been sunning myself on a beach somewhere in the tropics, enjoying the palm trees and a fruity drink served with a paper umbrella. I was a well-educated, successful entrepreneur who'd made, lost and regained fortunes. I'd never run afoul of the law beyond a speeding ticket when I was sixteen. I drank very little and was not a drug user.

Unless, of course, Ilana's stories were accepted as truth.

Ah, Ilana. My beloved arrived shortly after group therapy on day four. My social worker, Lisa, had gathered a lot of background information from my family and friends during my stay. She met with Ilana and I to discuss my discharge plan, a comprehensive approach that would monitor my recovery and prevent another suicide attempt.

The meeting was in some ways fortuitous. For the first time ever, I was given a diagnosis: severe clinical depression. My psychiatrist, Dr. Brad Johnson, a handsome, middle-aged man with bright, intelligent eyes whom I nonetheless found inordinately chipper for a guy named after a line of sex toys, explained that I'd been clinically depressed most of my life.

All of a sudden, things made much more sense. That was why I couldn't stop myself from going under, locking myself inside my home to sleep for days on end. That was why I struggled with an overwhelming sense of worthlessness no matter how much success I created. That was what caused me to destroy my own happiness. That was why I always felt sad and morose even when nothing sad or morose was happening.

Although I didn't quite understand the diagnosis or the full impact of its effects, I did feel the first glimmer of hope. With the help of this wonderful team, I could begin a new chapter in my life. After all, if a guy's peers could consider him a successful professional regardless of how large Doc Johnson dildos were, couldn't I triumph over severe clinical depression?

As Lisa led Ilana and me through the discharge plan, I dared to feel optimistic. *It's not all in my head*, I thought, *and it's not all my fault.* Now I could understand my actions from a different perspective. For decades I'd felt like I were living in quicksand, never able to gain enough momentum or energy to feel good about anything. People all around me lived happy, productive, prosperous lives. For me it was a struggle just to get out of bed.

A chemical imbalance in my brain caused all of it. It had been beyond my control before but could be managed with daily doses of medication. I wasn't sure if that last part was good news or not. Being medicated for the rest of my life wasn't something to celebrate. Dr. Johnson said it was no different than a diabetic who required insulin every day.

"Would you ever ask a diabetic to stop taking insulin?" he asked.

"No," I mumbled, lowering my chin to my chest.

He ran the numbers. A person who'd experienced one depressive episode had a fifty percent chance of suffering another. Someone with two depressive episodes had a seventy percent chance, and three episodes upped the odds to ninety percent.

Since I had suffered three episodes, each of which had led to a suicide attempt, medication would likely be required for the rest of my life. With proper dosing and outpatient psychotherapy, though, I could expect to live a long and happy life.

A happy life. What a foreign concept. I couldn't remember ever having a happy life. At that moment, meeting Dr. J's professional, nonsexual gaze, I dared to have a tiny ray of hope. I could commit to any discharge plan that would point me toward this happy life. After Lisa read off a list of activities, requirements and therapy sessions, a familiar look came over Ilana's face.

I held my breath. Yes, I loved Ilana. Even after everything, God help me, I still loved her. But Ilana was evil. She could not allow me the smallest morsel. She had to keep the coyote locked in the trap.

When Lisa paused to adjust her glasses, Ilana said, "You know...I'm not prepared to take Greg home until he admits to, and deals with, his drug addiction."

The earth stopped rotating. Everything went blank. I couldn't see, couldn't feel, and couldn't smell. Unfortunately, my hearing remained razor-sharp.

"He's a heavy meth addict," she said. "I think this issue should be a major part of his treatment."

With a thunderbolt of clarity, I knew that everything I'd been through the past few days was for nothing. I didn't need a discharge plan. I would not be discharged that day. Gob-smacked!

I at last began to understand the depth to which Ilana would sink, the betrayal of which she was capable. Still reeling, I did what any other reasonable person would have done.

"I don't do drugs and you know that!" I shrieked. Spit flew from my mouth. I might have started foaming.

"Come on, now--"

She got no further. I launched myself across the table and landed on her chest. My hands were around her throat. God, did it feel good. We fell and the back of her chair, or maybe the back of her head, hit the ground with a satisfying thud.

"Code black! Code black!" Lisa hit the panic button. "Patient out of control!"

"Beep Beep!" I howled. "I am the coyote! I am Wile E!"

I never let off choking her even as the door banged open and people poured into the room.

* * *

The next thing I remember, Keeper Tom was standing over me. He tightened the restraints that kept my legs and arms strapped to the bed.

"There you are," Lisa said gently. "Welcome back. How do you feel?"

I could hear her voice but couldn't see clearly. Several people stood around my bed. I recognized their faces but their names escaped me.

"You attacked Ilana," Lisa explained. "She says you have a drug problem. You should have told us. We can't help you if you're not honest. We'll talk more about this in your team meeting tomorrow. For now, try to get some rest."

She placed her hand on my cheek. "If you promise to behave yourself, Tom is authorized to remove your restraints. Can you do that?"

"Yes." I looked away. I couldn't stop myself from crying.

For the first time I began to think that maybe, just maybe, I did belong in a lockdown ward. If I actually paid attention, I might learn something useful. For now I had to wait, to play the game. I'd tell them anything they wanted to hear.

Attacking Ilana hadn't been a wise move but at least I'd taken action.

Not the gnaw-my-own-leg-off, self-destructive kind, either but action aimed at the problem. Now, though, I had to work extra hard to prove I was ready to go home.

CHAPTER SIXTEEN

I ate dinner by myself at a corner table, glaring at anyone who even looked like they were going to sit down. By then I knew the ropes. I had two sandwiches on my dinner tray while all the new inmates only had one. A few days before I'd noticed one of the long-timers balancing two hamburgers on his tray.

"How'd you get so lucky?" I asked.

"You just have to ask," he said.

OK, I thought, *that's simple enough.*

On the very first cruise I'd taken, I hadn't found out until the last day that when the waiter asked, "Would you like steak or lobster this evening?" you could say, "Yes," and receive both. Here, doubling up, especially for someone as dangerously thin as me, was not only acceptable, it was encouraged.

On the cruise I'd felt cheated, as if there was a secret handbook I hadn't received until the last day. For the appetizer, you could have escargot *and* shrimp cocktail. For dessert, chocolate mousse *and* peach cobbler. Who knew?

At Indio, I felt triumphant. I was in on the secret. I was gonna get everything I deserved. I mumbled my request to the nameless Food Keeper and received two helpings of the main dish every meal. I then shook my head at the new inmates. Amateurs!

As I lay down one night, I wondered if I really wanted to return to the chaos that was my life. The structure and routine of my temporary home was strangely calming. I was told when to get up, when to smoke, when to eat, when to whatever. There was comfort in not orchestrating the myriad details of life—mine or anyone else's.

Then the screams of other inmates jolted me from my reverie. Structure or not, I had to get out of there.

* * *

Thanks to Ilana, my dedicated team of professionals was very concerned about the ramifications of my drug use. They provided information on Narcotics Anonymous. Attendance at their ongoing meetings was a requirement of my discharge. That and weekly meetings with Dr. Kylie Westwood, the therapist I was referred to.

I also had to meet regularly with Dr. Johnson. He would monitor and prescribe my medications until we found the right dosage to treat my depression. I had a flash of him handing me giant bottles of sugar pills named *Lovin' Large* and *Kwik Wick* while a wall of sexual aides buzzed and vibrated behind him. He must have noticed my strange stare because he gave me that smile people reserve for simpletons.

Reluctantly I agreed to everything. Hell, I would have eaten *Kwik Wicks* by the handful if they'd told me to. Freedom was what I wanted. Freedom and that thing called a happy life. I would have agreed to anything for that.

I also knew Doctor Johnson gave a damn. That was pretty important, especially considering that my most recent try at suicide had been based on miscommunication. Trazodone was an antidepressant, the one I'd refused to take after my second suicide attempt. I had thought it was a muscle relaxer for back pain. So much for the hospital's diagnosis and treatment plan. The only way to die with Trazodone was to be hit by the truck that delivered it.

And that was just too messy a way to die. Bloodstains on the Armani? Road rash on the corpse? I think not.

* * *

I was released the first week of July on a sweltering Coachella Valley Thursday. Cathryn and Ilana arrived to drive me home. Although confused and numb from the new medications, I remember hitting my head on the roof of the SUV as Cathryn hammered one of the deep swales that crossed the road.

I barely noticed. I barely noticed anything, except that I was no longer a prisoner. Well, at least not a prisoner of the state of California.

Once we got home, Ilana went to bed. For days. Her drugs had run out. I had written off her bouts of sleeping to her manic depressive behavior. It was more socially acceptable to be manic than a junkie, and I had kept the fantasy intact for many, many months for both our sakes.

The hospitalization had taught me a lot, and not just about myself. My feces-throwing, self-cutting, hair-pulling, head-bashing neighbors at Indio had taught me the difference between drugs and disease. Now I stood at the bedroom door, face to face with reality.

Ilana was not mentally ill, I was. Ilana was a junkie, I was not. Both statements have been true for some time. It was up to me to deal with my half of this reality.

* * *

The prescriptions for anxiety and depression kept me in a thick fog. Doc J had said this was a typical early side effect, so aside from conserving my energy, I tried to cope. Cathryn stayed at the house for a few days to help out. The twins had mysteriously disappeared, leaving the guest room minus a few knickknacks but otherwise not entirely trashed.

Cathryn ordered me not to worry and gave the room a thorough cleaning before she settled in for a long few days. Ilana slept through it and I was dazed the entire time; we later referred to it as "the lost weekend." Cathryn made sure we both had meals and clean clothes. She fed the dogs, watered Ilana, picked all the brown leaves off the houseplants, and ordered every one of us around whenever we moved.

It was perfect. Keeper Cathryn duplicated something of the regimented existence I'd come to rely on during my stay at in the 'nutcracker suite'. Even better, I could talk with her. I trusted her, and some part of me was reaching out for help in a new way.

I wanted someone to listen, of course. More than that, though, I wanted someone to tell me the happy life wasn't just an institutional fantasy dangled in front of patients to motivate them. I wanted someone real, someone who'd succeeded in a real way in the real world to say, *Yes,*

Greg, click your ruby slippers three times and you, too, can come home to Kansas. Just leave those ratty mutts behind.

I knew it would take more work than that but I wanted to know the fight would be worth it. So I talked. And talked. I talked so much that half the time I couldn't remember why I was talking. Sometimes I'd keep talking and watch Cathryn's face for a clue…was I on track? Was I insane? She always seemed open and patient, never condescending. I kept yakking, desperate to put myself in order.

Inevitably, Ilana arose from her protracted beauty sleep to offer excuses. But she was a meth addict who'd collapsed after a binge. There was only so much a body could take. It had become a somewhat regular occurrence since the foreclosure, cycling through every four to six weeks.

She'd spend a week in bed, moaning about what a horrible life she had, talking of suicide and making it very easy for me to fool myself into diagnosing bipolar disorder. Then *poof!* Like that phoenix I'd thought she'd been when we'd married, she'd wake up, shower and dress, score more drugs, and be off like nothing unusual had ever happened.

We'd reached a mutual unspoken agreement to pretend it didn't exist. The week at Indio cured me of pretending ever again. But what could I do? I felt like the hapless cartoon coyote. The roadrunner's—I mean Ilana's—sharp mind, quick reaction time and a mountain of luck kept her two steps ahead. I was always left caught in my own trap.

One afternoon during that lost weekend, Ilana presented herself for lunch. She was still groggy and unwashed, muttering of suicide and wallowing in self-pity. After eating, she planted herself in a chair in the great room and wept daintily, all the while mumbling incoherently.

"Jesus, Greg," Cathryn said as we watched from the dining room. "Can't you get her in for some help?"

My eyes narrowed. "It's about time you knew the truth," I said. "Ilana's addicted to methamphetamine."

"What?"

Aha! I thought. *So I'm not the only bright, capable person who can be taken by surprise!*

Cathryn was, to say the least, incensed. She didn't do drugs, period. Ever. She didn't associate with people who did drugs, ever. At least not knowingly. When she rose from her chair, she looked like a Greek Amazon in full battle mode. Gus and Gizmo took off for the safety of the dark space behind the sofa. Cathryn stalked into the great room and planted herself directly in front of Ilana.

"Just what the fuck is going on here?" she thundered. "Yeah, you, Ilana! Don't just sit there curled up and boo-hooing in that chair. Talk to me. And for once in your miserable life, be honest."

Her icy tone cooled the entire house twenty degrees. The frost penetrated even Ilana's drug-addled cocoon. She sat straight up and tried to gather herself, sniffling and grabbing for tissues.

"Have you been doing drugs, you motherfucker?" Cathryn yelled. "Is the bullshit I've been living this week, looking after you and cooking for your sorry ass, because you've been high as a fucking kite? I left Jackson, my business and my own home for *that?*"

Ilana didn't have a lot of room to maneuver. A muffled and rather soggy, "Yes," was all she could manage before Cathryn launched a second volley.

"Well, listen to me," she growled, "and listen well, because I'm only gonna say this one time, your sorry Royal Highness. Do *not* think for one nanosecond I don't mean every word." She held up her finger and waited until Ilana focused on it.

"I'm giving you one pass, and today is it. If I ever, and I mean ever, even *think* you're doing drugs again, you're out of my life completely. You'll have no opportunity to redeem or explain yourself. The relationship will be O-V-E-R. Am I clear? Do you understand?"

Ilana sniveled loudly and reached for another tissue.

"If you lie to me, or if I *think* you're lying, same rules. You're gone. You have now blown any trust, belief or reliability you had, understand? Blown. Sky. High. And if there's any redemption, the work is all yours. I just don't give a shit. You're nothing but a shot-loose junkie who lied, manipulated and deceived me. This one time is all you get. *Understand, Ilana?*"

I smiled, knowing I finally had an ally. Ah, smugness. What short-lived satisfaction it was.

Cathryn rounded on me and said, "Don't think you're exempt from this, Greg. You can wipe that shit-eating grin off your face. Same rules apply to you. Got it?"

"But--"

"But nothing! I saw your discharge papers. I know you've been using meth, too. No wonder you lost all that weight! You're supposed to attend NA every week. If I hear that you've skipped a single meeting, there won't be any psychological handholding or feeling bad because you've lapsed. Our friendship will be over. Understand?"

Boy, did I. I had no doubt she was serious. It was pointless to argue that I hadn't been using drugs so I nodded and smiled and agreed. I could be drug free—I already was drug free!

Ilana cried, sniveled, sniffed and sputtered even more loudly. Then she agreed to Cathryn's rules...just like she'd agreed to mine. This time, though, I though maybe she could get clean and stay clean. Cathryn was a lot like the pair of rottweilers she and Jack owned: fiercely loyal, intimidating and nurturing all at once. Maybe her no-bullshit attitude would work where my supportive, compassionate husband effort had so miserably failed.

And if nothing else, the dirty little secret wasn't a secret anymore. Ilana returned to bed. I sat back to relax and process the many thoughts running through my head. If I hoped to get better, the chaos had to stop. For that to happen, Ilana had to get clean. If she were clean, we could pull together to pay off all that debt she'd built up buying drugs. For the first time, I had what looked like a plan.

Bring on the happy life.

* * *

I couldn't sleep. I still had a lot to figure out before I could get my own life straight. That left Ilana mostly to her own devices, which in the past had landed us both in a lot of trouble. I had to figure out a way to rebuild both our lives if I wanted that elusive happiness. No wonder I couldn't sleep.

Finally I rolled out of bed. Dawn was just stretching out over the desert so I decided to take advantage of the cool morning for a little mindless therapy commonly known as picking rocks. Until I'd moved into this house, I hadn't know that rocks would continually emerge from the sand unless covered by four inches of concrete. Since my yard wasn't yet fully landscaped, I could harvest rocks every day.

Nothing in my life was calm or simple. Digging rocks became a routine, my new obsession. It was a tangible activity that actually served a purpose. Rocks are expensive. I needed hundreds of them for landscaping. Every day when I stood back and looked at the latest pile, I could feel good about having accomplished something. Rocks were manageable. I was in control.

The man-door to the garage creaked open. Cathryn emerged, still clad in pajamas, and handed me a steaming cup of fresh coffee. She cocked her head and asked, "How are you doing? I mean *really*. Really *doing*?"

I didn't know what to do or say. Cathryn scared me. Because of Ilana's lies, her perception of me was all wrong. I didn't want to lose her friendship. She was the one person in my life who actually gave a damn… other than Doc Johnson, of course, but his role was somewhat limited.

Still, I was annoyed that she'd interrupted my project. I just wanted everyone to leave me alone. *How am I doing?* I thought. *Fine until you bothered me, so get lost.* Then I thought, *What the hell.*

"Nothing ever changes," I said. "Nothing in my life with Ilana will ever change. I can't take all this chaos anymore. I'm supposed to be resting. It feels like Ilana has to one-up me every time. I've always taken care of her…when is she gonna be strong enough to take care of me? I just got out of the hospital, for Christ's sake. They told me I have clinical depression. I don't even know what that means. I thought everyone felt the way I did, that I just wasn't handling things well. Maybe I really did need to be in Indio."

Hopefully that was what she wanted to hear. Now she'd leave me to my rocks. Instead she settled onto the edge of the patio table. The $5,000 patio table that reminded me of how I'd not only let Ilana screw up my own life but let her manipulate everyone else I loved, too.

"Well," Cathryn said, "I always live by 'fake it 'till you make it.' I've been taking Prozac for ten years, did a couple of years of talk therapy, and I'm doing OK."

I couldn't believe what I'd just heard. This person, this powerful, tough, dynamic, smart, energetic, take-on-the-world woman was depressed? The one who'd ripped into both Ilana and me takes Prozac? Wow! I didn't know what to say.

"The earliest part is the toughest," she said. "It takes a few weeks for the antidepressants to ramp up and therapy feels weird at first. But stick with it. People who do both fare better than those who set up only one. And if you ever need anything, let me know. The road isn't easy but you can walk it."

Jesus, I thought. *That* kind of depression I could handle. I felt something strange in my stomach, something loose and light. With a jolt, I realized it was hope...full-fledged, blooming hope. It felt good, better even than strangling Ilana had felt.

I sat down at the table. We chatted for over an hour as the sun came up and the birds sang in the bushes. Cathryn talked about her own battle with depression, including some of the things that had worked for her and some of the things she'd learned to avoid. Although she'd never tried suicide, she had been incapacitated by the illness in the past. She'd gone down, too.

The most shocking thing was her attitude. She talked about depression as if it were a minor irritation. She'd gotten through the hard part, the integration of treatment and medications into her lifestyle. Now it seemed like that part of her life was easily managed.

"I'll promise you this," she said. "I will personally kick your ass if you ever miss an appointment with your therapist or forget your meds."

I felt like crying. But for once they were happy tears. It was absolutely overwhelming to know she cared about me so deeply. Blinking back the waterworks, I nodded. She gave me a quick hug and we went back inside.

CHAPTER SEVENTEEN

I didn't realize how comforting the regimented hours had been until Cathryn left Monday morning. Suddenly I was thrust back into my chaotic life. By the time I arrived at the small building with medical suites for my first therapy session, some of the shine had worn off that hope. But I kept remembering Cathryn's motto, *fake it 'till you make it*. Maybe this therapist could help me make it.

After checking in at the reception area, I climbed a short flight of stairs to Dr. Kylie Westwood's office. I was immediately struck by how homey the room felt. It was small and the window was shaded for privacy. The artwork was pretty average; not bargain-basement kitsch but not gallery quality, either. I selected a comfortable yet not overstuffed chair and settled in.

Dr. Westwood, or Kylie, as she preferred to be called, made an unremarkable first impression. She was very quiet, very self-contained, and I got no sense of who she was. The one exception was the strong, comforting sense of well-being she radiated. Not a sloppy, soupy, emotional sympathy but a calm serenity.

She was shorter than me, blonde, about my age, neither gorgeous nor unattractive, and carried a few extra pounds. Not perfect. As unremarkable as the decor. She sat in a chair facing me, looked me straight in the eyes, and asked, "How did you come to be in Indio?"

She held my gaze for a long time. She didn't glance away or show any sign of impatience. Instead, she made sure I knew she wanted to hear the answer, and that she would listen to every word. Amazing…she wanted to *hear* me.

I launched Rocket Ship Greg. I told her about Indio's food, the facility, about the keepers, the despair, about the horrors, the other inmates, about Ilana and the loneliness, about my team, the doctors, the therapists, the activities, the weather, the heat, the smells, the sounds, everything. In minute detail. For half an hour. Until she was bored. Until I was finished.

"Yes," she said smoothly, "that's all well and good but you never answered my question. How did you come to be in Indio?"

Uh-oh. I was confused. She was supposed to nod, smile, and say that my chatter was good, very helpful, and I was recovering nicely. Suddenly, I was not at all sure this so-called doctor had any idea what she was doing.

"I just told you," I said.

"No, you told me what it was like. I know what such places are like. What I want to know is about you. What brought *you* to a place like *that.* Which is a whole different question."

I had no idea what to say, where to start, where to finish, or how much time we had. Did I even want to work with this woman? What did she want to hear? I was quiet for an eternity. She never interrupted the silence, she never moved. She just sat there, radiating that damned solid serenity, encouraging me to look inside myself, to see the dark places I had buried deeply then vehemently avoided my entire life.

With time to fill, my driving need to please others took over. I said the first thing that popped into my head.

"Well, I guess it was depression. That's what they told me in Indio. I'm clinically depressed, have been for years, and have never been diagnosed or treated."

That sounded better but it felt as if I were talking about someone else. I was just repeating what my dedicated team had said.

"Good," she said, "that's a start. How did you feel when you heard that?"

Another long pause. I was never sure how I felt at any given moment. Life had always been such a struggle just to get through, I'd never taken the time to figure out how I felt. All I could do was guess at what she wanted to hear.

"Relieved, maybe? Like it wasn't my fault? Like it might not last forever?"

Panic set in. I waited, hoping she would let me know if I was on the right track.

"OK. So why do you think you were depressed?"

SHIT! Another opportunity to give a wrong answer. I was doing this alone. I thought long and hard before speaking again.

"Well," I said tentatively, "it might have something to do with my family? As a child? My life with Ilana is nothing but chaos." There, I'd said it. Out loud, to another person.

That was as much a question as a statement.

"Good. Here's something else for you to think about. You said your entire relationship has been nothing but chaos. Where, in all that running around, is there any time for Greg? How are you supposed to recover amid all that chaos? Do you really think that's a safe and healthy environment for you?"

I blinked. I was dumbstruck. A safe and healthy environment? It was the only environment I had. Health had nothing to do with it. Maybe it wasn't safe or healthy but what was she suggesting I do? Leave? And go where?

Our time was up.

"I have faith in you," she said.

"I'm glad somebody does," I said as I walked out the door.

* * *

I arrived home spent and exhausted. The session had been absolutely draining. I really wanted nothing more to do with that strange woman who stayed so calm while she probed the most painful spots in my psyche. How had she known so quickly? Was my life that transparent a mess that she could pierce right to the core during our first visit? Maybe I was in bigger trouble than I realized.

But there was no rest for the weary. Ilana appeared, sniffling and bedraggled, finally out of bed and fairly coherent. We talked for a while. She clearly understood the gravity of the situation. Her drug use was becoming her, and our, undoing. She absolutely had to quit. She knew it,

I knew it, our friends knew it, my therapist knew it. Together we'd get through it.

She wandered back to the bedroom to sleep some more. I estimated she probably would need another few days of rest but she'd get stronger the entire time. I just needed to keep food and water moving into her system, and into mine. After fixing a quick meal and serving her in bed, I collapsed into the most comfortable chair in the living room.

I clicked on the TiVo and settled in for my daily fix of talk shows. While in Indio, the only time the other inmates had settled down for a few hours had been during the afternoon plather of hosts who clutched their mikes with tender earnestness as they shoved their meat hooks around for more juicy details.

I had lost my taste for the confrontational shows; I didn't like it in my own life, so why watch it in everyone else's? The softer programs were soothing. They were filled with tears and pain but always ended with redemption: a parent reunited with an estranged child, a couple reconciled, a trauma released.

It was magical, the flow of sixty-minute fixes, and endless. The men and women who orchestrated the magic worked their way into my head. They listened, they patted shoulders, they gave hugs and cried along with their guests. They seemed to have some secret, some golden key to life, to the happy life, and they shared it unselfishly with everyone.

I was hooked. I imagined myself on stage, bravely holding back tears as I spilled it all: Ilana's drug use, Ilana's bipolar disorder, Ilana's brothers, Ilana's failing real estate business. My lower lip would tremble but I would sit unbowed by the weight of my marriage, my efforts to carry the both of us into the light. The audience would sigh and the hostess would *tsk-tsk*. Applause, warm and welcoming, would bolster me as Ilana promised to be forever good, to stay forever clean.

I looked around the house. Dust lay thick everywhere. I hadn't had the energy to clean up and Ilana certainly never did any housework. Why was I doing this? The lie she'd told to keep me locked up, the one that now tainted the friendship that was my sole support, was unforgivable. How could I trust her? Maybe I was crazy. Was Ilana ready to do the tough stuff?

I tried to visualize the possibilities—drug free, drama free. A real life.

Who was I kidding? The only way to have a drama-free life was to extricate myself from Ilana. But how would I make a living? The only assets I owned were a five-year-old truck and the house. I'd cashed in my 401K, blown through my savings, and even cashed out my burial policy.

The only way I could generate any money was to take out a second mortgage or downsize to a smaller house. The capital gains taxes would chew up so much of the profit it would leave me worse off than before in a house with zero equity. I was a prisoner in a marriage where I was my own warden.

Then a thought occurred to me. *What would Oprah do?*

That made me think things through in a different way. I thought about Ilana's life, about what might have brought her to this state of chaos. And from her point of view, things looked pretty rotten. Brothers who were criminals and only ever after her money. Parents too removed to visit. The weight of the family's legacy and fortune riding on her shoulders before she even had benefit of the money. And a husband who was unable to help because he was clinically depressed.

Well, maybe she had reason to sniffle and boo-hoo. She was bipolar, after all. And it was pretty common that people suffering bipolar disorder tried to self-medicate their low periods by taking drugs. Since being cranked up on meth probably was pretty similar to the manic states, being high all the time probably felt more normal than the severe mood swings.

So, again: What would Oprah do?

Why, be compassionate, of course. Reach deep for that extra bit of sympathy. Be strong like Cathryn, yes, and lay down the law but temper it always with a soft hug and supportive words.

At last, a plan. A treatment plan for Ilana.

The telephone rang. I was feeling so good I actually answered. It was Jeff.

"Where's Ilana?" he panted. "Put her on quick."

"She's not available."

And truly she wasn't; she'd passed out again and trying to wake her would take long minutes of waiting that Jeff was not likely to enjoy, minutes for which he would make me pay.

A stream of obscenity thundered through the line. "I will cut off your legs with a band saw!" he screamed. "You get Ilana on the phone *right fucking now!*"

I hung up. I was shaking. He'd made threats before, usually leaping from pleasant into murderous the second I didn't hop up to do whatever he asked. But the threats had never affected me like this before.

Ilana had to be cut off from the influence of these people she thought were her friends. If there was any hope she'd stay clean, everyone from her past must vanish. I had to protect myself, too. I was in no condition to deal with career criminals. Jeff and Kevin would undoubtedly show up at our house. If Jeff were calling from San Bernardino, they'd show up in about an hour. If they were already in town, they'd arrive in minutes.

We had to leave. Fast. Cathryn had said if I ever needed anything, she'd be there. Shakily, I dialed her number. The timing, for once, was perfect. She picked up the phone.

"I know you only just got home," I said, "but Jeff and Kevin will be here soon, I just know it, and if Ilana even just talks to them let alone sees them she's never gonna get well, I don't know who else to call what should I do call the police lock the doors I just don't know if I can take all this I want to run and never look back just leave and leave Ilana to deal with this for a change they're her family not mine!"

It actually came out in one long sentence. I was frantic.

Cathryn said, "Hang on a sec. Just calm down. I'll be right back with you."

I listened closely, desperate for her voice. I heard her talking to Jack. Seconds later, she was on the line again.

"OK. Get the dogs, get some clothes, and get your fat asses over here. See you in ninety minutes."

We left immediately. Ilana lay flat out unconscious in the back of the Blazer. Socks, underwear, and a few necessities were piled up around her with Gus and Gizmo settled on her chest. My heart was in my throat the entire drive.

The house Cathryn and Jack had rented was a typical southern California brown stucco in a subdivision where everything looked eerily the same. So much the same, in fact, Cathryn was unable to find her own house. In desperation she'd started hanging those seasonal flags on the porch...a grinning pumpkin at Halloween, a jolly snowman at

Christmas. The neighbors loved the show of "community pride" but it irritated Cathryn beyond measure.

The interior was more to her taste, purely utilitarian. The furnishings in the living room were a mishmash of desks, office chairs and filing cabinets. As the largest space, it serviced the thing that consumed the largest part of their lives: the business. The family room allowed for a little down time. Assuming, of course, that humans would actually dare to boot either of the rottweilers or the equally large cat off the furniture.

When we arrived, Jack and Cathryn helped Ilana to the guest room on the lower floor while I brought in the dogs and our belongings. I'm not even sure Ilana knew she wasn't in her own bed. Although my system was still pumping adrenaline, I was totally exhausted.

Finally Cathryn, Jack and I sat on the patio bathed in the warm evening breeze. I'd made the right call. We were safe and protected here, among family. An hour later I padded down the hall and fell into bed.

* * *

Sunday was calm, quiet and uneventful. Ilana slept, except for when she was eating, and I got to spend some quiet time with Jack and Cathryn. I was still overwhelmed and wanted to focus on my recovery. But we all agreed that Ilana's situation was of immediate concern. A residential treatment facility, if we could get her to agree to it and if I could figure out how to pay for it, would be the best bet.

It all seemed so easy. Drug problem? Plenty of solutions. Check into a treatment facility, get sober, then spend the rest of a happy, recovered life in a church basement trading phone numbers with other people who can feel your pain. Depressed? Oh. Um…how about exercise? Do you eat well? Get enough sleep? Oh. Umm….

Ilana's situation took priority. Ilana could be helped. There was something tangible to do for her and it could be done immediately. Greg's depression would have to wait.

The next morning we headed to Jack and Cathryn's office, dragging an increasingly active but still fairly incoherent Ilana along for the ride. She insisted we take the dogs so I threw their bed on the passenger's seat. Our strategy was to call the one "normal" person in Ilana's family, her older brother Jeremy. He might be willing to foot part of the bill or he might know how to lay his hands on some of the family money.

Over the course of an exceptionally brief phone call, we learned that this would be Ilana's third voyage on the sea of formal rehabilitation. Both prior cruises had been financed by Jeremy personally. Both had sunk to the bottom. Our request for a third launch was ever so politely and ever so firmly refused. I didn't even bother asking if he could pry a little money loose from Ilana's mother.

We then rang every recovery center in southern California trying to find a bed at a county facility. The best we could do was a ninety-day waitlist. Finally, we called the world-renowned Betty Ford Center in Rancho Mirage. They had room but would only speak to the person enrolling in the program. We could listen on the other extension but the conversation had to be between the intake worker and Ilana.

I roused her from the Blazer, dragged her inside and sat her in front of the desk. Slumped over, barely audible, she listened to the intake worker and answered all the questions in a whisper. Name? Address? Phone number? So far, so good. Birth place?

"Chino, California," Ilana said.

My eyebrows shot up. Cathryn had precisely the same expression. Chino? Ilana had always said she'd been born and raised on her grandparents' estate in Manzanillo, Mexico. The rich Russian émigrés of royal lineage, remember? Related to Anastasia. Last name, Romanoffsky.

Chino must have had some other meaning for Ilana. Either that, or even Ilana's history had fallen to her drug-fueled fugue. At that moment, I didn't care. She was setting up an appointment with the world's best addiction treatment facility and I wasn't about to derail the train.

When the conversation was over, Ilana dropped the receiver and said she wanted to lie down. I took her out to the Blazer and settled her comfortably in the back. Gus grumbled at me, as if he understood that our lives had been upended and were still being shaken to see what fell out.

I returned to the office to thank Cathryn and Jack. I had no idea how we were going to pay for the treatment but if I got lucky I could sell one of the properties quickly. Once Ilana was a little more coherent, she could sign her power of attorney to me just long enough to take care of things.

It would mean selling below market and paying extra fees to another agent but I'd do whatever needed to be done.

When I got back to the truck, Ilana was gone.

"Ahhhhhhh!" I screamed.

Gus didn't like that particular sound. He attacked me, actually managing to nip my nose, and I fell backward to the pavement. I sucked in another breath and tried for some actual words.

"Ilaaaaaaaaaaana!"

Jack and Cathryn rushed outside. I pointed at the empty back seat and gibbered. She was gone. Vanished. Cathryn grabbed my shoulders and shook me hard enough that I bit my tongue. Blood dripped off the tip of my nose and coated my tongue. It caught my attention and I calmed down enough to take orders.

We each headed in a different direction. How someone barely able to stand could vanish was a mystery. I drove the truck around the block as Jack and Cathryn trotted between the buildings on foot. Ilana could have fallen, or simply lain down, or could actively be hiding in a rush of paranoia. I looked between buildings, under cars, behind bushes and up trees…anywhere and everywhere.

Finally, I caught a flash of a tall, lanky figure wandering aimlessly around a gas station parking lot. It was Ilana, remarkably unharmed, totally confused, and looking for a restroom. I bundled her back into the Blazer. She used the restroom at the office, got settled in the truck again, and we headed for Rancho Mirage.

Eventually my heart stopped racing. I was still clutching the wheel, though, and tried to pry my fingers free. It wasn't easy. I realized I was actually looking forward to dropping her off—with many loving words, of course—and returning to an empty house. Alone and blissfully wrapped in peace, I would finally get some rest. I would finally be able to focus on my own recovery.

We were halfway there when Ilana's head wobbled into sight in the rearview mirror. "Greg," she whined, "where are we going?"

"To the Betty Ford Center, just like you asked. You rest now. We'll be there soon."

"Oh, no!" She jolted wide awake. "Please take me home. I can only do this at home with you by my side. I don't want to be locked away from you! I need you! You have to be there for me. I promise I'll do this for you. Please, please, please, please, please take me home!"

She was beside herself at the thought of being locked up. I knew exactly how it felt to be in the same situation, of course. I'd felt the same terror at the ER and during the ambulance ride to Indio. She continued begging, an endless stream of pleas that grew louder with every minute.

I was too tired to fight. The past few days would have been exhausting for someone in good health. Since I'd been freshly released from the psych ward, the events were overwhelming. If she wanted to do this at home, I had nothing left with which to argue.

I flipped the car into a tight u-turn, nearly making a dump truck plow into the side of the SUV. I never flinched. Once home, we both collapsed into bed, bone-weary, bedraggled and spent. I had stepped back into my own trap and hit the trigger, just like poor, stupid Wile E.

CHAPTER EIGHTEEN

The next morning, life took on a different complexion. Ilana was past the worst of her withdrawal. She bathed, made coffee, and asked to have a serious conversation with me. Her demeanor was one of exhaustion, resignation, and an inkling of hope.

"Look," she said, "I know I've screwed up big time and I don't deserve to be believed. I've lied to you and been using you for a long time. I lied about your drug use because I couldn't face that it was me and that I'd destroyed this relationship. I'm begging for you to give me one more chance."

She began to shake. I'd never seen her that upset before.

"I have to do this," she said. "I'm gonna die if I don't. I'm gonna screw up everything we've worked for. I love you and I can't imagine my life without you. I can only do this if you're with me. I'm gonna tell my friends I can't see them ever again. Please, please, say you'll be with me on this."

She looked down at her coffee, untouched and now cold. She seemed utterly broken, beyond defeat.

"You don't have to give me an answer right away," she said, "but please think about it. This time, it's different. It's life or death. I'll do whatever I can to make things right. Just think about it, please?"

Her humility was stunning. I wasn't sure how to deal with this entirely new side of her. Ilana could be shrewd, brilliant, competent, totally self-assured, and one of the most magnetic creatures ever to bless this planet. Modesty and humility were not in her repertoire. She was the light that drew the moth, and her light had always been on high.

Now it was flickering. Did she, at long last, get it? And could she do what she was promising? A pretty speech indeed but I needed time to mull things over.

I headed into the garage, hoping that working on one of my projects would help clear my head. Through the closed door, I heard her talking on the telephone. Sure enough, she was calling her druggie acquaintances. She told them she was quitting for good and that she couldn't see them anymore. The finality in her voice was unmistakable.

I collapsed on the step by the door so I could hear every word. By the time she'd finished the last call, I realized the depth of her commitment. How could I reject this wondrous woman who at this very second was doing what she'd never done before?

I walked back into the kitchen, put my arms around her and said, "OK, we're in this together."

Great! that voice in the back of my head screamed. *Now how are you gonna get out of this mess?* My head didn't believe a word she said. My heart was desperate to believe. She was saying and doing the right things, going through the right motions. I didn't need to shout "Roll tape" this time. Ilana was playing the part of a responsible person. I couldn't have scripted it better myself.

* * *

The next few days were joyous. Ilana and I really were a couple again. I still felt overwhelmed yet was guardedly optimistic. Ilana worked her tail off getting her side of the office whipped into shape, updating the files I'd managed to organize, and drawing up new plans for the real estate business...plans that included me. She got up early, went to bed early, ate regular meals, was productive, and was not using drugs. I knew it, I could see it, and the difference was remarkable.

I breathed a sigh of relief as I headed off to my next appointment with Dr. Westwood.

* * *

Kylie kept asking me why I felt the way I did. I kept reaching for a deeper understanding yet all she ever said was, "Good...but why did you feel that way?"

We were talking about stuff I haven't mentioned to anyone in years—my grandfather's depression, my uncle's horrifying spousal abuse (also probably in response to undiagnosed depression), Kenny's suicide, and my years of being sexually abused. I wasn't sure how much deeper I could go.

If she just told me what she wanted, I would have gladly fessed up. My feelings about my mother? The details of Kenny's career? The glamour and too-high expectations ingrained from living on the same street as America's favorite space heroes, the NASA astronauts? *Tell me what you want to hear, damn it!*

All I wanted to do was sleep. Anything else seemed too difficult. I was tired of being tired. No one seemed to understand what I was going through, not even Cathryn. Hell, even I didn't understand. A recurrence of the cancer would have been preferable. I would have had real evidence of something wrong, symptoms that could be quantified and diagnosed, assigned a course of treatment with the surety of an eventual solution.

Depression, though, was a silent, slow-moving monster that crept in. It had no real beginning; it slowly took over. No one realized anything was wrong until it was far too late. One day, I simply couldn't get out of bed. I could have been dying of thirst yet there wasn't enough energy, will, or desire to actually get up and walk into the kitchen for a glass of water.

"Don't you have an appointment today?" Ilana asked as she brushed her hair at the mirror. "Dr. Westwood or something?"

I pulled the blanket over my head and moaned. Yes, I had an appointment but I still had no idea what to say or how to answer her questions. I finally pulled myself out of bed and fumbled into my slippers. She would have to see me in my pajamas. I didn't have the time or energy to shower and change. Besides, I would head straight to bed as soon as I got back.

Ilana, meanwhile, struggled to maintain the façade that our life was on track. Our finances were, as always, extremely precarious, and I, as always, was completely in the dark. As the desperation in her life increased, the quality of her performance deteriorated. Potential clients smelled her desperation and backed out the door as quickly as they'd arrived. They had no idea her concerns had nothing to do with the properties but they wouldn't risk being suckered into a bad investment.

Ilana stayed sober for maybe two weeks. Then she went back to her old ways. Since drug abuse was a deal-breaker with me, Jack, and Cathryn, she worked hard to hide her secrets. For a time, she was remarkably successful. I suspected something...she was up all night again, gone all day, and her brothers called incessantly. But I didn't confront her. I couldn't. Expending that much energy would have killed me.

So, I did what had always seemed to work in the past when things didn't fit into my new vision for my life......*Roll tape*.....

Finally we located a way to relieve a little of the financial pressure. We planned to sell one of her properties to a couple we knew. The condominium was a modest two-bedroom ideally suited for Mark's aging parents. For several weeks, much of Ilana's time was spent in negotiations and contract details. That kept her out of my hair...always a good thing.

* * *

"How's your therapy coming along?" Cathryn asked.

She'd stopped by for lunch while Jack picked up a few things for one of their local jobs. We'd made a few referrals for them in Palm Springs, which meant Cathryn popped by now and again.

"How do you like Dr. Westwood?" she asked.

"I'm not sure," I sighed. "She keeps asking me how I feel about things."

She laughed. "That's her job, you goof!"

"I know but...."

I frowned. I was very unhappy with how therapy was going and I thought Cathryn would understand.

"I just don't know what to say. I don't know what she wants."

"It's not about what she wants." Cathryn put down the apple she'd been nibbling. "Don't you get that yet? It's not about what the doctors or therapists want, or what your parents or wife wants, or even what I want. It's about you, Greg. You have to figure out what you want."

"I know what I want." My voice was so close to a yell I surprised myself. "I just don't know how to get it."

"You don't know what you want then." She shrugged, ever unflappable. "Not really."

"What the hell does that mean? Don't you pull that psychobabble bullshit on me, too!"

Now I *was* yelling. That wasn't good. I didn't want to alienate my only friend but I couldn't control myself.

"Well. The pussycat has become a lion." She seemed amused.

"What's so damn funny?"

"You, Greg. You remind me of me when I was in therapy. You've got to keep pushing. Until you figure out what's really down in that muck you've wallowed in all your life, you won't get well."

"Jesus, now you sound like Kylie!"

"Maybe that's because she's right." She picked up her apple again. "You've spent all your life smoothing out things, making them orderly and logical. Now you're being force to bite deep, to rip out all the stuff you've piled up to hide the rotten core. It's called emotions, Greg. It's messy and it's juicy. Get used to it."

She took a huge, slurping chunk out of the apple.

Crap. I had to change the topic if I wanted to keep her as a friend. I paid Kylie to make me miserable; I didn't need to get pressured by Cathryn for free.

* * *

Ilana went to northern California to take care of her mother. The last time she'd headed north, she'd hung out with her brothers making and doing meth (the so-called Arizona trip to buy our vacation property). I really didn't give a crap where she was going or what she'd be doing so long as I finally had the house to myself.

I looked forward to getting up in the morning, sitting peacefully outside drinking coffee, reading a good book, curling up on the sofa with Gus and Gizmo, or simply contemplating my future. I could nap in the sun after breakfast then dive into one of my many projects—raking rocks, fooling around in the garage, tinkering with the car.

Afternoons would bring more quiet time with additional reading and another nap. A leisurely, home-cooked dinner would be savored while the sun set over the mountains. Maybe I'd even dig up one of Nick's favorite recipes, something I hadn't fixed in a while. Dessert and coffee would pair well with the warm evening breezes as I counted stars. I would drift off to sleep knowing that for the moment, the chaos was elsewhere, gone.

I had a lot to think about. There were decisions to be made about how I was going to live the rest of my life and on what terms. OK, so my situation with Ilana wasn't healthy. Ilana herself wasn't healthy. What would I do about that? Leave her? Force her into rehab?

However unhealthy our life together had been, our relationship still tied us to each other. We were entangled in complicated ways, emotionally and financially. Simply walking away wasn't a real option.

It was a lot to process. I put it out of my mind for the first day. I needed total rest, complete relaxation. Then, when my mind was a little more calm and my body relaxed, I could think closely and clearly. Everything in my life was jumbled together, knotted and tied with miles of tangled string. I would cut some things and pick others apart. By the time Ilana returned home, I'd have our life plan laid out.

If she joined me, fine. If not, I'd have a plan for that, too…it's called divorce. I didn't have a clue about how I'd survive financially but something would come. Even if I had to sell the house. It would be a terrible sacrifice but I was through sacrificing myself. If it meant reclaiming my life, I'd cut the title into pieces myself.

The first evening alone was lovely. Even the dogs seemed to take advantage of the peace and they snuggled together on my lap.

* * *

The next morning, Ilana's brothers banged on the front door. I'd just stepped out of the shower and had a towel around my waist and a toothbrush in my mouth. I melted into the wall, hoping they'd go away. The last time I'd had a conversation with them was when I'd tried to get the police to remove them from the premises. Maybe they'd come to enact their revenge when Ilana wasn't there to interfere.

"Greg," Jeff sang. "Oh, Greg! We know you're in there. Come out and play!"

I was biting down on the toothbrush so hard bristles floated in the foam. Then a palm slapped the bedroom window. It was Jeff, by now pretty pissed.

"Open the fucking door!"

I swallowed the foam, gagged on the bristles, and unlocked the deadbolt. The pair brushed right past me, as usual. I closed the door before the curious neighbors could get too close a peek at my overly pale chest.

"You gonna put on some clothes, Prince Charming, or you gonna flash the neighbors while we move?"

I pulled the nearly bald toothbrush out of my mouth. "What?"

"Ilana hired us to pack everything up and move it out of the house. See the big truck outside?"

I looked out the window. How could I have missed the orange behemoth backed onto the lawn? I was being evicted? Again? From my own house? *By my loving wife?*

I dialed Ilana's mobile. As we started to discuss the situation, we were disconnected. She never called back. Every call I made went into her voicemail. Meanwhile, her criminal brothers roamed around discussing how they were going to crate up and haul off all our belongings.

The phone rang. I snatched it up hoping Ilana was calling on the land line. It was Cathryn.

"Thank God!" I hadn't realized I was shaking. I put my hand against the wall for support. "Jeff and Kevin are here trying to get me out of the house. They say Ilana sent them but I can't reach her and they won't leave."

"That's great," Cathryn said. "I was wondering how you were gonna handle all that stuff by yourself."

Now I was really confused. I was being evicted by my contractor? My best friend? I really was stuck in a cartoon, only the roadrunner had demonically possessed all the other characters in the episode.

"What are you talking about, Cathryn?"

"Didn't Ilana tell you? We're doing your floors while she's out of town. Everything has to be moved out of the house. There can't be anything on the floor anywhere. Jack and our guys are on their way with a trailer full of equipment. That's why I'm calling. Didn't Ilana tell you?"

"No." Why was I not surprised? Ilana's storm was brewing. "Are you sure, Cathryn? This doesn't make any sense."

"Of course I'm sure. Ilana and I worked everything out. Jack should be there in an hour. You guys have one week to move everything out and get the house ready. It'll take about three weeks to complete the work once we get started."

So much for peace and quiet! One week to move, three weeks to complete the work, and another week to move everything back in. Where was I supposed to live for the next five weeks? Tropical storm Ilana was perilously close to becoming a full-fledged hurricane.

I sent the twins out to find boxes and kept calling Ilana. She never answered, so I just kept packing. For three days. No one had lined up a storage locker and I certainly couldn't pay for one big enough to hold all our stuff. Instead we moved everything into one of the vacant condos. I didn't know what else to do.

I wasn't even sure how Ilana planned to pay for this. The floors would cost thousands. Even if Ilana had closed on that small condo, I hoped Cathryn and Jack had cut us a huge discount. There never was a chance to ask. I had my hands full making sure the twins didn't rob us blind.

Even with me running between rooms and accompanying them on every trip to the condo, I wasn't at all sure how much of our stuff would end up at a pawn shop. Although it was a lot to handle, and absolutely the last thing I needed to think about so soon after Indio, I really had no choice. As I packed, I mentally worked out the details. Put aside the money issue; Cathryn herself said she and Jack and Ilana had worked all that out.

I had planned to take advantage of Ilana's absence and go through some of that paperwork in the office. To keep that very important item on my to-do list, I needed to stay close to the house. I could set up my bed in the garage or sleep at the condo. Kevin and Jeff were working well enough under my supervision. They weren't sophisticated enough to hide a grudge so I didn't think I was in for a beating any time soon.

Hell, maybe they were just used to Ilana. They'd grown up with her, after all. After we packed and moved the last two bedrooms, it would take only a few days to prep the house. The twins would help during that stage as a cost-cutting measure. If I could keep them in sight during that time, I should come out all right. And then, finally, I could rest.

That cinched it; I'd stay in the garage. I wouldn't be able to use the house but the office had a bathroom, a coffee maker, a tiny microwave and a mini-fridge. Between that and a whole lot of takeaway, I wouldn't starve. I'd still be able to sit on the patio every morning and watch the sun come up.

It wouldn't be as private with all the workmen coming and going but I'd have nicer surroundings than at the condo. And, somehow, it made me feel safer. Not that I was paranoid about leaving the house. I had a sneaking suspicion Ilana had deliberately orchestrated this mess. For what reason, I just couldn't guess.

When I mentioned it to Kylie, her eyes got wide. "Greg," she said, "is this a good situation for you to be in right now?"

I nearly snorted. To spare her feelings, I merely rolled my eyes. "Obviously, the answer is no. But there isn't any choice."

"What about having the contractors reschedule?"

It was my turn to look at her. I hadn't thought about that. Honestly, how could Ilana know the precise push it took to keep me off balance?

"Well," I said, "the contractors are our friends. It would really be putting a load on them to reschedule."

"What about canceling?"

I shook my head. "Ilana paid for everything. I don't have the right to send back something I didn't buy."

"It's your house, Greg. You have the right to say what happens there as much as Ilana."

I sat there as that sank in. Now I was glad I hadn't snorted.

"You know," she said, "ever since you were abused, you've put a lot of effort into organizing and ordering your life. What you couldn't control in the external world you simply controlled through your fantasies. You pretended everything was fine." She leaned forward to make sure her words hit the mark.

"Life can't be charted on a graph, Greg. It's full of emotions, and emotions are messy. You've got to dig deep. You've got to deal with those messy emotions if you ever want that happy life."

Wait. Hadn't Cathryn already told me that? And hadn't I basically snorted in her face?

Shit.

CHAPTER NINETEEN

Things went surprisingly smoothly. The twins and I got the last of the belongings moved over to the condo with a minimum of fuss and no disasters. All the closet shelves were covered in sheets of plastic and sealed with tape. More equipment arrived along with truckloads of topping, colorant, sealer, and other ingredients for the new concrete floor.

At the very start of the design process for the house, I'd decided that I eventually wanted the floors to have the same finish as many of the luxury model homes in Palm Springs. The treatment required a new, thin layer of concrete to be applied to the existing concrete slab. The top layer would then be ground, acid stained and sealed to protect the finish and give it an everlasting shine.

To add to the look, stainless steel transition strips would be imbedded into the concrete. The designs would enhance each space individually and also flow into the next to pull the entire floor plan together. It would look similar to the terrazzo floors preserved in older public and government buildings. Jack and I finalized the plans and the full crew arrived from San Diego.

The project entailed a lot of hot, dusty, dirty work. The mess was unbelievable. A thick layer of fine concrete dust coated every surface, including the walls. To keep the crew from having to commute, Jack and Cathryn had rented a furnished condo with a fully equipped kitchen from a timeshare company.

The crew worked on the floors every day then headed back to the condo to eat and get cleaned up. I had evenings to myself. I tinkered with different projects in my garage and actually enjoyed the schedule imposed on my activities. I did miss the daytime talk shows, though. I'd really gotten hooked, especially on Oprah. She was the one thing I wasn't going to give up.

Every day around 4 p.m. I checked on the workers. Usually they were wrapping up by then. If they left in time, I could pop into the office and watch the portable TV/radio we kept in there. I'd dance around, helping the guys put things away and trying not to look too anxious for them to leave. I really did appreciate all their hard work but I needed my daily fix of wisdom.

Cathryn and Jack started to step in. I was too embarrassed to admit I wanted to watch Oprah but I really liked to hear her introductory comments that first minute or two of the broadcast. That set the tone for the show and helped me understand what her guests were going through. In listening to their stories, I was slowly learning how to deal with my own.

I knew Cathryn would never approve. She'd probably laugh in my face and tell me to bootstrap myself into my own life. But I needed some kind thing in my life, some soft spot to lie on, and Oprah gave it to me for an hour each day. I didn't have to figure out how to answer any questions and I didn't have to impress anyone with how strong I really was. I could just listen and cry and eat ice cream the entire time.

Then, when it was over, I went back to rebuilding my orderly world while the lessons sank in. *What would Oprah do?* I asked. Save that marriage. Improve that house. Salvage that business. Oh, what a wonderful woman.

"Greg."

Jack waited for the last of the workers to step off the front walk. I was hovering at the door, knob in hand, wriggling like a kid who had to pee. It was already one minute past four. Oprah would be walking on stage, settling herself on the couch. I had exactly twenty seconds of applause left before she began her opening monologue.

"Yes, Jack?"

"Lay off the dummy dust, will ya?"

For a second, I thought he meant to be careful not to inhale too much concrete dust. I was living there, after all, and a great deal of dust managed to sift into the garage every day.

Then I busted out laughing. He was making a joke. Maybe not one in the best taste, which I never would have expected from him, but a joke nonetheless. A concrete contractor's joke. Dummy dust. Drugs. Ilana's history as an addict. The entire place looked like a cocaine factory had exploded inside my house.

"Jesus, Jack," I said, still laughing, "you are full of surprises."

He gave me a very long look. I stood there, still smiling, less anxious for him to leave but still ticking off those seconds in my head. Finally he turned around and headed for the van.

I tried not to slam the door too loudly and sprinted through the house, out the back and into the office. Oprah was talking with Maya Angelou again. Oh, what pearls I would gather!

* * *

As the days clicked by, I was pleased with the progress on the floors but couldn't figure out why Cathryn, Jack and their staff acted so strangely. Whenever I popped my head into the house to eyeball the progress and picture how great the floors were going to look, the crew wouldn't meet my gaze. I guess they were worried I was going to criticize their work, so I always said, "Great job, fellahs!"

They'd give me a cursory smile and nod before turning back to their work. Jack stayed completely professional, talking to me whenever he needed to adjust something in the process but disengaging whenever my babble turned to private matters. That wasn't terribly unusual; he was a pretty quiet guy. But whereas before he'd at least humor me by listening, now even that was gone.

I wrote it off to him trying to keep the project on track. The schedule was already a little behind because they'd had to special-order the color I picked. There was no way to make up the time; the crew was already working at full bore. Cathryn seemed preoccupied so I tried to stay out of her way, too.

By then, I had other things on my mind. Although I was still rebuilding my strength and tired easily, I'd finally relaxed enough mentally to tackle the paperwork in the office. I spent a few hours sorting through the desk drawer.

I thought about the knife Ilana had left. I'd set it in plain view on the dining room table the same day I'd found it. She'd taken a warning shot. I'd returned fire, unwilling to let her know how much her threat had shaken me. But where had she gotten it? From her brothers?

The more I thought about her connection to them, the more I realized that Jeff and Kevin weren't capable of planning all the different things they'd done. Ilana must have told them what to do, when to arrive, even what to steal. And if that was true then I hadn't only married a roadrunner who'd turned my life chaotic; I'd married a conniving, manipulative woman who was taking me for every penny, every ounce of energy, and every wisp of my soul.

The thought hit me so hard I suddenly needed to vomit. I rushed to the bathroom and emptied my breakfast into the toilet. When I came out, Cathryn was standing in the doorway. She peered closely at me.

"I brought you lunch," she said. "Made it myself at the condo."

I rubbed my stomach. "That's kind of you but I really can't eat right now."

She set the foil packet on the edge of the desk. "Maybe you'll feel like eating later. You really need to take better care of yourself."

I nodded and smiled weakly. I didn't want her and Jack involved. If I was right, anything I shared would put them both at risk. "Don't worry about me," I said.

She nodded. "OK. But Greg, get some help."

"Got that covered."

And it was. I was meeting with Kylie again the next day. Cathryn nodded and left.

The second she was gone I headed for the large filing cabinet. It also had a lock. I searched everywhere for a key but couldn't find one. Finally I cut through the backyard to the garage, found a crowbar, and humped back to the office. The pry bar was too thick to fit into the space between the drawers so I went back for a hammer and a chisel. After carving out a big enough hole, I shoved the crowbar into the gap and started prying.

"Greg?"

I turned to see Jack in the doorway. He was holding a stick with some dried stain on the tip.

"The colorant came in for the top coat. This look like what you wanted?"

Still holding the crowbar, I went over to look at the stain in the sunlight. "Perfect!"

As I turned back, he asked, "Everything all right out here?"

"Oh, uh, yeah! Just lost my damn keys." I shrugged. "You know me. Nothing ever goes as planned."

He left me to my business. I watched through those tall glass walls as he talked to Cathryn. They bantered for a bit, shooting looks toward the office now and again. Finally she shook her head. Jack went back to work and Cathryn headed out to the van.

I'd explain the odd activity later. After I'd figured out Ilana's schemes, after I knew it was safe to tell them whatever I'd eventually discover. For now, I had a job to tackle.

* * *

What a gigantic job it turned out to be. Nothing was filed properly. Fistfuls of contracts were jumbled out of page and date sequence then piled, stuffed, and crumpled together. There were contracts for the purchase and sale of properties I'd never seen. Most were in Ilana's name but some were in her brother's names. The files went back years, the oldest nearly eight years.

Mixed into this were incorporation papers for some other business. I couldn't tell if it was for one business or many; pieces of the documents were scattered among different files. It almost looked like Ilana had used them for scrap paper while making notes for her properties. Names of people I didn't know had been scribbled in the margins along with phone numbers that might not even have been in this country and long lists of cryptic codes…bank accounts? PIN numbers? Charge cards?

I shoved all the furniture against the walls and spread everything out across the floor. Properties were grouped in one section and everything else went into another. Each section was subdivided by year then by address. Multiple owners were listed on different contracts for some of the properties, and many contracts stipulating different deals had the same date. Once I got everything sorted, I hoped to follow the trail of Ilana's life before we'd met.

The door opened. A strong breeze blowing across the yard scattered dozens of scraps.

"Shut the door!" I hollered as I threw myself across the piles.

"Sorry." Cathryn stood gingerly on the piles closest to the door. She didn't have a choice; there was that much paper spread around. "What 'cha doing?"

"Sorting out Ilana's files," I said. "She's smart but she doesn't have the patience for this kind of work. Some of this stuff goes back a decade."

"Looks like quite a job." She surveyed the papers quietly. "Greg, are you still seeing your therapist?"

"Of course!" I smiled broadly. "Don't worry, you don't have to kick my butt. I haven't missed a single session!"

"And you've told her how things are going?"

"Well, mostly we've been talking about my childhood. You know, figuring out why my adult world is so screwed up."

"How's that working out?"

"Not so well," I sighed. "We haven't made much progress, I guess. But you were right. About that emotional stuff. I'm sorry I didn't listen to you before."

She nodded. "Well, are you being totally honest with her?"

"What do you mean?"

I was getting a touch annoyed. Not only was she interrupting my work—and believe me, it was work to remember which pile had what kind of papers—now she was psychoanalyzing me. Sure, she'd been through it and sure, she'd been really helpful so far but I wasn't in the mood to stop right at that moment and have a session.

"Are you telling her everything?" Cathryn said. "I mean *everything*."

She was giving me that no-bullshit look. That was more irritating than anything else. Now I really was getting pissed. Who the hell did she think she was? She couldn't just bust in and demand an explanation. Like I even knew what she was demanding an explanation for! My life? My health? My choice of décor?

I was about to blast her with a piece of my mind when Jack poked his head out the back door. "Ilana's home!" he shouted.

I froze. What the hell? She wasn't supposed to be home for…another week, almost! Why the hell had she come back early? Shit! I'd never get through all those papers. She'd store them somewhere else or burn them. Anything to keep me in the dark.

By the time she flounced through the back door, I'd regained my composure. Cathryn looked from her to me and opened the door as Ilana approached.

"Cathryn," she said as she stepped in.

Her perfectly clad, overly-pointy shoe-of-the-season crinkled against the papers. She stopped. She stared at the explosion of contracts, notes, faxes and files. She turned pale. Putting one trembling hand to her mouth, she said, "Greg. Oh, Greg."

Tears came to her eyes. Then she whirled and was gone, racing into the house and down the hall, kicking up a cloud of cement dust like desert sand. Finally, the roadrunner was in retreat.

"Aren't you going to go after her?" Cathryn asked.

"No."

I felt smugly satisfied. The truth was going to come out and I was going to be the one who dug it up. I bent over the papers again as Cathryn went back to the house. When I looked up again, I could see Ilana pulling from a fresh box of tissues as Cathryn patted her on the back.

Gotcha, I thought, and continued sifting.

* * *

When I finally went back inside again, the crew had packed up and left for the day. Ilana turned on me. She accused me of using drugs.

Oh great, I thought. *Good for you, Ilana. The best defense is a good offense.*

I just rolled my eyes.

"Jack and Cathryn told me all about it," she said. "They have proof."

"What proof?"

"Your bizarre behavior. Your breaking into our own filing cabinet. Your 'filing project.' That's all drug-fueled, Greg. You're always so hard on me about my past addiction and here you are using!"

Suddenly everything made much more sense. If Cathryn and Jack actually believed I was using drugs, it would explain why they and their crew had been treating me like I had a contagious disease.

"I've scheduled a meeting with them this evening," she said. "There's a lot to discuss since I've been out of town for so long."

"Good. We can get this cleared up."

"You're not invited."

"Why not?"

"It's for business. You aren't part of the business."

That was news to me. Up until then, I'd been negotiating with them to move me out of the management position up to a full owner. After Indio, Cathryn had been so compassionate I'd talked through everything with her. She'd said there was no way she'd hold any of that against me. If I were doing drugs, though, they naturally wouldn't want anything to do with me.

I insisted on attending the meeting. I was going to confront Jack and Cathryn directly. Ilana, I believed, was somehow behind the drug-use story. After all, she'd made the same claim to my social worker while I'd been locked up. Although my loving wife put up a good fight, I didn't back down even when Gus gnawed on my ankle. I slapped a bandage on my leg and we got in the car.

CHAPTER TWENTY

It was a beautiful desert evening when Ilana and I arrived at the condo. The temperature was a pleasant seventy-five degrees with a light breeze. *The perfect climate for a showdown,* I thought as we headed up to the second floor. Since the crew started early to beat the worst of the heat, everyone except Jack and Cathryn was already asleep.

After a few whispered pleasantries, we headed to an empty bedroom. Ilana released the dogs from her Prada and began the meeting by asking for an update on the status of our floors. They discussed the details for about thirty minutes. I got tired of waiting and dropped myself abruptly into the conversation.

"I hear you think I'm a drug addict," I said. Loudly.

Everyone stopped. The heads of three deer were caught in my headlights. It was almost funny to see them freeze in mid-gesture. Even Ilana looked surprised. She must've thought I'd chickened out. After they exchanged glances, Jack spoke.

"Well, yes, Greg. It's pretty obvious."

"Why would you say that?" My voice was quiet. I stayed calm.

"Come on, Greg. Everyone knows you're using. Even the crew is convinced."

"I'll ask you again. What have you seen that would give you that impression? And if you're so convinced, why didn't you say anything to me?"

"I did say something, Greg. I said, 'Hey, you should probably lay off the dummy dust.' Don't you remember?"

"Yes, Jack, I remember. I thought you were joking. Do you remember what I said?"

"Sure. You looked at me in a funny way then you laughed. That's proof enough for me."

"How is that proof? I thought you were kidding. You should've approached me more directly, in a way that made clear you had serious concerns. That would've been reasonable."

"And say what? Greg, I think you're doing drugs. Knock it off?"

"Yes, that would've been a good start." Anger slipped into my voice.

"Come on! You were in no condition for a direct conversation about anything serious. You were obviously overwhelmed, exhausted and strung out."

"Now, wait a minute!" I yelled. "If I was in no condition to have a serious conversation, exactly how did you expect me to understand that your joke wasn't a joke? That doesn't make any sense. It's not logical!"

"You should've known I was serious by the tone of my voice."

"OK, let me get this straight." I held up my hands. "According to you, I was in no condition to have a serious conversation. But that's when you decided it would be a good idea to confront me about drug use. And you decided the best way to do that would be to tease me, expecting me to notice the *particular* tone of your voice *and* interpret your comment as serious."

I dropped my hands to my sides and looked him straight in the eye. "You can't have it both ways."

There was a long pause. "Well," he said, "that's not the only reason I thought you were using."

"OK." My voice was calm again. "What are those other reasons?"

"For one, you never ate. I looked in the fridge in the garage. There was never any food in there. And candy wrappers were everywhere. Everyone knows that someone on meth doesn't eat except to satisfy their sweet tooth."

"Of course there's no food in the fridge. I don't have a functioning kitchen! Why would I keep food around that I can't cook? I've been eating at fast-food restaurants. I got takeout a few times and heated it up in the microwave in the office. What leftovers I had were in the mini-fridge, also located in the office." My hands started waving.

"If you were so intent on looking for evidence, you should've looked in the trash! You would've seen all the bags from Del Taco and Jack-in-the Box. And Jack," I bellowed, "the candy is Tony's! Your employee! I don't eat candy!"

"Well, Greg, I'm just telling you what I know. Plus, you were supposed to be there every morning to let the crew in. Twice Tony had to jump the fence and bang on the windows before you woke up and let them in."

"Yes, Jack, you're right." I shrugged expansively. "I was still sleeping. I'm living in a recliner chair in the garage with no alarm clock. I overslept. If I were using meth, I would have been up, overexcited, and met Tony at the door saying, 'Good morning, Tony, I've already ground the floor by hand with sandpaper, what else needs to be done?'"

I leaned over and, God help me, wagged my finger in his face. "Did it ever occur to you there could be some other explanation for what you saw? Why would you immediately jump to the wrong conclusion and think the worst of me?"

Jack looked at Cathryn then at Ilana. Although he was in the hot seat, Cathryn had come to the same conclusions. All orchestrated by Ilana, no doubt. The women weren't about to let me know it. They were letting the guys duke it out.

"Ilana's brothers confirmed it," Jack said. "They told me with a wink and a nod that you guys were up all night working to get the house ready. They made it very clear it was only possible because of drug use."

"I can't believe you!" I threw out my hands and spun around like Gizmo asking for a biscuit. I couldn't help it. I was utterly incensed.

"You're gonna take the word of two criminals who are known to use drugs, oh, and manufacture drugs, oh, and have done jail time, over me? How could you do that?" My bellowing had turned shrill. I was losing any control.

"I just know what I saw, Greg. I know you're using."

"No! You can't have it both ways! Nothing you've said makes any sense. What you saw isn't proof of anything other than your willingness to believe the worst of me. I don't need this shit from you, Jack." I whirled on Cathryn. "Or you. We're gonna resolve this right here and right now!"

"Don't raise your voice to me," Jack said. "You have no right to come in here and accuse me like this."

"At least I'm confronting you directly! You have the right to accuse me, try me, and sentence me, all without a single word from me in defense? Why don't you hold yourself to the same standards? At least you know why I'm upset. You just threw me into the Gulag without a word."

"Now wait just one minute." Jack's temper finally flared.

"Shut up, Jackson," Cathryn said. "He's right.

She stepped toward me. "Greg, we're sorry. We were wrong. We should've talked to you directly. Everything you're saying makes sense and is logical. We jumped the gun and came to wrong conclusions for all the wrong reasons. Can we just start over and go on from here?"

"I'm not sure, Cathryn. Can we? I'm not the one who caused this breakdown in communication. How can I trust that if something else comes up you'll discuss it with me? I just don't understand why neither of you said anything."

Cathryn's eyes bored into Ilanas. "Say something, Ilana. You're the one who told us Greg was on drugs."

Cathryn broke her gaze with Ilana to glance at at Jack. Jack looked straight at Ilana for a long moment. When he met my eyes again, his lips were pursed. He wasn't about to say it but he was letting me know exactly why things had gone wrong.

With the two of them, and me, staring her down, I thought her composure might slip. No such luck. "I don't know what you're talking about, Cathryn," she said. "I never said that."

A roaring silence filled the next moments. Ilana never came to my rescue nor did she support Jack and Cathryn. Like Switzerland, she remained neutral. Maybe Jack and Cathryn hadn't said anything directly to me because Ilana told them not to. At any rate, I had no doubt who'd planted the idea in the first place.

She must have been talking to Cathryn all during her trip. She knew I was on to her. My refusing to back down despite the knife had pushed her into full battle mode. While I'd expected a sneak attack through her brothers or some other criminal element, she'd caught me with a political move. She'd driven my friends from me.

The first ominous winds were blowing. Tropical storm Ilana had just been upgraded to a category four hurricane headed straight for me.

Cathryn and I continued to talk while Jack and Ilana went to the kitchen for something to eat. Cathryn told me about the conversations she'd been having with Ilana. The way I'd been treated was perfectly normal—if Ilana had been telling the truth.

The longer I knew her, the more evident Ilana's psychopathic traits became. She'd successfully made me look like a nutcase and a drug addict. I'd been dismissed as irrelevant, even by people who'd known me for years. Add my struggle with depression, the naturally slow pace of recovery and a couple of suicide attempts, and her job couldn't have been easier.

Ilana always had someone to blame. Her life was a giant Ponzi scheme where the newcomers heard how awful her former friends had been and how they'd betrayed her. What the newcomers, me included, didn't know was that they were being groomed for the position of scapegoat. Add crystal meth to that and she had hour upon hour to scheme, plot and connive new twists for her vicious game.

"I can't believe how angry I am," I said. "I'm more angry now than I've ever been."

"Good," Cathryn said. "Anger is a better feeling than depression."

"What? I don't understand. I'm pissed off at you and Jack, too, remember?"

"You know, I can't make you believe me. We treated you like crap. You have every reason not to trust us. Hell, you might even think we're in cahoots with Ilana." She walked over to the window and looked out at the street before turning back to me.

"Greg, you're my friend. You were my friend before I really knew Ilana. I didn't quite trust her at the start and I should have listened to that feeling more. I didn't. I know you can't forgive me right away. Just remember that I am your friend. Jack and I both are. We're here for you no matter what you decide."

My gut feeling was that they could be trusted, especially Cathryn. I just didn't know exactly what had happened or been said to dupe them so quickly. But Cathryn had told Jack to apologize for the way the whole drug use thing was handled.

"You're in a dangerous position." Cathryn pitched her voice low so no one else would hear. "Call me melodramatic but I think Ilana's a psychopath. She's a crook, for sure. If her house of cards is falling apart, she's only gonna get more desperate. Especially if you're digging under her flimsy foundation. That puts you right in her line of fire."

"Yeah, I guess you're right. Even if I didn't want to, or couldn't, face the truth before, there's no getting away from it now. I made really bad choices in the past and don't have the luxury of making the same mistakes today. There's just too much at stake."

Gus trotted into the room. He looked from me to Cathryn as if making sure he had our attention. Then he marched over to Ilana's handbag and lifted his leg.

"You know," I said to Cathryn as I let him piss into the Prada, "that dog's smarter than I thought."

* * *

"It seems to me," I said to Kylie, "that I've taken on things that weren't mine and ignored things that were mine. It started with Bruce. He was older, he had all the power, he was the bad guy, and I'm the one who ended up guilty and ashamed. I should've been mad! I spent so much time blaming myself and feeling awful, I couldn't feel anything new. I couldn't miss Kenny, I couldn't be married, and I sure as hell couldn't enjoy my success."

"You must have felt like you were in the ring with a world-class boxer," she said. "Each time you nearly shook off one punch, another landed."

"It was just...well...my life. Something to be endured. I was too preoccupied getting through each hour to think or feel."

"All that pain and anguish had to go somewhere, and it turned inside." Kylie tossed her notepad onto her desk. "That's what some people view depression as...anger turned inside. You kept on bending but never broke. Greg, that's enough to kill most people!"

I dared to dream. There was a place where I could feel good about myself. I wasn't going to find it chasing the roadrunner or hiding in bed or with a handful of pills. In my own quiet way, that day I became determined to achieve that feeling again—on my own, if need be. After all, the coyote can do just fine all by himself.

* * *

166

"Wow, Greg, you look fantastic," Cathryn said. "Your haircut makes you look ten years younger."

"I know," I said. "The long hair thing really wasn't attractive. Someone told me last week I looked like Kato Kaelin. I didn't take that as a compliment."

Besides, I hadn't cared what I looked like for quite a while. Personal grooming had been the last thing on my mind when I'd wanted only to end my life. Now I was ready for some real change; I was ready to live again. The haircut was more of a statement than anything else. Cathryn seemed to know that.

"Glad to see you're back," she said.

"Me, too."

The floor project was finally winding down but was stretching out a lot longer than planned. Ilana and I moved to a different hotel, into a large suite with a full kitchen, living room and separate bedroom. The extra space allowed Cathryn and me to set up an office in the main room.

We'd been working on a business plan for a new company that would buy land and develop housing projects. It was the perfect marriage of our strengths with Cathryn and Jack's experience. The finances, contracts, design work and scheduling would take a great deal of computing power, both in laptops we carried with us and a central processor. Since the requirements were so specific, Cathryn was building the computers herself.

Our living room looked like a warehouse with boxes stacked in every corner. Most of my time was spent at the house making sure the final steps for the floor project were implemented according to my design, so I paid little attention to what the ladies were doing.

It might not have been the greatest move considering what Ilana had already put me through. I thought Cathryn would keep an eye on her and let me know if anything else was about to blow up. I hadn't considered that my loving wife might have been working for a long time on other schemes that weren't even on my radar.

CHAPTER TWENTY-ONE

One morning I was ready to leave when Ilana's mobile phone rang. Cathryn and I watched as Ilana's face grew white then a pale grey.

She nodded slowly. "I understand," she said before hanging up.

"Who was that?" Cathryn asked. "What's going on, Ilana? Is everything all right?"

"No," was all she could manage.

"Ilana," I said, "talk to us. What's happened?"

She began to fidget. She looked as if she couldn't breathe. "I'm so sorry," she said. "I thought I could take care of this without you ever knowing. Greg...our home is in foreclosure. We need ten thousand dollars by noon or the house will be sold on the courthouse steps."

"You're wrong," I said. OK, I squealed. I couldn't seem to get enough breath, either. I'd heard what she'd said but I couldn't believe it was possible. The house was in my name. The mortgage was in my name. How could we be in default?

"What are you talking about?" I asked. OK, I screamed. "I make all the mortgage payments. We're not behind. I don't understand!"

"I took out a second mortgage, Greg, and I've never made a payment."

"How is that possible? The house is in my name. You can't get a loan on a house someone else owns."

Ilana looked as if she'd been slugged in the stomach. How I wished I could have actually done that. She looked at me and then at Cathryn who was also waiting for an explanation. Her eyes rolled once and she blinked rapidly. I knew that look; it meant the roadrunner was suddenly at full stride.

"I included a quit claim with the paperwork we signed for our business partnership." She looked peeved. God help me—and some higher power must have because I didn't smack her—she managed to be irritated. With me!

"You should have looked at the paperwork more closely," she said.

That was rich! She conned me and it was my fault for not paying more attention. By this time I knew she couldn't be trusted but I hadn't expected she'd steal from me. My heart seized in my chest. The damage was already done. We didn't have ten thousand dollars lying around…that I knew of, anyway.

How could I have let something like this happen? I'd been asleep for too long. I needed to wake up and pay attention. Ilana's admission was like a two-by-four hitting me upside my head. She had my full attention.

"Ilana, how could you?" My arms waved wildly. I would've given anything to have a single stick of that dynamite Wile E. always ordered from ACME.

"Everyone just calm down," Cathryn said. "It's ten-thirty. We need to move fast if we're gonna prevent this. Ilana, Greg, how much cash can you come up with? I'll call the office and find out how much Jack and I have in the bank. If we pull together, maybe we can take care of this."

At least someone was being practical. I was still trying to figure out how it had happened. Ilana claimed to have a few thousand dollars in her safe. We'd shoved that into a corner of our shower, the only place that wasn't part of the flooring project.

She gave me the combination then began making frantic calls. To whom—the twins? Her mother? Her older not-gonna-help-Ilana-ever-again brother?—was just as much a mystery as how we'd landed in this mess. I raced to our house, praying for a miracle. The fact that Cathryn was willing to help was my only comfort.

At the house, I ran straight to the bathroom. Crouched inside the shower, I punched the combination into the keypad six times. The safe wouldn't open. It was silly of me to think Ilana would give me the correct combination. Even sillier to think she had any cash. I sank to the floor and wondered what was going to happen next.

My mobile phone rang. It was Cathryn.

"Greg, don't worry," she said. "It was a false alarm. Ilana spoke with the mortgage company. It was all a mistake. Come back to the hotel and I'll explain everything."

A mistake? How could it be a mistake? Either we were in foreclosure or we weren't.

On the drive back, my mobile phone rang again. It was the plumber. He'd put a drain in the butler's pantry to accommodate an ice machine. The check I wrote bounced. He demanded cash immediately; otherwise he was going to the police.

Writing a hot check over five hundred dollars was a felony. The check I'd written on the business account was for thirteen hundred. There had been plenty of money to cover the check when I wrote it. Another mystery.

I was going to be charged, tried and convicted. I'd be locked up again, this time in a prison. There wouldn't be anyone shouting "code black" when my cellmate decided to relax by pounding on me...or raping me. My body would be traded for cigarettes and drugs. The only thing the guards would stop was any suicide attempt. That would trigger an investigation. What else could possibly happen?

I was shaking by the time I arrived back at the hotel. Jack had joined Cathryn and Ilana. I could barely keep myself from yanking every hair from Ilana's head. It must have been pretty obvious because everyone stopped speaking as soon as I entered the room.

I kicked a few boxes of computer parts out of the way and slumped into a chair. When Cathryn and Jack rose to give us some privacy, I waved them back to their seats. Ilana would have to explain herself in front of them.

"How much money did we come up with?" I asked.

"It doesn't matter," Cathryn said. "It was a false alarm."

"Yes, it does matter. The plumber just called. The check I wrote bounced. What happened to the money in our account, Ilana? I have to cover that check today or he's going to the police."

Ilana stared. She was struggling to come up with some answers. Her mouth opened and shut. I heard the click of her teeth like the dry snap of a beak.

"What about the money Jack and Cathryn owe us?" I asked.

"Huh?" Cathryn looked totally confused. "What money? We don't owe you any money."

"The money Ilana put in your account so you could get your mortgage," I said. "The money that pumped up your bank balance so the mortgage company would approve your loan. The twenty-five thousand dollars that got you approved weeks ago but which has not yet been returned. Congratulations, you got your house, now we're losing ours! When can we have the money?"

"Wait a minute," Jack said. "How did you expect us to pay for the labor on your floors, Greg?"

"So you decided to keep the money? Is that what you're saying, Jack?"

"No. But how else did you expect us to pay our staff?"

"Get a job, Jack. I don't care. Just give us our money!"

"I don't have to take this shit from you." Jack spun around and headed out the door.

I looked at the ladies. Ilana hadn't said a word.

"You're wrong, Greg," Cathryn said.

"How am I wrong, Cathryn? I'm just telling you what Ilana told me."

We both looked at Ilana. Still no word.

"Yes," Cathryn said, "Ilana put twenty-five thousand dollars into Jack's bank account to cover the mortgage requirements. I've been asking, on a daily basis, when she wants it put back into the business account. Want to see the text messages saying which account it should be deposited to?"

Ilana started to squirm.

"The deal Jack and Ilana made is that our staff, who've been working for weeks on your floors, were to be paid out of that money. So tell me, Greg, how do you think our crew is gonna be paid?"

"No," I said. "You two had this worked out already. You had the payments set up for the floors before work ever started!"

"We had the cost worked out, yes, but not the payments. Who pays a contractor up front, Greg?"

"We gave you a deposit. I saw the check."

"For materials, Greg. And since you added those metal strips, that went over budget right away. We only started seeing some money after

Ilana and Jack agreed the loan you gave us would stay with us. That didn't last long. And all of it went to the crew. None of it went to Jack or me."

I stared at Ilana. She remained silent but I could see her brain whirling. *Run faster,* I thought. *This time, you can't run fast enough!*

"And by the way." Cathryn's tone turned sharp as she looked at me. "Do you really expect me to believe you knew nothing about this? Get real, Greg. I saw the paperwork for the second mortgage myself months ago."

Ilana popped out of her desperate attempt at invisibility to attack. "Yeah, Greg. And what about the money from the cable shopping network? You told Cathryn that's worth eight hundred thousand in revenue."

"Where the hell are you getting that from?" I asked. "That fell through ages ago. The computer with the product designs mysteriously disappeared when you lost the *other* house in foreclosure."

I rounded back to Cathryn. "You know this story. I told you about it over and over right after it happened. I never said I'd had a contract. It was a good opportunity, yes, but Ilana's shenanigans made sure it went poof!"

She was looking at me like she wasn't sure whether to believe me. Meanwhile, I felt like I'd been dropped into a movie set without a script.

"Cathryn!" I shouted. "You know there's no income. My story has never varied, never! I always told you the truth."

Finally her expression slipped out of doubt and all the way over to shock. I had Ilana dead to rights. We both looked at her.

She'd been sitting next to me during the entire confrontation. Now she got up and moved across the room. She stood next to Cathryn and turned back toward me.

"I don't know what you're talking about," she said. "I never told you they owed us money and I certainly never said anything about your supposed contract with the cable channel."

I couldn't believe it. She'd been caught and now, moments after bringing up the nonexistent contract herself, she was lying again. Plus she'd "crossed the floor" like any experienced politician, aligning herself physically with the voter whose support she craved.

She sat on the sofa, smiling and looking quite satisfied. She was so busy giving me the beady eye she didn't notice that Cathryn was immobile. She looked from Ilana to me and back, trying to find some remote semblance of logic among the arguments and lies. She was finally realizing how expertly my loving wife had manipulated everyone, including her and Jack.

She took a deep breath. With any luck, she was about to piss in Ilana's Prada, too.

"I'm not sure what's going on here," she said, "or who's telling the truth. What I do know is…I don't want any part of it."

With that, she picked up her attaché and left.

Ilana and I stared each other down. I had thought I'd caught her in two huge lies but now I wasn't sure. Based on Jack and Cathryn's reactions, I might have been wrong. I'd felt so confident that I'd shown my friends how devious Ilana could be but it had left me with an empty feeling in the pit of my stomach.

All the stress hit me like a boulder dropped from a cliff. The coyote had taken his best shot and been hammered…again. I collapsed on the bedroom floor, curled up tightly, hugging my knees to my chest. The longer I sat, the more my emotions flowed. I was sobbing and trying desperately to catch my breath when Ilana appeared in the doorway.

"Get up, you sorry peace of shit. You disgust me. You're so weak. Look at you. You're so pathetically weak. I'm not sure what I ever saw in you."

To emphasize her contempt, she kicked me lightly with the toe of her pointy, dainty shoe.

That kick snapped me into a clarity more magnificent than any in Dante's cosmos. In a flash I realized just how deranged Ilana really was. She stood over me gloating as if she'd finally won by crushing me in the weight of her many traps.

I had no idea what was going to happen next. I had no idea what I wanted. I had no plan for how to move forward. But I knew what I did *not* want. I didn't want the chaos, the madness, the lies, the manipulation, the drama. I didn't want anything that had the slightest connection to Ilana or her life.

Every time I'd turned around, she'd closed another door in my life. I was trapped. I'd quit my job to partner with her but the real estate business was worse off than when I'd started. She'd pulled out every penny of equity to fund her drug mania.

Since working wasn't part of her lifestyle, the rentals sat vacant and the properties were never shown. There probably hadn't been enough money left in any of the properties to cover the closing costs, so why bother? For all I knew, the rentals were mortgaged at such bad rates we couldn't charge enough rent to cover the loans. No money was coming in yet cash was flying out the door like smoke rolling off a financial bonfire.

I'd made some horrible decisions. Now my entire livelihood was tied to an evil, scheming bird. I had thought my escape route would be the business with Cathryn and Jack. Until Ilana had stuck her beak in. She'd told me Cathryn had requested she write the business plan; she told Cathryn I'd asked her to write it. Then she'd let the idea molder, leaving me stuck in limbo.

Staring up at those beady eyes and that triumphant, hard smile, one thing was sparkling clear: Ilana and I were finished. She was crazy. She was a drug addict who'd do anything for her next fix. I'd thought our love would be enough to make her want to stay clean but the only thing she cared about was keeping her pipe filled.

For the first time in a very long time, my intentions were crystal clear. I had to pull myself together. I had to save what few assets I could and get as far away from her as possible. But I had to be careful. She was capable of anything. Given the right opportunity, my loving wife would dispose of me any way she could. She'd already made that clear.

As these realizations sparked in quick succession, the door clicked shut. Ilana had left. I had no idea where she was going and didn't much care if she ever came back. I walked down the hall to the suite Cathryn and Jack had rented and flopped onto the couch. Jack was pacing and muttering under his breath, incensed at my accusations. I wasn't even sure they knew I'd come in.

"God," Cathryn said, "I am so over this BS and drama. I want to get this job over with and get as far away from this insanity as possible. No offense, Greg."

She waved a hand at me. It did little to placate my own feelings.

"Jack," she said, "after you left, Ilana told Greg I've been asking about the money from the cable channel. Greg's told me that story a million times. There is no contract. I never asked Ilana about it and I have no clue what she was on about."

I nodded. I was tired but at least someone was on my side.

"Between you calling Jack a thief," she said, aiming her anger at me, "and me being some sort of patsy, I'm about done with the pair of you! Ilana's an interesting piece of work. I get the feeling she's behind all this but I couldn't prove anything. All I want to do is finish the floor, get my computer stuff out of your room, and go home."

"I know just how you feel." Jack spoke directly to Cathryn, as if I weren't even in the room. "How are we gonna pay the crew? Since we've been so busy on their job, we don't have much else lined up. We just might be screwed here."

"Ilana's claiming the foreclosure is a mistake. Hopefully, Greg will come up with the cash. There's really only a couple of days of work left, so we may as well finish what we started." She looked out the window for a moment.

"You know, Ilana was the one who wanted me here for the past two weeks. We were supposed to build the computers and get a bunch of the business stuff submitted for reimbursement and financing. Cash is an issue, yet I really had to push her to work with me on those invoices. You'd think she'd be desperate to get some money coming in, especially after investing so much in that equipment."

"Those computers are probably stolen," I muttered. "She and her brothers probably broke into a warehouse somewhere. They are their own little gang."

"I'm starting to wonder if anything she's ever said is for real. I thought I was gonna get a whole mess of work done and take a huge step to improve our lives, and I've done nothing! Ilana was always too busy, or on the phone, or not here, or at escrow or something. I've done about three hours of real work in ten days. The rest of my time was just wasted."

"Let's get your stuff out of their room," Jack said, "and go home. I think everything we've worked on for the last few months will amount to nothing. I don't know what part Greg has in this little passion play but I want out."

Cathryn nodded. "You know, he always seemed like a pretty cool guy. He always did what he said he'd do. He's been the reliable one. Now, he's just off his nut. Could anyone be that innocent?"

"Who cares? He called me a thief, remember? He lies, he's been depressed, he does drugs, he doesn't do drugs…whatever! He's as much a part of this crap as Ilana."

"Hello!" I hollered. "I'm right here! Don't talk about me as if I'm not in the room!"

"Sorry, Greg," Cathryn said. "This is just so much bullshit, you know?"

"Tell me about it. I just spent ten minutes curled up on the bedroom floor. Do you think my loving wife would offer comfort? At least try to lie her way back into my good graces? No. Her version of love is to kick me."

"She...what?"

"Kicked me! With her pointy toe! Her Prada-clad talon of a toe. Last season's, I might add."

"You're kidding, right?" Jack asked.

"No. I wouldn't kid about something like that."

"Well. Now we know who's evil."

"Yeah. And I guess I know who isn't a thief."

"And," Cathryn said, "I guess Jack and I have to admit that you're probably not nuts."

We all smiled. We'd each realized we'd been sucked into the same vortex. Our friendship was still tentative, though. We were like dogs circling, not knowing if we could trust each other but at least recognizing that none of us could trust Ilana.

Chapter Twenty-two

My loving wife and I stayed in the hotel while the flooring project finished up. Our only means of communication was through our mobile phones. Since the area had almost no cellular reception, the only way to receive a call or text message was to leave the phones on the bathroom windowsill. It made me feel even more isolated and desperate.

The days were a horror show, the nights worse. I pretended to be the same husband she'd pulped into roadkill while secretly scrambling for a way out. My attorney told me to keep quiet while he prepared for divorce proceedings. Once I'd untangled the mess with the quit claim, he'd file the papers. Her entire world would be blown to smithereens.

Meanwhile, I had to continue living with her. Sleeping in her nest was uncomfortable, to say the least. And Ilana started a new tactic to keep me in line. Anything she picked up threatened to become a weapon. Since I was still dangerously underweight, her ability to cause me grave harm was indisputable.

One evening she was chopping vegetables and abruptly turned toward me as I walked to the sink. The knife was aimed at my gut. If I hadn't jumped back, it would have sliced right through my belly.

"Greg," she said, "you're not thinking about leaving me, are you?"

For a split second, I thought she'd found out about the divorce. But that was impossible. I'd gone to my attorney's office in person. I hadn't written anything down or made any calls. There was no way she could know. Unless she'd followed me.

"Ilana," I said, "I'm tired. I don't want to argue."

"Because if you were," she said as she shook the knife with just enough absentmindedness to appear innocent, "I don't know what I'd do. I don't know if I could…control myself."

I backed out of the kitchen. Later I found that knife, the street-fighting knife she'd left in the filing cabinet, inside my briefcase. A bright pink sticky clung to the blade. *Love you,* it said. Beneath that was a picture of a heart.

A bleeding heart.

* * *

Early one morning, the phone squawked to herald a text message. I didn't want to wake Ilana, so I tiptoed to the bathroom and closed the door. When I read the message, it made no sense. Then I realized I'd picked up her phone by mistake.

How serendipitous, I thought.

The message was from Cathryn. When I realized what it meant, I read all the previous messages between her and Ilana. The correspondence covered the past three months, and most of it was about me. They talked about how crazy they thought I was, how far I'd fallen into drug addiction, how I never did anything right. They fed off each other, looking for the worst in everything that happened.

They'd also set me up. They'd planned different situations down to scripting what they did and said just to see how I would respond. In a recent message, Cathryn had given Ilana a moment-by-moment account of my interaction with Jack and his staff on the jobsite. She'd ended by saying, *He's not capable of filling a hole.*

I sat in the bathroom with my eyes glazed over. What had I done to deserve this type of treachery? I forwarded all the messages to my phone and marked them as unread on Ilana's so she wouldn't know I'd seen them. Then I deleted the messages from her sent folder.

Then it occurred to me—if they were communicating by text message, how else were they communicating? I drove to the house. Cathryn often used my computer when she was in town, so I'd set up her own login account. Since it was my computer, I was the administrator. I logged in as myself, removed Cathryn's password then logged in as Cathryn.

Dozens of detailed emails expanded on the text messages. Ilana had taken real events and put just enough spin on them so they were both believable and made me look unreliable or dishonest. She attributed her own lies to me. The scenarios were accurate, except the names had been swapped. It was like some bizarre scene in a 1960's cold-war spy thriller, except I was the sucker being led to slaughter.

Finally I had proof. If Cathryn believed any of it, she would've been putty in Ilana's hands. And why wouldn't she believe her? Ilana was, after all, my loving wife. The woman I'd married had been on a campaign to make me look like a crazy man. Not once, ever, did she say anything positive. It was exactly like what Bruce had done, twisted and distorted something good, except on an emotional level.

I wasn't a child anymore. I wasn't powerless. I abandoned any emotion for Ilana except one: contempt. This coyote was going solo. My den would be stocked with dynamite and mist nets. Ilana had declared war long ago. I was going to end it.

Of course, I couldn't help being disappointed in Cathryn. I'd thought better of her and was angry she'd gone along with the betrayal. But she'd been duped as thoroughly as I had. The only way I'd figured it out had been to investigate. If I could provoke Cathryn into focusing all her attention on Ilana and her claims, maybe my shaky ally would become a real one.

But I knew Cathryn. She was so stable and solid, it would take a lot to move her out of her current beliefs. The only way she'd teeter was if she were good and mad. So my first step was to really piss her off. I could stand up to any scrutiny. Ilana would crumble.

My mobile phone vibrated. Cathryn had sent me a text message. She couldn't reach Ilana and asked me to tell her something. My reply was simple.

I'm sorry, it read. *I'm not capable of passing on messages. I'm still trying to figure out how to fill this hole.*

She was furious. *How did you get Ilana's text messages?* she demanded.

I fired all the text messages I'd found on Ilana's phone to Cathryn as fast as I could. The barrage ended with a lengthy and carefully constructed email to both of them. I told them exactly what I knew and what I thought about their stupid little games.

Once Cathryn got angry enough to defend herself, we could finally compare notes and uncover Ilana's lies. All I could do in the meantime was wait. And pray. Soon Cathryn sauntered around the back of the house and casually wandered into the office.

"Thank God, Greg," she said, "Finally! See what Ilana's been up to? NOW do you see her for what she is?"

I took a deep breath, willed myself to stay calm, and opened my own script.

"Hmm," I said, "I think the question that's a little more to the point is what the hell were you and Ilana playing at? You're the one who was out of line here. All I did was catch you. You could've told me about this after the blowup at the hotel, you know. I'm really disappointed that you weren't honest with me. I expected better of you, Cathryn."

"Hello?" she said, totally calm.

She sat down, totally relaxed, in one of the plush guest chairs. She kept looking at me as if about to say something, but remained silent.

I stayed quiet. I wasn't about to be the first to talk. Finally she stopped in front of my desk and looked me straight in the eye.

"Yes, I've been in communication with Ilana all along," she said. "It's amazing how far she was willing to go to screw you over." She tapped the desk thoughtfully.

"I just couldn't believe what the evidence was showing," she continued. "I had to know what was real. So, when Ilana started communicating with me directly, I played along. Didn't it seem strange to you that Ilana was suddenly acting like MY best friend?"

Huh??? What was she talking about? This is NOT part of the script! And this scene isn't improv!

"Come on, Greg, THINK! Ilana's been out to set you up right from the start. I thought that was obvious. At least to me."

"Well, why didn't you say something to me, face to face? Isn't that what friends would do? Not all this game-playing."

She thought for a moment. "Would you have believed me?" she asked, gently. "I know this was risky, but I couldn't stand the thought of losing our friendship. I did what I had to do so that you'd see Ilana's true colors yourself. Telling you wouldn't have done any good. You didn't want to see.'

"I still don't understand," I said.

"Greg, let me be really blunt. Until now, today really, you only saw what you wanted or needed to see in Ilana. "Needed" is probably the better word. If I had gone after Ilana before this, you would have backed her up, and our friendship would have been over. I couldn't let that happen."

Although I hated feeling like I'd been manipulated, the wisdom of Cathryn's choices started to make sense. She was right; I would have blindly backed Ilana back then. Today was a whole different ballgame. I was much healthier now, and had a much more accurate vision, thanks to my treatment, and my own hard work. I was ready to claim my life back, starting NOW

I thought about what she'd said for a couple of minutes, and put forward a proposal. "Cathryn, maybe we can channel our frustration and anger into something positive. I need you're help if I'm going to salvage anything out of my life. Are you up for it?" I asked.

Her response took a quarter of a second. "Count me in. I have some amends to make with you. Jack and I will do whatever we can to help."

Yes! Finally, an ally. Except that she'd really been an ally all along.

"I just have to get one thing clear," she said.

Oh, shit, I thought. Somehow, some way, Ilana's work was going to wreck this. I waited to see what other trap was about to be sprung.

"Your discharge papers from Indio," she said. "They listed that you use meth. Ilana showed me those papers while we were looking for a holistic in-patient treatment center for you. What's up with that?"

Wham! Just when I was getting up, another boulder from Ilana slammed me back down.

"The only reason meth use shows up on my chart," I said with a steadiness I absolutely did not feel, "is because of lies Ilana told the day I was supposed to be discharged. She showed up hours late and in the middle of the discharge meeting blurted out some lie about me being a meth head. I attacked her and ended up locked up for another couple of days."

"You actually attacked her? Physically, I mean?"

"Yes. Not one of my best moments."

"I had no idea. I was there, you know, driving around the parking lot to keep the air conditioning going. That wasn't discharge day. Ilana told me she was just visiting. When we got home we looked for a residential rehab center for you. She even cashed in some of her stock portfolio to pay for it."

"Newsflash! Ilana purposefully screwed things up to keep me locked up. My worst vices are the same as yours—nicotine and coffee. Plus, there is no stock portfolio. That's been gone for a while now."

"It's even worse than I thought! She's nuts!"

"Welcome to my world. I don't even try to understand her motivation anymore. I think it has something to do with the crime ring she and her brothers run but I can't prove that and I don't really care. All I want now is to protect myself and my assets."

"She is unspeakably evil." Cathryn reached over and touched my arm. "I am so sorry for being so blind for so long. I'm having a hard time believing she's capable of so much destruction, and I can't even begin to try to understand the motivation. Actually, I don't really care at this point. She's on her own. You just let Jack and I know what you need. We love you, OK?"

I started to shake violently. I had no one but her and Jack now. I'd never really had her before; Ilana had made sure of that. But Cathryn was my friend now, truly my friend, and the relief flowed through me like a tide. It washed away all the tension and behind that came a wave of exhaustion. I collapsed in her arms.

She lowered me to the floor. We sat there as tears flowed, mostly from me but also more than a few from her. I hadn't realized until then how much stress the whole situation had put her under. She patted my back and rubbed my arms, nodding and making soothing noises. I felt like a child, like a boy and a man and a wrung-out doll all at once.

Then I was weeping again, gasping for breath and moaning as I panted. Something new was breaking loose, something old and dark and hidden. It cracked open like rotten pillions hidden in the ocean. Up floated bubbles of rot and decay, choking off my words.

"I...I..." I panted.

"OK, Greg, it's OK," Cathryn said over and over. "Tell me. What is it? What's wrong?"

It was her touch, the smoothness of her palm against my face, the sturdy curve of her arm around my shoulder. I'd finally found the one thing I'd searched for all my life: a comforting hug given with love. Not lust, like Bruce's touch; not greed or the need for control like Ilana's; not even the searching, frustrated grip my ex-wife had used in her attempts to drag me away from depression. In Cathryn's arms was love, pure and unadulterated.

"I…he…" I moaned.

"Take a breath."

She pressed her hand against my stomach. Her touch was warm and radiated calmness into my belly. I took a breath and let it out.

"Kenny," I finally said.

"Your brother."

I nodded. "He…."

"Tell me. It's OK. You'll be OK. Just tell me."

"My cousin. Bruce. He molested me every summer from when I was seven until I was twelve or thirteen."

Who said that? I sprang out of her hug, pacing the small office like a caged tiger, hoping it had stayed as a thought inside my head. Too late, it was out.

"Wow." Cathryn leaned back. "That does finally shed some light on why you've stuck with Ilana through so much. You can't feel too good about yourself with something like that lurking around."

I fell into a chair. I couldn't believe I'd told her. I'd never told anyone about my cousin, no one except Kylie! I didn't want my friends to look at me with sadness or treat me differently. Just like with the cancer, I thought private battles should stay private.

But I'd been wrong. I'd been wrong about so much. About the cancer, about Ilana, about the life I thought I didn't deserve and the misery I thought I did. Could I be wrong about this, too? Was it at all possible that I should tell…and not just about the abuse but the rest of it, too? That massive, sunken shipload of pus I'd deeply buried so long ago?

"Greg. Greg, are you all right? We're gonna deal with this, OK?"

I looked at her. She'd betrayed me then she'd done something more— she'd owned up to her actions and apologized. In all my life, I don't think I'd ever met anyone else strong enough to do that. In all my life, I'd never met anyone else strong enough to share my buried burden.

"That's not all," I said.

She moved close enough so she could hold my hands. She sat at my feet, looking up with an open heart. Her cheeks were still damp but her eyes were clear. "OK," she said. "What else?"

"The molestation…that's not the real secret."

She waited. There was much more to the story but I stopped with the ship only halfway to the surface. Dredging up the past and all those emotions might not do me any good. Regardless of how hurtful and damaging the events had been, regardless of how horrid the feelings had been, at least they were familiar. There was no telling what new emotions would rush in once the old ones were gone.

That unknown, the unfamiliar turmoil to come, terrified me. But the hatch had already blown off the lowest, most putrid decks. An overpowering stench leaked into every fiber of my body and soul. I felt like I would vomit from utter disgust. I didn't want to feel that way. I wanted to get up and run, to disappear into a dark cave in the desert. No matter where I went, I would take the stench with me. Putrescence consumed me; it *was* me.

I'd never before felt emotional torment as a physical pain. Yet there it was. My head pounded like it was about to explode, my limbs felt alive with a creepy-crawly itch that made me fidget constantly. I was a mess. I had to pull this terrible treasure to the surface if I ever wanted to be free. But I couldn't. Before long, it would drag me down with it.

"Whatever happened," Cathryn said, "it's over now. I'm here. You're safe."

She squeezed my hands. When she reached up to touch my face again, the darkness broke through to the surface.

"The molestation," I said, "isn't the real secret."

CHAPTER TWENTY-THREE

I'd hated it when Bruce touched me and I certainly hadn't wanted to touch him. Slowly, though, my body responded.

It was purely physical. My mind was in overdrive, feeling the tingle of sensation where he touched. I didn't want him doing anything but there was a pleasure to it, to the basic mechanics of the movement.

Bruce must have sensed the change because one night he crawled under the covers and started sucking me. It made me feel so ashamed, so dirty, yet the physical sensation itself was enjoyable. Even as my mind screamed for him to stop, my blood rushed and my skin grew hot.

I'd been betrayed by my own body. Repeatedly. I knew what we were doing made me feel dirty, but I was powerless to stop it. Later, I hadn't wanted it to stop. Yet my shame was exponential. I didn't know what was wrong with me. Why was I finding enjoyment in something I knew was dirty and shameful?

A few years after the abuse started was when Kenny had professed his faith in front of the entire church. How I'd envied him. He really seemed to be comforted by his decision to "accept the Lord into his heart." He changed after that, settling into some radiant peace he said came from knowing God. Hoping for that same peace, I headed toward the altar a year later.

But I didn't feel better. Trying to open up to some higher power only added to my guilt and shame. I was a fraud. I couldn't tell anyone about Bruce. I thought the abuse was as much my fault as his. In trying to make things right I'd become a liar, telling people I was born again. I had damned myself as surely as if a divine finger had branded a curse on my forehead.

As this struggle gripped my every waking hour, life sped up for my family. I had finally decided to tell my parents about the abuse when Uncle Conrad died of cancer. That same year my great-grandmother, Mama, was also diagnosed with cancer. When the doctor told Papa, he said, "I can't live without my Rita Jean," then collapsed with a heart attack.

He was hospitalized in a semi-private room with Mama in the other bed. When he woke, he told us he'd had a horrible nightmare that Rita Jean had cancer. We told him it wasn't a dream. He closed his eyes, said, "I can't live without my Rita Jean," and died instantly from a massive heart attack. Mama wasted away for another year before she finally succumbed.

It hadn't seemed right to burden my parents with more trouble, what with the funerals and all. A few months after Mama's death I finally got up the courage again. I spent a week rehearsing what I was going to say. Dad always made pancakes on Saturdays so I picked the time after breakfast for the conversation.

When I got out of bed that morning, the house was eerily quiet. A note in the kitchen explained that our next-door neighbor, a family friend we called Aunt Betty, had died the night before. My parents were at the funeral home.

Aunt Betty had been like a grandmother to me and she was gone, too. I lost the courage to ever try speaking to my parents about the abuse. Being touched by a cousin made me feel awful but didn't hurt me physically. It seemed so insignificant compared to all the deaths.

I began to think that somehow all those deaths were my fault. My entire family was being punished for what I did with Bruce, for deriving pleasure from something so wrong. I went through a real rough period where I refused to visit the farm alone. Mother and Dad thought I was grieving but I knew someone else would die if Bruce and I did "it" again.

Eventually I stayed at the farm again but I never really lost the fear that something really bad, even death, would descend. I remained powerless to stop Bruce while secretly enjoying the sensations. My entire life was taken over by my dread of and longing for those furtive summer nights.

* * *

"When Kenny died," I said, "all those feelings came back. The utter emptiness of knowing I couldn't tell anyone. No matter how bad the depression had become, no matter how much I'd suffered because I'd never told as a child, I also couldn't tell anyone as an adult. My depression had been pushing me toward that but even an unconscious effort to deal with it made someone else in my life die."

"That's some mighty strange magical thinking," Cathryn said. "Because you're bad, others get punished? The world just doesn't work like that. People die. They get sick. They kill themselves. I'm not making less of your loss but...."

"I know." The tears welled up again. "It was just so unexpected. So sudden. Like all those deaths when I was a kid."

"Suicide usually is sudden, Greg. For the friends and family, anyway."

"And--"

I had to stop. The sobs were choking off my words again. Cathryn rose onto her knees to hug me. I fell forward into her arms and we sank to the floor together.

"It was so sordid!" I wept freely as I spoke. "Kenny disappearing, the note that explained nothing. And the waiting! I never knew whether to pick up the phone. It might be the police saying they'd found the body and then he'd be dead for sure. But it might be him! Sometimes I still think it might be him."

Cathryn smoothed my hair. "Greg. Look at me."

Her eyes were gentle. I felt the strength in her gaze, the love in her hands.

"Your brother is dead," she said. "He threw himself off a bridge and drowned. He's not coming back, ever. By now, even his body has gone back to the earth. You know that, don't you?"

I nodded. Fresh tears were clouding my sight but our gaze remained locked.

"You are not responsible for his choices," she said.

"But--"

"But nothing. You couldn't protect him then because you were too small. You couldn't help him as an adult because he wouldn't let you."

"What do you mean?"

"He could have called you. He could have asked for help. He didn't. You're not his keeper, his bodyguard or his therapist. You didn't kill your relatives back then and you didn't kill Kenny."

God, how I'd needed to hear someone say those words. Someone who knew me, someone who gave a damn about my life and my health and my wellbeing. Kylie had said it plenty of times, Doc Johnson had said it…hell, even I'd said it. Somehow it had always felt hollow. Caring, honest, true, and hollow. When Cathryn said the same thing, it was like a revelation of love.

All I could do was hang in her arms and sob. It was the kind of cry that had been years, decades, in coming. She handed me tissues until I ran out of tears. I felt better then, like after throwing up. The body still feels like shit but the stomach isn't in so much pain. Now that my dirty little secret was out I felt a bit better. I also felt a whole lot worse but in a different way.

We talked for another half an hour until I convinced her I was OK. I just wanted to go to bed, which is exactly what I did. She made me swear I'd see Kylie right away, even if I had to book an emergency appointment. I did.

I had something to ask her. Something I couldn't even ask Cathryn.

* * *

"So now you know the real secret." I stared at Kylie. I didn't want to miss any little flinch or twitch that might tell me her true feelings when I launched my big question. As evenly as possible, I asked, "Do you think it means I'm gay?"

There was that silence again. Kylie wore that peaceful look of total calm and acceptance. I felt so strange. I was emptied out yet not deflated, exhausted but not weak. And even though I nervously awaited her next words, being gay wouldn't crush me. It was just another scary unknown. But I'd have to wait to discover the truth. First Kylie wanted to set me straight (insert crazed laughter here).

"First thing's first," she said. "There's a couple of things I want to be really clear about, and you're just gonna have to take my word."

She leaned forward and put her hand over mine.

"Your body's response to what Bruce did is perfectly normal. It's nothing to be ashamed of, and is fairly common among people who are sexually abused. It can even happen with rape victims. It's nothing more than a physical response. It's nothing to be ashamed of or feel guilty about. The body is hardwired to respond certain ways to certain stimuli. Repeat a stimulus enough and primitive reactions take over. It doesn't mean you asked to be abused or enjoyed being molested."

She waited until I nodded. Then she sat back and folded her hands in her lap.

"The second thing is this. Being gay is not determined by what happens in your life. You are born that way. Just like you're born straight. Events can't make a straight person gay any more than they can make a gay person straight. You're not attracted to men at all, are you?

"No!" the answer sprang to my lips easily. I found women attractive, not men. Sex with women was exciting. But still…how my body had reacted…Then it all began to come together for me. It had been just my body reacting, exactly like she'd said. It wasn't who I was, and it didn't mean I was gay.

She waited until I nodded again. I needed some time to assimilate this new information. She continued where she'd left off.

"You know," she said, "that's an awful lot of stuff for a young boy to keep to himself. The events alone were pretty horrific but the feelings that went with them must have been unbearable. I would really like it if you could cut yourself a little slack. You were just a boy. You respected your parents and put what you thought were their needs ahead of your own. You experienced loss and grieving. That's a heavy burden for a healthy adult to bear."

She opened her hands like a flower blooming. "You survived all that," she said gently, "and went on to have successes in your life. Put aside the feelings for a moment, if you can, and recognize just how absolutely remarkable your survival and your success really are."

Me? I thought. *Successful? Yeah, right. Locked down in the nutcracker suite after trying to off myself. Three times. Living with a junkie I can't shake. No future.*

All the pressure coalesced in that single moment. Although she was trying to help me, I blew.

"What makes you think anything about me is either remarkable or successful, for Christ's sake?" I yelled. "I tried to kill myself three times, and failed miserably, by the way. I'm depressed, my wife is a drugged-out crazy person, and my life is completely out of control. So tell me, what's remarkable about that?"

I was on the verge of tears. If I started crying, I might never stop. All the feelings that had been so carefully packed and stored away threatened to drag me deep into the muck.

Kylie held both my hands and stared straight into my eyes.

"You're alive," she said. "You're here. You're *not* crazy. You *are* a *good* man. You have morals, principals and ethics. You're brave enough to talk about the past. You want something better for yourself. You're doing the hard work. You want to get well. You *will* get well. That, Greg, means you're pretty remarkable."

I shook my head.

"The first thing I want you to do," she said, "is to cut yourself some slack for what happened in the past. Forgive yourself for being a kid. Forgive yourself for not being perfect. You did the absolute best you could with the tools you had at that time. And you did good, OK? Can you get that?"

I'd spent so much of my life feeling guilty and ashamed, and become so good at feeling those emotions, I wasn't at all sure about forgiveness. That was way outside my comfort zone.

Maybe, though, forgiveness would dampen that putrid stench. Maybe the smell would finally vanish. And as for acknowledging my success, well, that just might lead to self-confidence. What was it Cathryn had said? Fake it 'till you make it. I knew I could fake it. Maybe that meant I could make it. With luck, before Hurricane Ilana made landfall.

Kylie called the next day to see how I was handling everything. I promised I was fine and would see her in a few days for my next visit. At that point, I was scared to go back but more scared not to. I had laid my soul bare. I needed Kylie and Cathryn to help me put my life back together.

* * *

Our next few visits ran together in my memory. Kylie talked a lot while

I vacillated between screaming and crying. It didn't feel like much of an advancement but at least I wasn't in bed or curled up on the floor.

Then Kylie said she wanted me to do an exercise. I'd done the role-playing she'd set up before. At first I'd been reluctant. I didn't see how pretending would solve anything. Hadn't pretending gotten me into this whole mess of a life in the first place? But acting things out helped break the hold my past had on me.

This time Kylie asked me to get comfortable in my chair. She wanted to do a guided meditation. By leading me through a visualization, she'd help me release some of my guilt about Kenny. I wasn't quite sure that was ever going to be possible but because Kylie had asked, I'd try.

I concentrated on my breathing. Instantly, I heard a loud, forceful sucking sound, like a vacuum cleaner hose that was clogged. I felt as if I were being drawn through that hose to a place deep in my past. I stood on a turn-of-the-century railway platform dressed in an old-fashioned suit of black, heavy wool. People brushed past and the steam engine belched thick clouds into the damp air.

Porters with wheeled carts delivered luggage to baggage cars on various rail lines. Women wore long dresses with bustles, and the men were dressed like me. Bells clanged, conductors yelled, and life swirled in a beautiful cacophony.

I looked down at my stout black boots and saw two suitcases on the platform beside me. One was small and light. It had been packed well and held neither too much nor too little. The other bulged and was cumbersome. Bits of its contents poked out from either side.

I immediately recognized the smaller case as mine. The larger one I wasn't so sure about. In a strange way it was familiar, yet I knew it wasn't mine. It was placed close to me, though, so it had to be mine. Didn't it?

As I stared, I became ever more certain that this large case was *not* mine. A knowing swept over me, as crystal clear as my revelations on the hotel floor. This case and all its contents didn't belong to me. I'd been carrying it for quite some time but it had been an unnecessary burden. It was time to return it to its rightful owner.

A stranger detoured out of the crowd. He picked up the larger case and walked slowly away. When he reached the end of the platform, he looked over his shoulder and tipped his hat.

Kenny smiled from under the brim. I smiled back. After giving me a wink, he turned and walked away. I slowly picked up the smaller valise and walked in the opposite direction.

My eyes opened and locked on Kylie's face. Just like I'd feared, that tidal wave of emotions rushed in—relief, sorrow, elation, sadness, forgiveness, and everything in between. Rather than drown me, though, I felt cleansed. As the emotions continued to roil and release, I felt more and more buoyant.

Maybe there is something to this psychobabble crap, I thought as tears welled in my eyes. A gasping sob escaped me. For the first time, I wept for the loss of my brother and best friend.

Kylie handed me tissues until I was cried out, which took quite some time. "You OK?" she asked gently.

"Wow." I wiped my eyes a final time. "Every time I've thought about Kenny, it's been so complicated, you know? I always felt guilty, like I should've done something or known how he felt. Or I felt ashamed, like everyone knew and blamed me. This is the first time I've been plain old sad and able to just miss him. I feel like I've lost a hundred pounds!"

I managed a wan smile. I wasn't exactly sure what had happened but I knew how I felt. My muscles were loose, like I'd just run a marathon, and the stench was gone. I felt better than I had in years. From that day on, I'd only get stronger. I'd finally started to heal. Of that, I was sure.

* * *

As I was getting myself together, Kylie leaned back in her chair. "Greg, we spent some time talking about what happened with Ilana and your friends."

"The Prada kick," I said wryly.

What would Oprah do if Maya Angelou kicked her? Probably settle her on the couch for a special four-hour broadcast. I was beyond talking. I was all about action.

"I've asked you before," Kylie said, "whether you thought you were in a healthy situation."

"Say no more. Remember that great haircut I got after being released from Indio?"

She looked at me strangely but nodded.

"A few weeks ago that salon went up for sale. They have six stylists and provide spa services like massages, facials and tanning. The owner wants to stay on as a stylist, so whoever buys the place will have a built-in expert. I might buy it."

My friend Donnie had been cutting hair at the salon for almost ten years. Michele, the owner, left much of the daily business operations to him. Donnie had already agreed to stick around if I bought the place. Since Michele wanted to stay on with her book of clients, everyone won.

"People always need haircuts and pampering," I said. "I'll be able to focus on growing the business while Donnie manages the place. Since the spa's been around for a long time already, it's a stable operation. Precisely what I need to free me from Ilana."

"Sounds like it," she said, "but can you afford to buy the business?"

"Ilana owes me a lot of money. She never paid me anything for all the work I've done on the real estate venture. If she agrees, financing will be no problem."

"Now that's worrisome. Ilana has already shown you she can't be trusted. Although I can't offer a professional diagnosis because I've never met her, she certainly sounds like she's presenting psychopathic personality traits. Since you've been under her control for so long, she's not likely to want to let you go easily."

Kylie leaned forward to make sure I was listening. "Trying to trick her could be very dangerous. At this point, Greg, my instinct says to just run."

"No. Not yet." I might have messed up my entire life so far but that was over. From here on out, it was the new Greg and a new life.

"It's too soon," I said. "I have to create an escape route. Obviously I can't count on a business future with Ilana. Any possibility of a business future with Jack and Cathryn might also be shot to hell. Cathryn said she feels like she's in the middle of an earthquake. I need to create financial independence for myself, by myself. Then I can break from Ilana forever."

"I still don't like it," Kylie said. "But if you can get what you need to move out of her life then go for it."

As I left, she called, "Be careful!"

I nodded. The coyote was on full alert.

CHAPTER TWENTY-FOUR

The seemingly unending floor project was winding down. I desperately wanted to move back into the house. To my home, my sanctuary, my salvation. Getting Ilana off the title would be fairly easy, considering the questionable method she'd used to get on. Once that was done and the salon purchase closed, I could completely extricate myself from her clutches.

The floors were gorgeous, really worth the wait. The metal strips and layers of stain and sealer produced a fantastic result. It was precisely the right finishing touch for my house. Jack, Cathryn, and their staff had long since decamped to San Diego. The remaining work, the final coats of sealant, was being handled with day trips.

As the men spread the final top coat of urethane, I headed off to the local drive-through deli. The entire crew deserved a celebratory lunch. Besides, I would be really happy to see the end of all those people who, although they acted polite, were most definitely not my biggest supporters.

When I returned, Cathryn's vehicle was parked in the driveway. She'd planned to oversee the final day's work. We were going to celebrate later by having dinner together. While I parked beside her vehicle, a Lincoln pulled to the curb and a middle-aged couple got out.

The woman was short, stocky, and intensely red-headed. She looked like Ethel Merman, younger yet having lived a less-forgiving life. As I opened the front door, Ethel waved a sheaf of papers at me and charged across the lawn. Her companion, a thin, dithering man slightly older than her, stumbled to keep up.

"What are you doing in my house?" she barked.

"I beg your pardon?"

"This is my house." She shook the papers at me. "I bought it at a foreclosure sale. What are you doing in *my* house?"

"There's been some mistake." My heart was clutching at my chest but I stayed calm. "This house is not in foreclosure."

Cathryn heard our conversation and came to the door. "Is everything all right?"

"This woman seems to think she bought my house." I managed to smile while I focused on my breathing.

"Street trash!" Ethyl yelled. "Hobo! Bum! You're trespassing! I'm calling the police!"

One of the neighbors poked his head out his front door. Cathryn, ever the professional, smiled gently.

"May I have a quick look at the paperwork?" she asked. "You don't have to hand it to me. Just hold up the relevant pages."

As she scanned the documents, I watched her face draw tight. "One moment, please, while I get someone who can help you."

She hauled me inside and closed the door in their faces. Jack was standing in the foyer. It was astonishing how much space he could take up when he wanted to. He was so pissed, he wanted to take up all the space I might use to escape. And he did.

"We've completed thousands of dollars worth of work," he growled. "We've been paid only a fraction and Ilana doesn't own the house anymore? That'll put us into bankruptcy, too!"

"Just wait," Cathryn said.

With both us men trailing her, she strode into the master bedroom where Ilana was surveying the work.

"Ilana," Cathryn said expansively, "there you are! A woman at the front door says she just bought your house at a foreclosure sale. You need to talk to her. *Now.*"

The first chink in Ilana's armor showed. A look of absolute horror flitted across her face before she composed herself.

"Oh, don't worry," she said. "There must be some misunderstanding. I talked to my lender about that weeks ago. We got it all sorted out. There was no sale, the house is mine, don't worry about a thing. I'll explain everything."

Jack, after throwing me the dirtiest look I'd ever gotten from a man without being punched immediately afterwards, went back outside to organize the empty sealer containers and other debris they had to remove. I was surprised at how much noise an angry person could make throwing around empty sealant containers.

"I believe that woman," Cathryn said to me. "She has the paperwork. You're screwed and we're screwed. We aren't gonna get paid for this job. And I don't want to be part of whatever game Ilana's playing. It's just not right."

"Cathryn," I said, "I have a plan. I'm going to get out of this mess soon, I promise. When I do, you and Jack will have your money. I swear. It might not be right away but I'll pay back every penny."

Cathryn thought for a moment. Finally she said, "I guess we'll finish the job. There isn't that much left to do, so we might as well get it over with. I just don't know what you're thinking, Greg. After that whole blowup at the hotel, I'm confident all the drama is Ilana's making and that you're just, well, naïve."

I flinched but stood steady. She was right; I had been naïve. Worse than naïve, really, because I'd suspected Ilana of using drugs again. I also should've suspected that her brothers' criminal activities might have had more to do with her than them. I deserved to take a little knock from the truth, and Cathryn deserved to be the one to deliver it.

"It's hard to believe anyone can be that slow on the uptake," she sighed, "but you've been dealing with the whole depression thing. I know exactly what that can do to your life. I believe you, Greg. I may be your biggest supporter but I'm done playing games. When Jack and I finish the sealant, we're getting the heck out of here."

Al and Sonja Peterson, the couple who'd bought the house, returned to their car. Ilana led them out, chatting and laughing the whole time. Everyone seemed relaxed. Except I knew Ilana's composure was a front. Everything about her was a front.

My loving wife returned and told me that the sale had been a mistake, that the Petersons had seen it was an error and agreed it would take only a few days to sort out the paperwork.

So not to worry, no problems, everything was fine, just please don't peer too deeply into the papers or the proceedings or Ilana's entire house of cards. I just smiled. She was lying, and I knew it. I had her dead to rights. How could I have been so blind for so long? For every lie I knew about, for every game I'd uncovered, how many lies and games have been going on that I know nothing about?

Cathryn and Jack kept their word. They finished the floors and left. While Ilana was back in the office, the three of us stood on the lawn to say our goodbyes.

"You know," Cathryn said, "it's sad. I don't think I'll ever see Ilana again. I sure hope you're gonna be all right, Greg. But there's nothing we can do as long as you're with her. You've gotta get out of this one on your own."

"Yep," Jack said. "We've done all we can. As long as you're with Ilana, we're stuck. You know, Ilana made her choice—she chose drugs. Now we'll see what your choices are gonna be."

Cathryn was in tears. She hugged me and held me for a while. Finally she wiped her eyes and said, "I'm so sorry, Greg. I hate leaving you alone but I don't know what else to do. I can't allow Ilana to cause more problems for us. Our business is really struggling because of her games. I wish you could get out tonight. Please be careful, OK?"

"I'll be careful Cathryn. I appreciate your concern. I also understand you have to do what's best for you. I don't blame you for running. If I could, I would. But I have some things to take care of before I can be done with Ilana."

Boy, talk about tough love. A baseball bat upside the head would have been more subtle. On the one hand, I did understand. Why should they stick around and suffer just because they were my friends? On the other hand, I wasn't sure they still were my friends. Wouldn't friends stick around and provide moral support?

As they drove off, I wondered if I would ever see them again. In the days that followed, they didn't call me and I didn't call them. They loved me and would do anything I asked, if I asked. I loved them too much to do that. I was going to fix this mess by myself.

* * *

An earlier call to my attorney garnered some fast answers. He had hired the Petersons to purchase the house at auction in partnership with me. It couldn't have been more simple for them. All they'd had to do was pay off the second mortgage, be paid a hefty fee, and the remaining proceeds from the sale of the house would come back to me. I couldn't stop the foreclosure, and I couldn't afford to keep the house even if I could have gotten it back. At least this way, I'd at least get most of the equity out of it when it sold. And, to all public appearances, I'd lost the house. Ilana would never know. The coyote finally got one up on the roadrunner.

I had to regain control and watch out for myself. Yet I was exhausted. I needed time for more therapy, to process new emotions and finish grieving Kenny. If things would only go well for a little while, I could get back on track. But my life had been reduced to a fight with a meth-head over the one and only asset I had left. I had won the battle, but the war was far from over.

"Greg."

Ilana's voice echoed in the empty house. I turned to see her standing in the doorway to the bedroom. Something shiny was nestled in her palm. I assumed it was her cell phone.

"What, Ilana?"

When she tucked her hair back, I realized she was holding a gun.

"Greg. You believe me, don't you?" She was breathing hard and her eyes were glassy. She was as high as a supernova and about as explosive.

"It's important that you believe me," she said. "You're my husband. A husband should love his wife. You love me, don't you?"

"Of course, Ilana."

My voice shook the tiniest bit. I hoped she wouldn't notice. I didn't want to piss her off at that moment.

"Because if you didn't love me," she said, "if I ever found out you were thinking of leaving me…."

Her hand wavered. The gesture looked like she was at a loss for what to say but the gun did all the talking.

"I'm not going to leave you, Ilana."

"I can't live without you," she whispered. Her voice was hoarse with sorrow over the imagined abandonment.

"I won't." She snapped to attention. "I won't live without you!"

"You don't have to."

I spread my arms slowly. She wobbled then fell forward into a hug. She felt limp but I knew she was capable of attacking at any moment. When her arms dropped off me again, she kissed my cheek before turning away.

"I'm going to take care of the house," she said. "Don't worry, Greg. As long as we're together, you don't have to worry about anything bad happening."

She stopped at the front door and looked back. "You'll be here when I get back."

It was clearly a command.

"Of course," I soothed. "Why don't I make dinner tonight? We'll stay in. Just the two of us."

She peered at me closely then nodded. Slipping the gun into her oversized bag, she walked out to her car. As she pulled down the street, she gave the obligatory double beep. This time the blasts were long and abrasive, more like threats that echoed through the house even after she'd turned the corner.

I leaned against the wall, relieved and released. That was it. I wasn't going to sink into the pity party pool and let Ilana drown me. I was going to face reality and deal with the situation head-on. No more wallowing, no more conning myself. I would deal with exactly what was in front of me, and I'd do it one day at a time. I wouldn't be overwhelmed.

I would, however, be very, very careful.

CHAPTER TWENTY-FIVE

By keeping my head in the sand, I'd allowed Ilana to spend every penny of our assets on drugs. By refusing to acknowledge my depression, I'd lost jobs and a good marriage. By refusing to deal with decades-old abuse, I might have missed an opportunity to help a brother who might have been denying his own abuse. I'd made bad choices then compounded them with even worse ones.

If that were true, if I'd helped place myself in this awful position, then I could also change my situation by making different decisions. That was a lot of power to wield, and it felt good. The question was whether I was strong enough to carry through with my new decisions. I had doubts but I also really didn't have any other choice.

It had been a while since I'd gone to bed and shut out the world. Going under had always given me a safe place to hide. Even the idea no longer held any appeal. I could no longer live in my head, in a make-believe fantasy world. For the first time in my life, I was out from under the debilitating depression.

God, did it feel good. And God, did it feel scary. I was a coyote navigating the new day, squinting in the sunlight and far from any den. But the air was crisp and I could smell freedom. I could smell the happy life. Step by step, I followed my nose.

I made an offer to buy the Sun Salon and Day Spa. Michele and I had a very positive meeting. We worked out the price and how ownership would be transitioned. She promised to show me the ropes while she grew her book of clients as a stylist. By the time we opened escrow, the entire staff was excited about the change.

Ilana was selling one of her properties and agreed to pay for the salon from the proceeds. As she looked over the papers, she stopped with the point of her pen on the most important clause.

"Why is ownership in your name only?" she asked.

Because, I thought, *I'm running for the hills the second I have some financial independence.*

"This will help balance our assets," I said. "Remember? All the properties are still in your name. Rather than sign them into both our names, it's cheaper to just put new ones into my name until everything evens out."

I didn't mention how she'd cheated me out of my own home or how she hadn't paid me enough to buy a cup of coffee at the quickie mart. I hoped she'd decide her façade of loving wife and successful real estate agent was too important and she'd go along with the plan.

After an agonizingly long moment, her pen began moving down the page again. She signed off on the bottom. When I took the paper, my heart soared. Then she looked me in the eye.

"Remember, Greg," she said softly, "I won't live without you."

* * *

Ilana wrote a check to Michele for fifteen thousand dollars. By the time I found out, a few days had passed. I was furious. The check would bounce if Ilana's property didn't close in time. I called Michele right away and told her to hold the check. If she would just wait a little while before depositing it, everything would be okay.

It was too late. Michele had her own needs and plans, and had been waiting for the initial payment. She'd immediately begun spending the money. Suddenly her own life was on a crash course.

"Ilana!" I hollered as I trotted through the house. "Ilana! Why did you write Michele a check you knew we couldn't cover?"

"Well," she said as she shoved a set of files into her Prada knockoff, "you told her I would write the check. So I did."

"But you knew there weren't enough funds to cover it!"

"But Greg, she said you'd said I'd write the check."

"Later! After your property closed and the money was available!"

She shouldered her bag and fixed those beady eyes on me. "Don't blame me," she said. "I didn't know what kind of con you were pulling on her. I just did what you said to do."

And there I was, dynamited by my own ACME bomb, my fur covered with soot. She never had that conversation with Michele. She knew a hot check would make negotiations messy, if not impossible. I just hoped there was enough goodwill left with Michele to work this out.

The moment I thought things couldn't get worse, Ilana called the electric company. She claimed to be Michele and asked that the service be transferred to Ilana Harding. Somehow she'd obtained the personal information she needed about Michele to pull that off. Now no matter who owned the salon, all she had to do was cut the power or stop paying the bill. It was a crazy way to try to control someone but that was Ilana—crazy and controlling.

Since Ilana and I were business partners and married to boot, Michele naturally assumed we were working together to cheat her out of her business. Explaining why Ilana had nothing to do with the business when she was paying for everything was, of course, difficult.

Following the advice of her attorney, Michele asked me to leave the salon. I could return only after the situation was resolved.

* * *

To say the atmosphere at home was tense would be an understatement. I did everything in my power to stay out of Ilana's way. I couldn't bear to look at her. Every time I saw her the coyote inside bared its teeth. She was hell-bent on destroying my life and any chance at independence. I wanted to stuff her pretty little head into her Prada knockoff and cinch the straps around her neck. Tightly.

Appearances were critical in this game. I played the loyal husband. Unhappy, yes. I even managed to look a little chastened whenever she ordered me to do some household chore to test my obedience. But she had to think I was under her control so completely I'd given up any hope of breaking free.

Ilana put on her own act. She was up early...or never went to bed. I was never sure which. Even though all-night work sessions meant she was doing drugs again, I didn't give a damn.

I should have. I was the only project she had left to work on.

One day, she was in full swing by the time I roused myself. She was geared up in her best designer knockoffs and talked nonstop on her mobile. I headed to the kitchen and ignored the chatter. She joined me at the table as she hung up.

"That was my attorney," she said. "I told him about what happened with Michele. He advised me to turn myself in to the local police and cooperate. That way Michele won't get into any trouble for writing bad checks. It's the right thing to do."

"So…is your attorney arranging this?"

"He's going to accompany me to the county sheriff's office. I'll turn myself in and we'll appeal to the district attorney's office for leniency."

I was a bit skeptical but the charges she could face over that single crime were real. Maybe this was part of her game…she'd been too savvy to actually let me own the salon but she also knew she had to dance around the courthouse. She'd probably end up with a slap on the wrist and I'd still be dependent on her.

She shouted, "Wish me luck!" and slammed the front door.

I stood in the foyer. Was she really heading for jail or was she busy with the twins cooking up some other disaster? I headed out to the side yard to harvest more rocks. It had been a while since I'd spent the day mindlessly digging and being soothed by the work. I grabbed the rake and stepped outside.

As the tongs bit into the sand, I was struck by the absurdity of the action. I'd always found comfort in tasks that required very little thinking and lots of manual labor. It was my version of finger painting. That day it was just hot, back-breaking work. I soon exhausted my nervous energy and retreated from the heat.

Funny how things change. Those old habits just don't have the same calming effect anymore. I wasn't sure if that was progress or if it left me without an outlet for my anxiety. For now, it didn't matter. I took a long, cool shower. I thought about nothing the entire time, focused only on the flow of water over my skin. Refreshed physically and mentally, I headed to the office where I could do something productive.

As the day progressed, I began to worry about Ilana. If she'd been telling the truth, she could be in trouble or already in jail. Part of me actually felt sorry for her. Not long ago, she'd been the love of my life. The rest of me couldn't have been happier. I felt like a little kid who sees a bully finally getting spanked…gleeful. My gloating brought a twinge of guilt along for the ride but I enjoyed it nonetheless.

Around eight o'clock that evening Ilana sent a text message. She was about to be booked and jailed. She wanted to let me know she was alright and that she wouldn't be able to communicate for a while.

As I sat in the office, unsure whether to believe this new missive, Jeff cut behind the house and waltzed through the door.

"Where's Ilana?" he asked as he dropped into a chair.

"In jail."

"What? No, really. Where is she?"

"I'm serious. She turned herself in for a hot fifteen-thousand dollar check she wrote."

"Ilana's not in jail."

"Yes, she is."

"No, she's not."

"Well, if you know where she is, why are you asking?"

He rubbed his face with one hand. It was the first time I'd ever seen him turn serious…not counting the times he'd threatened me or blown up at someone, of course.

"Greg, Ilana's not in jail. I don't have time to tell you the details right now. I just stopped by to ask for gas money. I promised my friend I'd drive him to work. He has to be there in less than an hour. Do you have some money I can borrow? I promise to come back and explain everything."

"Ah, sure. How's forty bucks?"

"Perfect. I shouldn't be more than half an hour."

"Alright, Jeff, but you'd better get back here and explain this or I'll come looking for you. Understand?"

"Yeah, right, like that's gonna scare me," he said with a grin. "Relax. I promise I'll be back."

It took about an hour but Jeff actually returned. He showed up with a friend, a young woman I'd never met before. We moved into the great room where he introduced Cheryl.

"Tell Greg what happened tonight," Jeff said.

Cheryl looked uncomfortable but began describing her evening. She'd been at home when someone banged on her door. Three men, seedy thugs, were looking for her son.

This young man had been running with some street hoodlums and gotten involved in a stolen car ring. The men at the door were trying to recover a vehicle he'd stolen. When Cheryl couldn't tell them where her son was, they forced her into their car at gunpoint.

"There was a young woman in the back seat," Cheryl said, "working on a laptop."

As she described the woman in great detail, I formed a picture of Ilana.

"The laptop," I said. "What color was it?"

"Red. Like fire engine red. And it had a Ferrari logo on the front panel."

I knew that computer. Cathryn had set it up for Ilana. I still couldn't quite believe it.

"You're saying Ilana was looking for a car thief?" I asked. "How did you end up with Jeff?"

"The men had driven around so much they needed gas. After they filled up, they made me go inside to pay. The second I stepped inside the mini-mart, they drove away. I called Jeff to come pick me up. He's the only person I know who could protect me."

"Why should I believe you?" I shook my head. I wasn't about to be duped by Jeff, too. "Ilana's in jail."

"Greg, look at me!" Jeff yelled. "Have I ever lied to you? I've stolen from you, I've given you lots of grief, but look me in the eyes and tell me if I've ever lied to you."

Gus jumped onto Jeff's lap. He stared at me with that look, the one that was patient. *I'm waiting,* it said. *I'll wait forever until you finally get it.* Even Gizmo circled Jeff's feet, whining and licking his ankles.

The dogs were right. Jeff was a convicted felon, had conveniently neglected to tell me things, had threatened to cut my legs off with a band saw and had made my life miserable but I couldn't think of a single time when he'd lied to me.

"OK," I said. "But this is just too weird. What would Ilana be doing in that car? Maybe she was being held against her will, too. There has to be a logical, rational explanation, right?"

"There is," Jeff said. "She was with…let's just call them her business associates."

"And what business might this be?" I asked wearily.

"Car theft. She's the ring leader. Sorry, Greg. I told you Ilana wasn't in jail. She's been screwing with you since the beginning."

"Why are you telling me this now?"

"Because I'm tired of watching her hurt innocent people."

"You steal cars, too!" I waved my hands wildly. "How does that not hurt innocent people?"

"We only steal nice cars." His grin returned. "People with nice cars have big insurance policies. They get a new car and we get our cash. It's a win-win."

"Did you steal my car?"

"Ilana did."

"I suppose she took it apart and left the frame in San Bernardino, too."

His face clouded. I didn't especially want Jeff angry with me but it was too late; the words had been spoken.

"Look, Greg, I had nothing to do with your car." His fist balled up on the arm of the chair. "Ilana did that with her other buddies. She asked Kevin and I to hit your car but I wouldn't do it."

"Oh, come on. You expect me to believe you'd turn down easy money?"

He laughed. It wasn't a pleasant sort of sound. "Jesus, Greg, you're totally fucked in the head." He rubbed his face again.

"You have no reason to trust me, OK, fine. But Ilana must have really fucked with you if you think I'd steal a car from someone who'd just tried to kill himself."

That took me by surprise. "You knew about that?"

"That, and the pills you took, and the *other* pills you took. Oh, and the cancer."

"You knew about the cancer?"

He nodded. "She told me everything."

"Everything?"

"She told me she screwed you out of the house the day she had you sign the papers. She told me about faking Nick's will and the settlement she got. Hell, she even bought me a pair of silk socks to celebrate!"

"She did?" Ilana had never bought me a pair of silk socks.

"Look, the point is, I kept waiting for you to catch on. You finally have, and so have I. She double-crossed me on a contract."

"What kind of contract?" My heart went cold as I thought about Ilana's knife and gun. It must have shown on my face because both Cheryl and Jeff sat back.

"Christ," Jeff said, "a *car theft* contact. You know me better than to think I'd kill someone for money!"

Yeah, I thought, *the 'for money' part being the critical difference.*

"She cost me," Jeff growled, "cost me big. You don't need to know the details but basically she stole an entire warehouse full of cars from me. I can't deliver my contract now. Hell, if Kevin and I boosted cars from LA to San Francisco for the next two days, I still couldn't fill that contract."

For the first time, I realized Jeff was nervous. Not scared; guys who know how to make napalm aren't ever really scared. But he was fidgety and angry, and hadn't cracked a single joke at my expense since he'd arrived. Something really did have him worried. We both knew who was responsible.

"Are you…going to be all right?" I asked. Not that I could help him but it seemed like he needed a little moral support. After all, I was the expert at knowing when people needed moral support.

He grunted. "Yeah, I'm gonna be fine. I've just got to get this straightened out. My reputation is shot right now. I've got to clear it all up and find a way to make the buyer happy. Damn Ilana! She doesn't care about anyone but herself."

He looked at me. I flinched before I realized he wasn't angry with me.

"You've never deserved the way she's treated you," he said. "I know it's a lot to take in but Jesus Christ, Greg, open your eyes! She didn't buy those computers; she had someone break into a warehouse and steal the lot! She didn't turn herself in; she's been hunting for Cheryl's son with a car full of gang bangers!"

I was unbelievably frightened. I didn't know what was true. Maybe if

I talked with Ilana I could figure out if things really were that bad but she wouldn't answer her phone or the text messages I'd already sent. Besides, what was I supposed to say? *Hello, dear, how's your day? Say, can I have some of that carjacking money for groceries?*

"Hey," Jeff said, "if you're gonna be OK, we're outta here. I don't want Ilana to find us here. It'd be better if she didn't know about our conversation."

I nodded. She and her brothers were clearly in the middle of some type of turf war. I didn't want to end up in the crossfire.

"If I were you," Jeff said as he rose, "I'd get out of town."

"I can't," I said. "I've got things I have to take care of – me, primarily! She can't know I'm on to her."

He shrugged. "It's your life, buddy. Your choice."

With that, he was gone. I crossed through the house to watch through the window. When I saw Kevin sitting in the driver's seat of their car, a chill swept my belly. He never let his brother get more than a few feet away. The only time those two had ever been separated had been during Jeff's stints in jail. If Kevin had stayed in the car, it could only be for one reason: he was a lookout in case Ilana came home.

If she had two streetwise criminals running scared—or feeling threatened, at least—I was in much more danger than I'd thought. But how was it possible that Ilana could be involved with street thugs? Riding around in a car, armed with guns, kidnapping mothers and hunting a car thief? Ridiculous.

And vintage Ilana.

CHAPTER TWENTY-SIX

That familiar feeling of panic started to creep in. I began to pace. Jeff had said I should disappear. Where would I go? My life? Really? But I had nothing. Should I take the dogs? If I ended up homeless, maybe I could sell them.

As I spun around to pace back to the window for the twentieth time, my eyes fell on the bookcase. Dust! Why was there dust on the shelves? I had to clean up! When I plunged under the kitchen sink for a rag, I froze. My mind flashed on Ilana leaving the house. Cheryl's voice and her description of the ringleader rang in my head.

The laptop with the Ferrari logo. When Ilana had left, she'd taken her computer. Who takes a laptop to jail?

I called the sheriff's office. They had no record of an Ilana Harding or Ilana Marks showing up, much less being booked. As I stood there with my hand resting on the phone, Ilana called.

"They released me," she said, "but I need a ride. I'm at the Rite-Aid store on Palm Canyon Drive."

It was ten-thirty.

"How'd you get there?" I asked. "The jail is in Indio. How did you get from Indio all the way back to Palm Springs? That's twenty miles!"

"A county bus takes inmates to the bus station on Indian Canyon Boulevard. Are you coming to get me or not?"

"I'll be right there."

On the drive I tried to think of what to say. I was frightened but I had to keep my cards close to my chest. As I pulled into the parking lot, Ilana stood by the store with her laptop case. She seemed exhausted and angry.

"I still don't understand how you got from the bus station to Rite-Aid," I said. "It's six blocks. Why didn't you have me to pick you up there?"

"What are you saying?" she snapped. "You don't believe me? I don't have to take this shit from you!"

Damn. She'd gone from zero to eighty in a heartbeat.

"Ilana, what's wrong with you?"

"I don't have to take this from you, Greg. Not after the day I've had. I just spent hours in a dirty jail trying do the right thing and all you can do is ask me a bunch of stupid questions. If you don't believe me, there's nothing for us to talk about!"

"OK, suit yourself. I'm just trying to understand what's happening."

Nothing was said the rest of the drive. We lived nearby so we didn't suffer the silence for too long. When we arrived, Ilana immediately crawled into bed and was asleep in seconds. She'd been up all the night before, so that was no surprise.

Before collapsing, she'd stashed her computer bag in the office. I quietly closed the bedroom door and headed outside.

In her bag was a folder stuffed with pink slips for an entire battalion of vehicles. There were owner registrations for vehicles I'd never seen, cars I knew Ilana didn't own. I even found the pink slip to my car. And then I unearthed THE gun.

This wasn't the little gun she'd waved at me before. This was much bigger and had a big clip loaded with big bullets. Little guns were for scaring off rapists and muggers. Big guns were for killing.

I felt as if a ton of rocks had dropped into my stomach. I ran to the bathroom and threw up. As I hovered over the toilet, I knew Jeff and Cheryl had told the truth. My wife was mixed up with thieves and street thugs. What else didn't I know about her?

I had to get out. I had to run fast and far.

But not too far. I stood up and wiped my mouth. Now I was pissed. Scared, well, that was the sensible thing. But I was also getting really angry. This woman, who I'd loved with all my heart had pillaged and plundered my life. She'd taken me for all I was worth and wanted more. She wanted to beat me, to grind me into a pit of humiliation so deep I'd never climb out.

She *liked* playing the roadrunner. She enjoyed flicking that tongue at me while I got caught in trap after trap; she loved to race away with the wind in her hair only to return, to stand tantalizingly close, to tease me with the nearness of a good life before she sped off again.

Her time was up. The Year of the Coyote had begun.

* * *

Although the purchase of the salon had been shot to hell, Donnie was still my friend. He only knew Ilana by sight and had never really talked to her. He hadn't wanted to. When I told him about the bounced check, he said he'd always gotten a weird vibe off Ilana and had stayed away.

Donnie was a farm boy by birth but had done a lot of living. Although he wouldn't be considered a criminal by even the most prim of church ladies, he was street-smart. He had a lot of plain old common sense and lived a quiet, moderate life.

Privately, that was. I'd known him long enough to peek behind the curtain dividing his public life from the stuff he kept hidden. At the salon, he was a short, pudgy guy who wore lots of leather. His hair was dyed an ever-changing rainbow and his effusive, effeminate charm kept his clients panting and tipping heavily.

The minute he got home, everything changed. He threw on jeans and a roomy shirt before disappearing into his studio to pursue his true passion—art. Working as both a painter and a metal sculptor, his internationally acclaimed works were sold under a pseudonym through the more exclusive galleries on El Paseo in nearby Palm Desert.

He rarely granted interviews and never allowed himself to be photographed. His double life was so compartmentalized that no one at the salon even knew where he lived. His apartment, a nearly bare single room, boasted a New York-style kitchen alcove with a hotplate, mini-fridge and a few storage shelves; a tiny bathroom with a shower but no tub; and a view of the communal laundry facility. Perfect for the single guy with two lives.

He had a great radar for people. Just by chatting me up while cutting my hair a few times, he'd figured out I was one of those few people who could actually keep a secret. Not in a spy-novel sort of way but by being a loyal friend. The same trait, in fact, that had caused me so much trouble with Ilana. If anyone could be trusted to provide a hideout, it was Donnie.

I definitely didn't want to drag Cathryn and Jack into this mess again. Besides, Ilana would probably look for me at their place. That would put them in danger, too. Donnie was my only option. After I'd explained as much as I could, he was nearly as stunned and confused as I had been. But with both of us working on this little problem, we quickly got things sorted out.

Since Ilana didn't know where Donnie lived, we kept it that way. We hid my car behind a strip mall a few blocks away and returned to his apartment. I was already on high alert, and my head rotated constantly looking for any sign she'd tracked me down. We turned off all the lights and sat on the floor discussing what to do next.

My mobile phone chirped. A text message had arrived. From Ilana.

Greg, where are you? We need to talk.

Other messages came in about every half an hour. The phone rang but I let it all go into voicemail. Finally, around 3 a.m., she showed me her cards in a longer text message.

Greg. I've been working to rid our lives of all the gutter-rats, starting with my twin brothers. Everything was going smoothly until tonight. There was a mix up but Juan has taken care of it. It's safe to come home now. I'll explain more when I see you. With love, Ilana.

Rid our lives of gutter-rats? I hadn't realized we had gutter-rats! Who was Juan? Plus, what did she mean she was starting with the twins? Was she having them executed? Jeff and Kevin certainly had acted as if she were capable. Had she put a hit out on them? Or would she try to do it herself?

With a certainty as cold as Ilana's heart, I knew she would come after me herself.

* * *

Finally I managed to get a few hours of sleep. It was nearly noon before I woke and got my first cup of coffee. When my phone rang, I almost didn't bother to look at the caller ID. I did, though, and snatched up the phone.

"Greg," Cathryn said, "are you okay? What's been going on? I've been so worried!"

"Why? What happened?"

"Ilana showed up here this morning, very early. She said you'd disappeared. She wanted to know if you were here. We told her you weren't but she wouldn't leave until she'd searched the entire house. And I mean the *entire* house, including the garage and the crawl space. She was here for an hour."

"Cathryn, you can't do that again. Ilana is very dangerous. You can't let her in your house anymore."

"We could tell she was cranked up on something. She was talking a mile a minute and kept yelling about you abandoning her. Where are you? Are you safe?"

Yes!!! My friends were back!!. With those words, Cathryn and Jack had both enveloped me in a huge, warm hug.

Cathryn and I talked for nearly half an hour. She never questioned a single thing, not even the most outlandish moments like Ilana waving the gun at me or kidnapping a woman over a stolen car. It was just that simple. She'd walked away because even if I couldn't untangle myself from Ilana, they'd untangle themselves. They were back in my life because I was getting out of Ilana's.

I hung up knowing I had yet another safe harbor. Cathryn said to call often so they'd know I was safe. They'd also promised to do anything they could to help. Now that the odds were a little more in my favor, I was ready to launch an attack.

It still felt like I was losing everything, though. I was hiding out in a tiny studio apartment barely big enough for the twin bed and bistro table Donnie had set up for himself. I was a wink away from homelessness. My worst fears could come true at any moment if Donnie decided to boot me out.

Yet my choices seemed so simple. There was only one option: run for the hills. Grab my belongings and get out...of the marriage, of the debt, of her life. How could I have stayed with her for so long? I couldn't even imagine a future with her anymore.

And that, I knew, was a very, very good thing.

* * *

My plan all along was to have the Petersons buy and quickly re-sell the house to recapture the equity. I'd built the place for just under half a million. The last appraisal had come in at one point three million. Sure, they'd get paid a fat fee, and there'd be some costs involved, but still, it was a difference worth fighting for.

Ilana had been in contact with the Petersons all along, trying to buy the house back. They told my attorney that Ilana was having trouble getting funding and so was reluctant to make a formal offer.

That, at least, was good news. I received the news, and felt somewhat strange. I felt…lighter. Stronger. If I kept this up, I might actually catch that damn roadrunner.

As I opened the door to my car, I thought I heard Gus barking. It was a gorgeous day, not too hot for a change, a perfect day for tourists or locals to be strolling with their dogs downtown. As I looked around, my tongue shriveled like jerky.

Ilana was skittering toward me. Gus and Gizmo were stashed in her oversized bag and Gus had spotted me. He was going ballistic, barking and snarling. I guess Ilana wasn't the only one who was pissed I'd abandoned them.

I ducked into the car and fumbled with the keys. When I dropped them, I swore. By the time I shoved the key in the ignition, Ilana had appeared next to the car.

"Greg!" she called through the window. "Talk to me. Greg! I love you! We have to talk!"

I cranked up the engine and peeled out of the spot. Ilana ran alongside, smacking the window with her palm and shrieking my name. I turned away from her and headed toward the exit. Her six-inch heels clacked alongside even as I accelerated. God help me, with those little skinny legs churning underneath her, she really was the roadrunner!

I hit the turn without slowing down. As I straightened the wheel, there was a thump. Ilana was splayed across my hood with her face pressed against the windshield. Out of the corner of my eye, I glimpsed the dogs.

The handbag had caught on the side mirror. Gus barked nonstop while Giz shivered violently.

"Greeeeeeeeeeeg!" Ilana wailed as plum lipstick smeared the glass.

I hit the brakes. She grabbed one of the windshield wipers in an effort to stay on. The wiper ripped off and she slid less than gracefully to the pavement. I swerved around her, stopped at the corner to gently deposit the dogs in a confused heap at the curb, then sped off before Ilana, now limping on one broken heel and waving the wiper like a sword, charged down the block.

"Holy shit," I muttered.

I guess Kylie had been right.

* * *

All my belongings were, of course, still in the house. Meanwhile, the Petersons had filed an unlawful detainer. They claimed it was just a formality to protect themselves down the road. They said they had no intention of evicting Ilana or seizing our belongings for auction. The paperwork was a legal formality in case everything fell through.

I confirmed all this with my attorney. Everything was going exactly as planned. When I found out Ilana was out of town for a night, I risked dropping by the house to pack some of my belongings. The sheriff had gotten there ahead of me and posted the eviction notice. The property and all its contents were now safely locked up.

As I drove off, I actually felt a sense of relief. With Ilana out of the picture, I thought the plan my attorney and I had put into motion might actually work. They were contracted to sell the house, get their expenses covered and their nice fee, which would give them over $100,000 profit for a very little work. The real estate market was still booming in Palm Springs. If they could sell for just under a million, I'd come out OK.

That, of course, still begged the looming question: what to do about my murderous spouse. A strategy to deal with Ilana? Humph. That would require thinking about my future. It'd been a while since I'd done that. But I didn't have the luxury of soothing my mind into a calm contemplation of my options. Ilana was unraveling at an alarming rate. Since she wouldn't stop until she found me, my schedule had shrunk to days rather than weeks.

In a way, that was all right, too. I'd wasted so much of my life already. One unexpected aspect of depression was that it had stripped me of logical thinking. Depression turned out to be a very narcissistic disease. It was self-indulgent; I'd spent all my time filled with negative emotion that was all-consuming. I'd felt sorry for myself constantly.

And it had gotten me nowhere except deeper in Ilana's tar pit. I hated that my life had been reduced to coming up with an escape plan and a backup plan. But at least I had options. If I stayed calm and thought it through, I knew I would be fine.

Run, coyote, run.

CHAPTER TWENTY-SEVEN

Hiding out at Donnie's place gave me a lot of idle time. I filled some of the hours watching Oprah. I thought it might create a little comfort, and that hearing other people's stories would give me some insight into my own situation. After all, she talked to abused and battered women all the time. Maybe one of their escape plans would be a perfect fit.

One day Oprah invited her friend and mentor Maya Angelou on… again. I liked her and all but really was getting tired of the same old coffee klatch. Then Oprah started complaining…there wasn't enough fluff to the pillows in hotels these day or some other terrible discomfort she'd suffered. Maya told her to stop feeling sorry for herself and to be thankful for something each day.

Oprah was a tough, dynamic, intelligent, beautiful, successful woman. Her success extended beyond a fabulous career and stunning material wealth. For her to reach a point where it was difficult to find things to be thankful for made me realize that we all have struggles. There was no magic list where accomplishments checked off in the margin added up to happiness. Success, sure. Money, definitely. Happiness? Not.

I decided that every day I would find something to be grateful for. The sunrise, the warm breeze, the fact that I wasn't living with a drugged-out criminal. Anger had allowed me to take back my power. But I didn't want to get stuck inside anger, either. If I could go from depression to anger, I should be able to go from anger to frustration. Compared to anger, frustration was another step in the right direction.

A formal offer was made for the house. The Petersons accepted and opened escrow. Ilana was living in a hotel room by then. We saw each other as needed but always at my attorney's office and always in the middle of the day. Even though the divorce papers had been filed, she still thought we could work it out. She even said how much she was looking forward to moving back into the house together once the deal closed. I'm not at all sure who she thought was buying the house, but it didn't really matter.

I just nodded and smiled. Letting her keep that illusion alive created the least amount of stress for me.

* * *

Donnie and I went to dinner to celebrate the opening of escrow. He suggested a restaurant next to the salon in the same strip mall where we'd parked my car. When we arrived, we cruised around back to check on the vehicle. Michele suddenly appeared and pulled her car around so we were blocked in. When Donnie poked his head out the window, she started yelling.

Those two had been friends for almost twenty years. Donnie had worked for her since the day the salon opened. Apparently all of that meant nothing now that her business was threatened. She accused him of betraying their friendship by allowing me to stay in his apartment. She thought Ilana and I were still conspiring to steal her company.

Minutes later, two guys showed up and threatened to kick our asses. Friends of Michele, I assumed. Donnie and I walked calmly into the restaurant. As we took a booth in the rear, he looked shaken. I was, too. I didn't need two different women sending thugs to beat me senseless. But for Donnie, it meant the end of a friendship plus the loss of a job. He was suffering because he'd decided to help me during this crisis.

I'd been talking with Cathryn several times a day. When she heard about the threats, she was really concerned for my safety. She was also afraid I might get back together with Ilana if Donnie couldn't help me anymore. She offered to let me stay in the extra room in their new house. With two rottweilers on the property, their home defense system was pretty much shored up.

Cathryn and Jack still wanted me to work with them once all the dust settled. Just then my hands were full extricating myself from Ilana's mess but it was nice to know I'd have somewhere to go. But since they'd never been paid in full for the floors, they had their own issues getting the company back on its feet.

I felt that old guilt, like I left a swath of destruction wherever I went. I started to think of Kenny again, of my still-estranged family, my ex, my lost job and destroyed finances, everything. I was sinking back into the muck, and it was a struggle to keep moving forward. I constantly asked myself, *What would Oprah do? What next?*

Whether it was this mantra or simply the need to fix, finally and forever, everything that was broken, I kept going.

* * *

Early one morning I received a text message from Ilana.

Good morning, Greg. Look outside Donnie's door. I LOVE YOU. Ilana.

A grocery sack sat on the stoop. I stared at it for the longest time. It sat their, squat and unmoving. I didn't hear any ticking but that meant nothing.

I touched it with one toe. Nothing. I tapped it a little bit harder. It toppled and I wet my pants just a little. Out spilled a single serving of apple juice, a box of Frosted Mini-Wheats and a half gallon of milk.

And a note.

My dearest Greg,
I know this is your favorite breakfast. You should be in the hotel with me and our puppies where you belong. Since you won't stay with us, at least we can have breakfast together. I'm sitting, alone, in my hotel room eating my breakfast.
Enjoy. I LOVE YOU,
Ilana

How had she found out where Donnie lived? Was the cereal poisoned? Was the apple juice really liquid nitrogen that would explode when I tried to pour it down the sink? God only knew. My safe house was no longer safe. Now Donnie was at risk, too. I left the food on the landing and went inside to pack.

Suddenly there was a banging on the door. I hid in Donnie's shower while he went to send Ilana away. It was Jeff.

He pushed inside. "Is Greg here?"

"Ah, no. He's gone out for a while."

"It's OK." I came out of the bathroom. "I can't hide forever. How'd you know where to find me?"

"I followed you." He shrugged as if it were the easiest thing in the world. "Have you seen Ilana?"

"I'm doing my best to avoid her these days. Why? I would've thought you knew where to find her."

"I do but she's not at her hotel. The bitch broke into our storage unit and stole our gun and knife collection."

I thought about that for a moment. I didn't like where my thoughts took me. Not one bit.

"Do you think she would do anything stupid?" I asked. "Like shoot someone? Like me, for instance?"

"Hell, yeah! But not with those things. She's gonna sell 'em for drug money. Kevin and I got that collection from our Dad. I was hoping to find her before she got rid of too many."

"Sorry to hear about that. I don't know where she is."

"No prob. You wouldn't have twenty bucks I could borrow, would you?"

"You never miss an opportunity to ask for money, do you?"

"You're usually good for it. So do you have twenty bucks?"

"Yeah, sure." I handed him a bill.

"See ya! Give me a call if you hear from Ilana." He glanced at the groceries on the way out. "You gonna eat this?"

"You don't want that. Ilana left it. It might be poisoned."

He laughed. "That's not her style, Greg."

He tucked the bag under one arm and was gone. Donnie and I just looked at each other.

"I'm sorry," I sighed. "I never meant for you to get hurt in all of this. I think we could be in some real danger now. There's no telling what Ilana might do. I'm just so sorry."

"Hey, no problem. I told you when you first came here we're in this together. I'm not surprised. Jeff and Kevin are criminals; Ilana is desperate. She can't stay in that hotel forever. I wonder how she's paying for it. How did you think this was gonna turn out?"

"I don't know. I just never thought it would come to this. Maybe I should find another place to stay. I have to start thinking about where I'm gonna live and how I'm gonna make some money."

"I agree. But until you figure it out, you're welcome here. I wouldn't worry too much. Ilana may be desperate but I don't think she'll do you harm. Besides, just because she knows where I live doesn't mean she needs to know you're staying here."

"What do you mean? Of course she knows I'm here. She sent a package to the door this morning and Jeff just confirmed I'm here."

"I know but you're moving out today! If anyone asks, I'll tell them you went back to Texas to lick your wounds and spend some time with your parents. If someone comes, you can hide in the shower."

It was a good plan…up to the last point. A shower curtain wasn't especially bulletproof and I'd be alone most of the time. I decided to take Cathryn up on her offer. The rottweilers would offer a lot more protection from anyone who came stalking around the house. Besides, their new place was nearly an hour's drive from where Ilana was staying. The tougher it was for her to find me, the better off I'd be.

At least, that's what I hoped.

* * *

The plan worked incredibly well. I stopped answering my phone and never answered text messages. I stopped answering email as well. Ilana was beside herself. I rarely left the house and left the TV and radio off when Jack and Cathryn weren't home. The longer I stayed invisible, the clearer I got about how to move forward.

I did have one shock, though. When Cathryn invited me upstairs one day to see how she'd decorated the top floor, I couldn't help but notice she and Jack were sleeping in different rooms. Everything looked neat and well organized, so I assumed they'd been sleeping apart for some time.

"Uh, Cathryn," I began. "I don't mean to pry but are you all right?"

"Right and tight," she said. "Why?"

"Well, it looks like Jack's stuff is all in another room."

"And?"

"Um…well, are you two all right? As partners, I mean?"

"Why wouldn't we be?" She leaned against the doorframe. "Greg, are you feeling OK?"

"I'm fine. But...."

I stopped. Maybe they were one of those couples who slept apart because one of them snored like a speedboat. Maybe they had an open relationship and brought "dates" home for overnight stays. Maybe, most shocking of all, they were one of those strange celibate couples. No matter what the answer was, I was clearly treading in private territory.

"I think the stress is getting to you again," she said. "Have you been seeing Kylie?"

"Yes. I'm fine. It's just...."

"What?"

I jerked my head toward the other bedroom. "Well, you and Jack."

"Yes?"

"Aren't you together anymore?"

"What are you...."

She stopped as some light flashed on in her head. She started laughing so hard she had to hold onto the doorknob to keep from sinking to the floor.

"You think Jack and I are a couple? A romantic couple?" she managed between howls. "All this time, you've thought...We...."

She couldn't talk after that. Just then Jack came upstairs.

"What's so funny?" he asked.

I shrugged and started to blush. I wasn't sure why but at least he didn't know what the joke was, either. Yet, anyway.

"Greg," Cathryn gasped. "All this time, he thought we were a couple!"

"Oh, Jesus." His tone was half mirthful and half what-were-you-thinking. "Greg, I'm gay."

"You're gay?" I squeaked.

"He's gay!" Cathryn roared as she buckled under her own glee.

"You didn't notice my boyfriend at your wedding?" he asked. "You remember Chuck. He helped me walk you down the aisle?"

"Oh, shit," I said.

"You never noticed that Cathryn and I never held hands? Never kissed?"

"I thought you guys didn't do that in public."

"You never noticed that Chuck and I hug? Walk arm in arm? *In public?*"

"Well, yeah." I was really blushing now. God, what an idiot I'd been. "I just thought you were…comforting him. That he was going through a hard time."

"Damn, Greg," he chuckled, rolling his eyes. "You really do need to escape."

"I…I'm really sorry." I was actually close to tears. I had something new to feel guilty about, and every ounce of it deserved.

"I've been so selfish and self-centered," I said. "I just couldn't see beyond my depression."

"Greg." Cathryn sobered and gripped my shoulder. "You were focused on yourself, that's for sure. You needed to be. But there's a big difference between being self-focused and being self-centered."

It took a moment but finally I nodded. When they were both sure I was all right, Jack grabbed my hand and slapped it dramatically to his chest.

"Greg," he proclaimed, "any time you need some *comfort,* not the kind of comfort I give my *boyfriend* mind you, you just let me know. I'll be there for you - you'll have more comfort than you know what to do with!"

I laughed. Cathryn laughed. She managed to mumble about my not knowing Jack was gay; the more she mumbled, the harder we laughed. Finally Jack left us in the hallway still giggling like schoolgirls.

It was exactly what I needed. I was feeling so much better about my life and feeling less and less negative emotion each day. The future, my future, was a concept I was actually beginning to anticipate. Only a few days had passed since I'd moved out of Donnie's but it seemed like months.

CHAPTER TWENTY-EIGHT

"How could I have been so gullible?" I muttered.

Cathryn and I were sitting on the back porch overlooking the lake. I'd actually slept well the night before. My sides ached from all the laughing we'd done the previous day and my belly was stuffed from the huge breakfast Cathryn had insisted I eat. Under her watchful eye, I was already regaining some weight. But I couldn't help picking at the huge scab that was my marriage.

"You didn't know," Cathryn said. "It's not that you saw everything she was doing and ignored it. Most of her shenanigans were hidden totally out of sight. She did the same thing to Jack and me. In fact, she told Jack different things than she told me. We never thought to compare stories."

"But I should have known. I was married to her. I lived with her day in and day out. It was like Kenny only different. He was my brother but we hadn't lived in the same area for years. I understand that I couldn't have known about my brother, and I accept that no one could have helped him. But my wife? Her criminal activities? I should have known."

"You don't look behind the door unless you've hidden there yourself." Cathryn looked up from her cup. "Jack said that to me when you first came here. I think that pretty much explains what happened with you and Ilana. Why would you expect her to lie about everything? You started a relationship after you were friends. You really thought you knew her. You expected her to be honest. Why would you look behind the door?"

"Even when I did look," I muttered, "I didn't figure it out. You know what I thought when I found out that nearly everything in her closet was a knockoff? I thought, wow, she really does love me. She's buying cheap stuff to save money for our business. Turns out everything about her was a cheap knockoff."

"Except you." Cathryn fixed her gaze on me. "You're the only real thing Ilana ever had and she blew it."

For a second, just for a second, I thought maybe Cathryn was coming on to me. Then she broke eye contact and stood.

"More coffee?" she asked.

I let her refill my mug. By the time she'd sat back down, I'd pushed aside any idea about kindling something more than a friendship. I'd also squelched the tiny flutter in my heart. I had no idea if that was what she wanted. I had no idea if that was what I wanted. Until I was free and my life was stable again, I couldn't risk losing her friendship.

* * *

The next day started like any other. I had errands to run, so I got ready to walk to my car. Although we didn't think Ilana would come back to the house, we kept my car hidden in the parking lot of an office complex on the south side of the lake. As far as everyone else knew, I was in Texas.

I looked around to make sure no one I knew was in sight. Then I slipped around the side of the house and took a path through the woods. Even though the trail was heavily screened from the road that circled the lake, I often checked behind me and watched the path ahead as best I could. I couldn't be too cautious.

The car was waiting, unmolested as usual. I didn't let my guard down much; I would keep to the side roads and smaller strip malls to prevent any accidental sightings. As I turned out of the resort's parking lot, a car that looked like Ilana's popped up in my rearview mirror. At a stoplight in the downtown district, I took a good look at the driver. Sure enough, it was Ilana.

I made a few unscheduled turns and circled the block to make sure she really was following me. She stuck close, using her turn signals when I did and turning sharply when I gave no warning of a turn. When we arrived back at the same stoplight, all my fear dissolved.

Now that she'd finally appeared, I felt nothing but anger. It was a good feeling. It burned away any thought except ending this now and forever.

I pulled over. Ilana pulled up right behind me. Before she could get out, I was at her window.

"What are you doing?" I demanded. "Why are you following me?"

Gus and Gizmo sat in the passenger's seat. Gus let out a mournful howl. He'd never done that before. Since he was the only man in Ilana's life now, he was probably as miserable as I'd been. *Sorry, buddy,* I thought, *this coyote's going solo.*

"I'm not following you," Ilana said. "I'm in town to visit some friends. Just because you don't have any friends doesn't mean I have to give up mine."

My hands itched. I wanted to strangle her so badly. She was the one who'd cut me off from everyone else, and she knew it. She was just trying to wound me. This time, I wasn't going to retreat.

"Where do these people live?" I asked.

"On San Jacinto. Not that it's any of your business."

"San Jacinto is in the opposite direction. Stop following me. Just leave me alone."

"You lied to me!" she yelled. "Donnie told me you were in Texas visiting your parents. Why did you lie? Why haven't you answered my calls?"

"I didn't lie to you. I never told you I was in Texas. We haven't spoken in weeks."

"Exactly! Why haven't you returned any of my calls or my text messages or my emails?"

"Because there's nothing for us to talk about. The only time I want to see you again is when we finalize the divorce at my attorney's office. So stop following me!"

I got back in my car and carried on. Ilana followed. I didn't know what she wanted or what she was capable of doing but I couldn't stop thinking about the arsenal of guns and knives she'd stolen from Jeff. As she stuck to my bumper, I became acutely afraid for the safety of my friends.

She'd fucked up my life and the lives of too many people around me. I wasn't going to let her hurt my friends again. I drove directly to the police station. Ilana pulled up beside me and rolled down her window.

"I know what you're up to, Greg. I know you're trying to steal the house and my properties and the entire business. It won't work!"

She pointed a gun through the window. The big gun. The one I'd noticed in the bottom of her laptop case. The one with the big bullets.

I took a deep breath and stayed calm. Maybe if I pretended to not see the gun, someone would walk by and she'd put it down.

"Ilana, how can I steal anything from you? The divorce is set up so we each keep what we brought into the marriage. That means you keep all the properties and condos. As for the house, that's already gone. It went into foreclosure because of you. If you want to get technical about it, you actually stole the house from me."

"That's not true!" she screamed. "It's not my fault we lost the house. I'll shoot you before I'll let you steal the house from me!"

"Whatever, Ilana."

I rolled my eyes and hoped she didn't notice how heavily I was sweating. She had to put that gun down. I couldn't make a move without getting shot. Hell, even the conversation could tip her over the edge. I had to bring her back to reality.

"I really don't care what you think," I said. "Do you see where we are?"

"Of course. In a parking lot."

"Do you see the sign on that building behind me?"

She looked. Her eyes widened.

"Oh, shit!"

She put the car in drive and left me sitting in the parking lot. I let out a huge sigh then calmly walked inside. I told the duty officer I was being followed and was in fear for my life. When I mentioned the gun, I was asked to have a seat in the waiting room.

I wasn't at all sure how I was going to explain any of Ilana's chaos to a police officer. I did know that I felt safer surrounded by police than on the streets while she was in town.

"Hello." A female officer with a clipboard came over. "I'm Officer Dallas. I understand you think someone wants to harm you?"

"Yes, that's right."

She escorted me to a small room with a table and three mismatched chairs. I ran through an abbreviated version of my life: my relationship with Ilana, her drug use, the desperation she felt because we'd been evicted, the pending divorce, her theft of the guns and knives, her aiming a gun at me in the parking lot, and, oh, yes, that one of her brothers was a convicted felon out on parole.

Her eyebrows rose when I mentioned the gun. When I mentioned Jeff's name, she nodded. "Please wait here," she said. "I'll be right back."

She left me alone in the small room. When she returned, she was accompanied by three detectives. Each detective was from a different department and investigated different types of crime. Each held a large file they plopped on the table.

This was beginning to feel more like an interrogation than an interview.

The first man wore a brown suit and a necktie pulled loose at the collar. "I'm Detective Williams," he said. "I've been working a car theft case and I'd like to ask you a few questions."

"I don't really know anything. I found a bunch of pink slips in my wife's laptop case but other than that, I don't know what she's up to."

"Do you or do you not know a man by the name of Jeff Harding?"

"Yes, I know Jeff."

He questioned me about what I did or didn't know about several stolen cars. "What about this report your wife filed accusing Mr. Harding of stealing her car?"

"Ilana's car has never been stolen," I said. "She did hide it in our garage for a time. Jeff was pretty upset when he found out. He told me then Ilana had claimed he stole it but I didn't believe him."

The next detective, a woman whose beauty hung on despite the wear her job had placed on her, opened a thick, well-thumbed file. The words *9 of 12* had been written on the cover. She asked me about checks written to Ilana's real estate company from large companies like Coastal Closets. One of the checks was for $16,000.

I told the detective I'd never seen the check before but I seriously doubted it was legitimate. Ilana's company didn't conduct the type of business that would require Coastal Closets to pay sixteen thousand dollars for anything. She dealt many more checks from other companies across the table. All had been made out to Ilana's company. All of them had been labeled as forgeries.

Each of the detectives went through their files asking me question after question before briefly outlining the various crimes Ilana had shoved her beak into. Then they turned the questions on me.

"We know who you are," Detective Williams said. His tone was less than pleasant. "We know you're Ilana's husband. We can't prove you're involved with your wife's criminal enterprise--"

"I'm not!"

"At the very least," the female detective said, "you knew about her behavior and ignored it until things got out of hand. Now you're trying to turn her in as revenge for having lost the house."

They actually knew about the foreclosure. They had all the documents! Ilana was chasing me, she had pulled a gun on me, and the police were interrogating me!

I talked and talked. I objected to their accusations and talked some more. Although I could have left at any time, I needed them to believe me. Even if they weren't going to be on my side, at the very least I needed them to lay off me. If it was going to be just me and Ilana out there, I couldn't have the police gunning for me at the same time.

Finally the female detective said something I could use. She explained that they and other police departments had been watching Ilana for over twelve years but none had been able to gather enough evidence to arrest her.

"You want evidence?" I asked. "I'll give you evidence. There's a paper trail. I was trying to sort it out when the house went into foreclosure. The files are a mess but Ilana apparently kept every document she ever forged, finagled or falsified."

They looked at me sideways. I realized I'd said *forged, finagled* and *falsified* in the same breath. I blushed but stayed strong.

"Why would she keep evidence that would incriminate her?" Detective Williams asked.

"How the hell should I know? Probably so she can relive her past conquests."

"She's pretty bright to have gone this long without being arrested even once. Maybe you're just trying to stall our investigation into *your* activities." Detective Williams tapped the folder. "Why should we believe you?"

"You don't have to believe me." I shrugged. "Look for yourselves. Call the Petersons and find out what they did with all our property. They're such cheapskates I bet they put every bit of it into storage to auction off later. Auction houses don't clean up the stuff, they just sell it as is. If you're fast, you might hit the mother lode."

All along, I'd thought I was dealing with a drug addict who'd turned to small-time crimes out of desperation. The police showed me Ilana had been a criminal since long before we'd ever met. I'd always hoped she'd finally see the light and get cleaned up. Now I'd seen the light, bright and piercing, like a ray aimed by Dali's angel. Even if Ilana kicked the drugs, she'd still be a criminal.

I didn't care what happened to the house, I didn't care about the stuff inside the house. At that moment, I didn't even care if the police would ever be able to charge Ilana with the crimes they knew she'd committed. I'd wasted too much of my life already. When the "interview" was finished, I walked out not caring if they called the Petersons. All I cared about was never seeing Ilana again.

CHAPTER TWENTY-NINE

I got into my car and called Cathryn. She and Jack had to know Ilana was around and how dangerous she was. For all I knew, the police would show up at their house to interrogate them next. I didn't want there to be any surprises. Cathryn ordered me home right away but I refused.

After a short debate, I agreed to stock up on whatever I'd need for a while and stick close to the house for the next few weeks. She knew someone at the police department and would demand they get their asses in gear about Ilana. There was a chance she could get a patrol to drive by the house now and again but none of us was going to count on that just yet.

I pulled out of the lot and drove around town for a while, watching the side and rearview mirrors for any sign of my obsessive soon-to-be-ex wife. She seemed to have disappeared, at least for the moment. I did my errands, loading up on groceries and whatever else I might need. As the hours passed, I finally relaxed. Ilana had taken off for good.

For the next few days I hunkered down at the house. Although I didn't exactly stay away from the windows, I did keep an eye on the woods whenever I sat out back. But the shoreline had been developed for private homes on either side so no one could get close without being in plain sight.

The police, meanwhile, did assign a patrol to the house. I never knew when the squad car would drive by or if unmarked cars were also passing through but Cathryn assured me her friend had taken care of that, at least. And after the files were recovered from storage, Detective Williams called occasionally to update me on the investigation. They now had enough to arrest Ilana.

But they couldn't find her. She'd checked out of the hotel the same day she'd pulled the gun on me. Her brothers insisted they didn't know where she was; judging by how much trouble Jeff was in with his "boss" over the double-crossed carjacking heist, I had no doubt he would have turned his sister over in a second.

Although she was still a threat, I reveled in the satisfaction of knowing that her life was crumbling now...especially because I'd been able to think clearly enough to guide the police to her cache of incriminating trophies. It was her turn to cower and my turn to roam free.

* * *

Eventually life returned to normal. Even though the police investigated all Ilana's known associates throughout California, they turned up nothing. The gang she'd gotten involved with recently had either helped her flee to another state or had taken care of her themselves. After all, an associate on a personal vendetta could expose the entire organization.

Although still very cautious, I started rebuilding my life. I began working with Cathryn and Jack in their business. It was ironic that from the beginning, Ilana had undermined our friendship in the hopes of cutting off my escape route. The end result was that not only was I working with them, I was also living with them. Not an outcome she would have predicted.

Because the company was struggling, Cathryn and Jack were too busy working to be making all the decisions. I took on the role of Chief Financial Officer. As the business, and my mental state, improved, they sought my advice more and more. Soon they were free to focus on nothing except landing new gigs.

A portion of my job involved working in the field. I had paid close attention to the entire process at my own house, so it was easy for me to step in on other projects. My body needed the physical activity. It felt good to work hard and come home physically exhausted at the end of a long day. I wasn't turning into a muscleman overnight but eventually I'd build my strength back.

I continued to see Kylie but found it more and more difficult to fill the allotted time. Eventually our sessions were scheduled for every other week. I felt better than I had in months. I'd established a regular routine of working, eating, sleeping and recreation. At last, I'd achieved a normal, boring life.

I found a small home directly across the lake from Cathryn and Jack. Sitting in their backyard, I could see across the lake to the back door of my new home. The place was much smaller than the Palm Springs house but big enough for one. The divorce wrapped up the same week I opened escrow. Finally, freedom was going to be mine.

* * *

Late one morning I watched the sunlight shimmer off the lake. Although things were going well, my body was only slowly recovering. I'd lost so much weight I'd been horrified to realize how much I'd looked like a war refugee. I had been a refugee, from a war unrecognized by any nation.

At any rate, Cathryn was pushing me to work a little less and focus on my health a little more. The moment she'd heard me sniffling the night before, she'd all but forced me to take a day off. We negotiated half a day, so I slept late and lounged around the patio drinking coffee and reading the newspaper. I'd even turned off the cell phone and left it on the bureau.

Finally I decided to take a walk. A breeze was coming off the lake and leaves flashed silver in the bright day. A trot through the woods would be very relaxing. When I reported back to Cathryn at the job site that afternoon, she'd be pleased. After finishing my coffee, I locked the house. The rottweilers stared through the patio door but knew I wouldn't take them along. I was still too weak to control one of those animals, let alone two.

I set off none too briskly. I really had needed time to do nothing and walking fast would have ramped me back up into business gear. Instead I dawdled down to the small beach area the neighborhood had developed for the homeowners. From there I picked up the narrow asphalt path that snaked around the lake.

The trees weren't terribly thick in some areas. The developers had left enough to screen the properties from the streets and reduce noise from the nearby highway. As the breeze moved the branches around, I glimpsed the road that circled the lake. A car patrolled slowly near the curb then rammed up onto the greenway.

It was Ilana. I only needed to see a flash of that pale face, that crown of feathery hair to know I was in terrible danger. I ducked behind a tree, wondering if she'd seen me.

"Greg!" The car door slammed and her voice rose into a shriek. "I see you! Come out and *kiss me hello!*"

Ah, shit, ah, shit, ah shit! I had to get out of there, and fast. I took off down the path back toward the house. Bullets chewed into the trees and splinters hit my face.

"Shit!"

I dove into the bushes. Branches tore at my clothes and my knee thumped onto a rock. I hardly felt the pain.

How many bullets did one of those clips carry? She'd gotten off, what, three shots? But how many were left? Five? Eight? I had no clue. As I peered through the undergrowth, I heard Ilana moving through the shrubs.

"Gree-eeg," she called. "My darling. My love. My *husband,*" she snarled.

She found the path and moved along it. Not running, not even jogging, but her long legs and angry stride sent her speeding my way. I was on the lake side of the path and poorly hidden. She'd round the bend and see me in a second. If I made a rush for the street, though, she'd see me move. I'd be too close to dodge the next bullet.

I pushed deeper into the undergrowth. The lake really wasn't very large and, since it was manmade, was only a few feet deep. The beach area was meant for kids and suntanning rather than actual water sports, so I couldn't just slip underwater and swim away. But the woods were crosscut by shallow irrigation channels that funneled runoff into the lake. If I stayed low, I might be able to sneak away.

"Greg!"

God, it sounded like she was standing right behind me. I crawled forward, slipping under the bushes and into a ditch. I lay flat and eased my head over the edge to check on her progress.

She was a leap away. She'd worn her Ferrigamo boots and a tight pair of Gloria Vanderbilt jeans for this expedition. I saw the bottom of a Prada handbag, a real one but tattered with age, slung over her shoulder. Then she moved on, closer to the house. She balanced on her toes so the sound of her heels against the asphalt wouldn't give her away. She hopped along, more like an angry roadrunner with every step.

As the breeze rustled the trees, I crawled along the ditch. As I'd hoped, the wind covered the sound of my movements. Ilana kept moving toward the house. Then I heard her voice, speaking low this time, and I turned to look.

"Find him," she said to Gus. "Find Daddy."

She placed the dog on the ground. He immediately charged back along the path. I scrambled through the ditch and burst onto the street with Gus yapping and nipping at my ankles.

Another few shots rang out. I ducked behind a car as holes appeared in its fender. Gus stopped yapping. As I hunkered behind the tire, the dog jumped into my lap and licked my face.

"You only love me when Mommy's on a rampage," I whispered.

He whined but it was a piss-poor apology.

"Greg."

Ilana had reached the edge of the clearing. She knew where I was. I had no weapon and no hope. Not a soul haunted the suburbs that morning; everyone was at work or in Starbucks having their third coffee break of the day. Ilana had to have at least two bullets left. I figured my time on this planet was down to about that many minutes.

"Greg!"

Her boots came closer. She didn't bother to disguise the sound; she knew she held all the cards. Tucking Gus under one arm, I crawled over to the other tire. A shot ricocheted under the car.

"*I love you!*" she screamed. "Greg!"

As she rounded the back of the car, I crawled around the front. A bullet thunked through the hood and into the engine block. Then there was a clatter as the empty clip hit the street.

I ran. I've never run so fast in my life. I shot out from behind the car and back into the woods. My feet knew the pathway and I kept going until another shot whizzed past my ear.

I ate dirt. Rolling into the shrubs, I lay still and listened. There was some rustling near the street then nothing.

I lay there for a long moment. *What would Oprah do, what would Oprah do?* I thought furiously. *Goddamn it, what would Oprah do?*

Then it hit me…Oprah wouldn't know what the hell to do. She had a bazillion dollars. She had dozens of bodyguards who'd tackle stalkers before they got within a mile of her illustriousness. She had her own private island, for God's sake. Despite all the things she might have been through, she'd never faced down a psychopath with a gun.

No couch-side chit-chat or earnest looks would stop a bullet. I had to be stronger than that. I *was* stronger than that. Any thought of Oprah was jettisoned as I focused on what I could hear.

Where the hell was Ilana? I had to know. If I moved an inch, she'd get me. I could feel her watching, waiting for me to raise my head into her line of sight. She'd exterminate me like a rancher taking out a pest.

Lying there wasn't going to solve anything. If someone did come down that pathway, Ilana would shoot them just to make sure she had every chance to kill me. I had to go on the offense. I had to figure out where she was.

I petted Gus until he stopped shaking. Rolling over very quietly, I set him on the ground.

"Find Mommy," I whispered.

His eyes bulged. Ever so softly, he whined.

"Find Mommy!" I tried to make my whisper sound cheerful.

He lifted a paw as if he'd already become a casualty in this war.

"No deal," I hissed. "Find Mommy! Now!"

He started shaking again but set off. Every few steps he stopped to look back at me. After I glared at him a few times, he resigned himself to the reverse tracking job.

He moved back down the pathway. I crept along on all fours right behind him. He stuck to one edge, as if ready to duck into the bushes at the slightest movement. So was I. We inched forward until he turned into the trees.

He threaded through the woods and back onto the street. I watched from the shrubs as he trotted down the strip of grass near the curb. Then he stopped behind a transformer box and looked back at me.

I slipped out of the trees and crouched next to the power transformer. My plan was to charge around the other side and jump on her. If I caught her off balance, I might be able to trap her long enough to get the gun. The rest of the plan involved me sprinting back to the house to call the police.

I wiped my hands on my pants. After a few deep breaths, I clenched my fists and leaned forward like a runner on the starting blocks. Gus stared. I took a final look around to see if a police car just happened to be driving by. No such luck. Gritting my teeth so hard they hurt, I charged around the transformer.

And tripped over Ilana. And went sprawling. She also fell but got to her knees faster. She put the gun to my head—whacked me with the barrel was more like it—and we wrestled in the slippery grass.

"Greeeeeeeeg!" she wailed.

"Ilanaaaaaaaa!" I yelled.

Both my hands were wrapped around the gun. I was surprisingly weak and was already panting like a mad dog. Ilana was surprisingly strong and made little peeping sounds as she tried to point the barrel at my chest. Her legs kicked against me, the heels of her boots raked my legs like talons, and I couldn't gain any leverage. Instead we rolled into the street. With every rotation of our bodies, the barrel moved a little closer to my chest.

A shot went off. Pain seared my thigh. Had she been aiming for my crotch? Shit!!

New energy surged through me. I stood, listing dangerously on the good leg, and dragged her up with me.

"I love you, goddamn it!" she hissed.

A breathy laugh escaped me. Gus, apparently made bold by my new strength, and stood on the curb barking. Gizmo had tumbled out of the Prada at some point and cowered behind Ilana, pissing and shivering. Blood streamed down my leg as I rapidly lost ground in the battle for the gun.

Gus launched himself off the curb and landed in our arms. Growling wildly, he cut into our hands like a blender. I'm not sure if he was after me or Ilana or both of us but I didn't let go.

Then he clamped onto Ilana's little finger. She shrieked and shook her hand as much as she could without releasing the gun but Gus was locked on. His growl was a continuous rumble and his jaws worked at her flesh until I saw bone.

"Let go!" she yelled. "Gus, let go!"

She wrenched at the gun so hard she stumbled backward. Her boot landed on Gizmo who cried like a rabbit squeezed in a deadfall. As Ilana looked down and gasped, I put everything I had into a hard twist to the left. Our hands broke apart, we both tumbled onto our asses, and I ended up with the gun.

I pointed it at her. She held Gizmo in front of her like a tiny shield. Somehow the dog hadn't pissed itself entirely before and peed a little now.

"Greg, you wouldn't," Ilana said.

"I would."

Just then a patrol car screamed down the street and skidded to a stop. I held the gun on Ilana until the officer jumped out and pulled his own weapon. As I made a show of putting the gun on the street, two more squad cars squealed around the opposite side of the block.

"Ilana Harding," an officer said as he brandished handcuffs, "you're under arrest."

Another officer put pressure on my wound while the third called for an ambulance. As the patrol car drove away, Ilana stared out the back, still wailing my name. I watched her leave. I took a deep breath and let it all out. The tiniest smile touched my lips as they turned the corner.

"Meep-meep," I said, and gave a little wave.

EPILOG

By the time the hospital assigned me a room, Cathryn and Jack had arrived. The nurse had contacted them at my request and they'd wasted no time driving over from the jobsite. Cathryn bustled in and stood by my bed.

"They said Ilana tried to kill you." She took my hand. "Are you all right?"

"The coyote always pulls through," I said.

She shook her head. "They've got you on some powerful painkillers."

I smiled and drifted into a peaceful, drug-buzzed slumber.

* * *

"Greg." Cathryn's voice pulled me out of my nap. "You ready to go?"

"Yeah, sure."

Jack was waiting with his car at the entrance to the hospital. After Cathryn got me settled in the front seat, I noticed a large cup filled with soda and ice cream tucked into the console.

"What's that?" I asked.

"That," Cathryn said, "is a root-beer float to welcome you home."

"You didn't have to do that."

"The correct response is thank you."

"OK, thank you, but you still didn't have to do that."

"Yes, I did." Cathryn leaned forward so I could see her face. "Jack and I have been talking. After this event with Ilana, we knew we were gonna take care of you again until you're well enough to be alone. It got us to thinking about the lost weekend."

"We never should have pushed you to take care of Ilana," Jack said. "You'd just been released from Indio. You needed help a lot more than she did. But she was the one we focused on."

"And look where it got her. And you." Cathryn reached between the seats to take my hand. "What kind of a friend have I been? I'm hoping I can be there for you now. So the float is a peace offering."

"I appreciate the gesture," I said, "but no regrets, OK? Let's just take it one day at a time and not worry about the past. Thank you for coming to get me."

"Sure, no problem. Do you want to talk about what happened?"

"Not really. If you don't mind, I'd just like to get home and sleep for a while."

Cathryn settled me in the guest room again. "This is your room for as long as you need it," she said.

"Thanks," was all I could manage. I was asleep before my head hit the pillow.

* * *

I woke the next morning as sunlight streamed through the window and panicked. Where was I? How had I gotten here? I had a vague recollection of something huge happening the day before but couldn't get a clear picture of the details. I fumbled with the blankets and saw my bandaged leg. Just then a gentle tap came on the door.

"Room service!" Cathryn called.

Then it all came flooding back. Cathryn opened the door and brought in a tray with a glass of apple juice, a bowl of frosted Mini-Wheats, and a steaming cup of coffee.

"I brought your breakfast, if you're up for it."

"Ilana attacked me!" I said. "I thought she was gonna kill me!"

"I know." She put her hand on my shoulder. "You don't have to deal with that. You don't have to deal with anything until you're ready. So eat, get rested, and tell us what you need. OK?"

She was right. I was stressed to the limit, overwhelmed...but not depressed.

I finished my breakfast and felt better, except that I could hardly keep my eyes open. I closed them and was lost for another twenty-four hours. I moved only to use the restroom and to swallow the meals Cathryn doled out, just like my keepers in Indio.

I woke the next morning and realized I was in dire need of a shower. Using the crutch the hospital had given me, I hobbled out to the kitchen to enjoy a cup of coffee. Cathryn came out of her office, clad in her pajamas, holding a steaming mug of coffee. She sat on one of the bar stools and asked, "How are you doing? I mean *really*. Really *doing*?"

I smiled. "You do realize you asked me that very same question almost a year ago? Man, you pissed me off. I just wanted to tell you to go away, get lost, and leave me alone."

"I wasn't there for you before, and I'm sorry."

"Hey, I already drank the root beer float. Apology accepted! Beside, you make good coffee and you always have my favorite cereal."

"All right. But no juice until you eat every flake. And this time you're not getting away with a partial flake or partial kernel excuse!"

Cathryn hung back in the doorway. Finally, she spoke, "Greg, I just have to ask something. Forgive me if I'm sticking my nose in where it doesn't belong."

"Okay," I said, nervously. What could possibly be bothering her now?

"Are you sure it's the smart thing to do to get that house across the lake? I mean, you know you can stay here as long as you like. I just don't see how you think you can afford it."

"Oh, is that all? That's your only concern?" I chuckled

She looked at me quizzically, not knowing why I was laughing. "Well, yeah. I know how much the company makes, and I know what you're making, remember? It isn't all that much right now, although things are getting better."

"Guess it's time I let the cat out of the bag then. Here's the surprise for you. The Petersons were working for me, through my attorney. They bought and resold the house, and got paid a fat fee for doing it. But I was their partner in the venture. The balance, less the attorney's fee, is mine. There's enough left to pay you and Jack what's owing on the floors, make the down payment on my new house, and give me a comfortable nest egg to start over with."

Cathryn sat, mouth open and stunned for a few moments. Finally, she shook her head as if not comprehending, and muttered, "But…but..how..when..I just don't understand?

"It's easy. I kept telling you, in my film the coyote always wins!"

I was going to be hounded by demanding, bossy women forever. It wasn't the worst thing in the world…especially not with Cathryn.

* * *

Finally I'd achieved the peaceful, boring life I'd always wanted. The surprising thing was that I wasn't bored. Without constant crisis, I enjoyed life in a way I'd only dreamed of before. I devoured books like candy, reading several each week. Golfing with Jack and his *boyfriend* Chuck become a regular activity.

The concrete business was doing well and I actually started getting ahead financially. Donnie still lived in his small efficiency apartment and eventually healed most of the relationships Ilana had destroyed. Michele sold the salon to someone else and continued to cut my hair without ever threatening to cut my throat.

Jeff took the Chihuahuas. He'd always been more attached to them than Ilana even though Gus bit him as much as he did me. The twins had actually been my saving grace that day; they'd called the police the second they'd found out Ilana was in town. If they had waited even a few minutes, the patrol cars never would have arrived in time.

As for Ilana…her arrest resulted in convictions on three felony charges. Nine were dropped in a plea bargain that avoided a long trail. Her prison sentence was reduced somewhat due to her mental state but at least she was getting treatment for her addiction. Based on the overcrowding in California's prisons, she was hoping to be out in a few months.

Fat chance. And if she did, this coyote was ready.